THE CORSET GIRLS UNLACED

ANNIE R McEWEN

First published in 2024 by Bloodhound Books.

www.bloodhoundbooks.com

Print ISBN: 978-1-917449-5-02

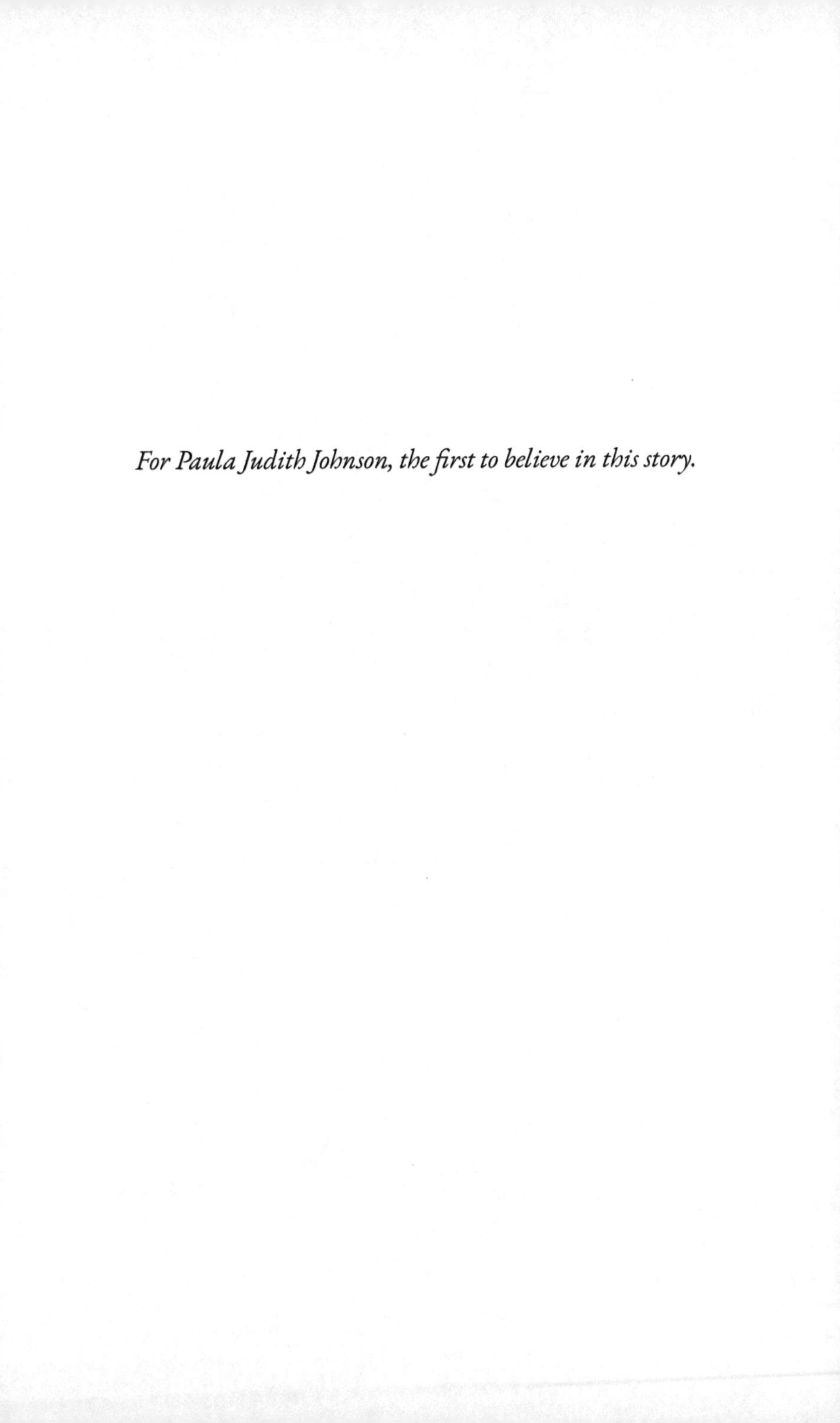

For Paula Judith Johnson, the first to believe in this story.

CHAPTER ONE
WHITECHAPEL, LONDON, 1892

'I didn't mean to kill him,' Jillian sobbed, 'it was an *accident.*' She rubbed her nose, then looked at her hand and gagged. Sir Hubert's blood stained her fingers.

Ada laughed, short and sarcastic. 'Spillin' tea in his lap – that woulda been an accident, Jilly. A carvin' knife across the gullet...'

Jillian slapped a fold of her skirt against her mouth to muffle a wail. Unstoppered, it would bring every policeman in a square mile.

Ada jogged her elbow. 'Listen, Jilly, he was forcin' himself on you. What was you gonna do, shoo him away with yer feather duster?'

Jillian wiped her eyes with the fold of black broadcloth, then squirmed on her half of the overturned wooden box in the filthy shed at the end of a filthy alley. 'I-I'd got away from him the other times,' she said thickly. 'Granted, he was staggering drunk, then. If I'd only told Cruikshank–'

From the other half of the box came, 'Baby Jesus in a satin nappy!' An Ada oath and mild, as hers went. They usually gave Jillian a laugh, but it would take more than a few chuckles to melt the frozen chunk of dread lodged in her chest.

Ada spat to the side before she went back to swearing. 'Bugger the butler and Sir bleedin' Hubert, too. Cruikshank woulda sacked you for whingin' and you'd have got no reference, neither.' She shook Jillian's shoulder. 'If you hadn't chivved His Royal Arseness first, I woulda got round to it sooner or later. And mind you, girl, I wouldn't have done him like you did, a tidy ha-ha across the throat like a French ex-ee-cutioner. I'd have cut off his tackle *slow* like, with a dull pair of shears.

'Besides,' Ada draped her arm across Jillian's shoulders and squeezed, 'he was askin' for it. What sorta eejit waves his knob at a woman who's holdin' a monstrous great knife? He deserved killin' on account of being cretinous.'

Cretinous. Ada had clearly been at her *Wilmott's Encyclopedia and Unabridged Dictionary*. When they'd fled Larches like minnows with a pike on their tails, the book was left behind with the rest of their belongings. Jillian vowed to buy her friend a new one. If she ever had wages again. Or wasn't hanged.

Ada stood. 'Wait here. I'll hawk the knife.' She took up Jillian's apron, now a tight, bloodstained bundle with a silver carving knife in the middle. Prying open the hinged plank that served as the shed door, she pushed through the opening. The plank thudded shut behind her and Jillian was walled off from the world.

Even with one less person in it, the shed seemed to shrink, crowded as it was with fear. And boxes. Boxes like the one on which she cowered filled the shed from wall to wall and up to its leaky roof. The boxes reeked of their former contents – rotting cherries, gone-off herrings, musty oats – all warring with and losing to the stink of the mildew that streaked the shed walls green and black.

The knife, the knife. It was utterly stupid to blame the carver for what she'd done, but Jillian couldn't help but feel the knife was the last, terrible 'if' in a list that led to murder.

If she'd had the full cab fare and not had to run the last mile back to Larches from her dawn trip to the docks to bid her ocean-bound brother farewell... If the kitchen hadn't been so frantic that Cook sent her, maid's apron in hand, straight back to the yard to retrieve the carver from the sharpening man at his wheel... If she hadn't returned with the knife by the scullery passage, where she ran smack into the master... If she'd been one of the other maids, not the one Sir Hubert had been trying to get his hands on for a year...

If, when he attacked her, she'd not been wild with fear and blindly slashed out with the knife... But she had. When Ada came upon her and the dying man, she'd grabbed Jillian's hand, and her apron, without a word and towed her away at a run. The carving knife, a third fugitive from the scene, was still in Jillian's other hand.

'*Lucky fer us,*' Ada said later, since otherwise they'd have had no resources at all.

Jillian started violently at a heavy thump from outside the shed. Since nothing followed it, the noise didn't herald a copper bashing his way in. Didn't mean one wasn't considering it from a stone's throw away, watching two rain-soaked women in maids' dresses coming and going for no good reason.

Minutes ticked by while her fear built upon itself in layers – a macabre trifle of possibilities. Capture, trial, notoriety, imprisonment, the noose. She sneezed into her sleeve, adding another layer, death by pneumonia. How long had her friend been gone? Five minutes? Fifty?

Ada said to wait. She was selling the knife – *the murder weapon, you hapless ninny* – and disposing of the apron, so Jillian waited, wrapping her skirts around her legs and shivering. There was nothing else to do, unless she threw herself in the Thames.

When she couldn't bear looking at the mould-painted walls of the shed any longer, she squeezed shut her eyes. Behind the lids, a gruesome sort of painting persisted. Her in her maid's dress, the bodice ripped where Sir Hubert had tried to wrench it off. Him in a dressing gown, pumping the last of his scarlet life onto the bricks of the scullery passage. The dripping carver, clutched in her fist. A white apron, lying next to the body and soaking up blood.

Still with her eyes closed, Jillian groped in the pocket of her maid's dress. Her hand closed around a small notebook, and she pulled it out. She needed to hold it, caress it, remind herself that she and it were still intact. There was comfort in the pebbled grain of the leather cover and the embossed word at the bottom. She spelled the letters by touch. *Journal.*

It had been Mother's, but was mostly blank when she died, so Jillian took it with her to the orphanage. They were allowed almost nothing at St Margaret's, but she would have left her shoes behind to have the notebook. She opened her eyes and angled her body to shield the little book from the rain that dripped through a hole in the shed roof.

The way she and Ada rocketed out of Larches with just the clothes on their backs was worse than the way she'd left home for the orphanage. There, the notebook survived only because it never left her side. Not after that vicious little harpy, Lucy Sholto, found it under her mattress and taunted her with it. Jillian, who'd never so much as raised her voice before then, struck Lucy in the face so hard it loosened a tooth. No one bothered her or her things after that, but Jillian kept the notebook within reach, even when she slept. It was bent at the corners and soiled from the years she'd kept it with her, on her.

Her fingers shook as she lifted the cover and felt the rough seam where the first few pages had been. Her mother's notations had filled those pages. Jillian memorised them, longing for any trace of her parents. After a few months at St Margaret's, the longing subsided, replaced by something serrated and dark. One day, in a spasm of rage at being landed there by those same parents, she'd ripped out the pages and burned them.

She couldn't burn memory, though, and it survived the purge. On the first page, there'd been a shopping list of notions, made elegant by Mother's penmanship. *Card of blue buttons. White glove silk. Needles.* Two pages of household chores followed the list. *Darn navy stocking. Black the stove door. Fill parlour lamps.*

She walked her fingers across the notebook's new first page, pausing on the title she'd pencilled six years ago at St Margaret's. *My Plan for Life.* Ada had her *Wilmott's* and Jillian had page after page of notes to herself and advice from deportment guides, a point-to-point course to run if she wanted a refined and orderly life. For six years, the book had been her magical steed, pocket transport to a future that had nothing to do with her grinding daily life at the orphanage and after.

There were a few empty sheets at the back. Had she been bright enough to take away a pencil instead of a carving knife from Larches, she could fill them. Point Eighteen, Decorating. *'A woman of refined sensibilities can render a prison cell attractive with furnishings and art.'*

More thumps from the alley jerked her back to the moment. She pushed the notebook deep in her pocket and wrapped her arms over her chest, trying for warmth. Failing. The cold seeped from inside her, flooding her limbs. Tucking her hands into her armpits at least hid the shivering.

With a curse and a stumble, Ada pushed through the plank flap. Rain and Whitechapel smells blew in with her – mud, horse piss, coal smoke. She nudged Jillian over on the box and pressed her wiry, work-toughened body close. Ada was shivering, too. It was a damned bitter April and there'd been not a single sunny day for months. They were both thin and lacked the right clothes to be out of doors, not that they had clothes for indoors, apart from the maids' dresses on their backs. Stolen maids' dresses, wet through and through. Their flight from Larches had been entirely in the rain and on foot, since neither of them had so much as a shilling for a cab.

Jillian couldn't imagine what they looked like to anyone else, but if Ada up close was any indication, they'd be mistaken for the lowest drabs in Whitechapel. At the best of times, Ada's curly dark hair worked its way out of the bun she kept it in for kitchen work. Now, tendrils were plastered to her forehead and cheeks like black moss, and her small, freckled nose was red and running. She'd been fighting a cough for days and her voice rasped with catarrh.

Jillian was no better off than Ada. Shoulder to shoulder, drenched to the skin, the two of them huddled and shook uncontrollably. All that being true, why were Ada's pale blue eyes sparkling with – joy?

'Three pounds.' She chortled as she flapped large, worn notes at Jillian. 'I tried for guineas, but he wasn't havin' it.' Jillian stared at the notes. Was that what a man's life was worth, three pounds? Not four, not four pound ten? She clenched her jaws to keep her teeth from rattling like castanets as she forced out words. 'Ada, I'm so, so sorry. You shouldn't be here with me. It's all my fault, it–'

'It ain't yer fault. It's Sir Arsewipe's fault.'

Somehow, Jillian was sure the police wouldn't see it that way. 'What did you do with the apron?'

'Sold it.'

'*Sold* it! But it was covered in–'

'Beef blood.' She speared Jillian with a look. '*Beef blood*, Jilly. I got tenpence for it. And a billy.'

Jillian took the folded linen handkerchief Ada handed over. It was moderately clean and nearly white. A constellation of tiny holes in one corner showed where someone's initials had been picked out. 'Thank you,' she said, trying for a smile. She tucked the handkerchief in her pocket and eased the conversation back to the knife. 'Ada, the carver. Are you certain it was a good idea to sell it? I mean, what if it's – traced?'

'It was a grand idea. First off, we need money, and we need it now. Unless you've got gold doubloons sewn in the hem of yer petticoat or a rich uncle somewhere, that knife was our only ticket to get any.'

No doubloons in the hem. No rich uncle. No family at all, since her parents had died within months of each other, six years ago. Her brother Pon, now Able Seaman Philip Erskine Morehouse in a brand-new Royal Navy uniform, was afloat somewhere. Maybe it was for the best they were all gone. If her parents and brother knew she'd become a–

Ada had a spell of hacking and wheezing, and Jillian rubbed her back. When her friend could speak, she went on about the knife.

'As to the rozzers tracin' it, no worries on that account. Silas and me, we go back to our misspent youth here in Whitechapel. He's got a smelter, see? The handle of that carver weren't hollow like the cheap stuff. Solid silver it were, and by now it'll be melted down and...' Ada's brow pleated, 'transfissured.'

'Transfigured,' Jillian corrected gently.

'Right.' Ada scrabbled in the pocket of her sopping, faded, and patched black dress. 'The blade weren't too shabby, neither. Sheffield steel, and Silas give me an extra ten bob for it.' She held out her hand where the shillings, dark silver, crossed it. 'For expenses as are immediate.'

What was more immediate were three loud knocks on the shed wall. Jillian's body twitched convulsively. Ada just nodded at her and went to the plank door, tugging it open and holding it for Jillian. When she didn't move, Ada beckoned impatiently. Dreading whatever was coming next, Jillian shot to her feet, clutching the torn halves of her bodice with both hands. She lurched into the alley, where she was instantly blinded by the sun that chose that moment to visit London. Her ears set up a clanging like church bells, drowning every other sound, and nausea charged up from her stomach.

Three steps. That's how far she got before the ground heaved and rose like a wave. Her feet were washed right out from under her and *whoosh!* she fell. Not the kind of falling, if she'd had any control, that she'd have preferred, artistic and graceful, a leaf spiralling to a pond. She went down frantic and fighting, a swimmer sinking for the third time, while a noise like *arrrg-gah* came out of her mouth and her arms windmilled. She, or the alley, tilted and whirled sickeningly. Wet hard dirt rushed up to meet her and everything turned black.

Jilly! Jilly! The words were faint and far away. Had she died? That would account for the distance. But then, the source came too near, too loud, and too Ada. 'Oi, Jillian!'

Her vision began to clear, in patches at first, and then completely. She couldn't have been unconscious for more than a few seconds, but it seemed like an age before her thoughts returned to the ranks. Unfortunately, clarity brought along deep embarrassment, like an unexpected tea guest when there weren't enough buns.

She was at least relieved to see that her splayed feet stuck out beyond the hem of her dress. She hadn't landed on her face. Or vomited on her shoes.

Relief was short-lived, terror on its heels. She was being held in someone's arms. Someone's warm, hard arms. Since Ada was crouching to one side and a yard away, the arms didn't belong to her. Jillian struggled. Ada reached out to help her, but before she could, a pair of large hands reached under Jillian's arms and yanked her to her feet. She teetered, upright but shaky, both glad and mortified that the hands stayed in place.

'She'll do.' The voice, hard but warm like the arms, came from behind and close enough she felt breath against the top of her head. Still steadying her, the large hands slid down to her waist and lingered there as the voice got even closer and the breath grazed her cheek. 'We call this place Whitechapel, but you don't have to go down on your knees to it.'

'Leave off,' Ada snapped, and swatted the hands from Jillian's waist, then began brushing her skirt, muddied by her fall. Jillian tried to help, but realised her torn bodice gaped, exposing her undergarments like a doxy showing off her wares. She grabbed at the ragged halves and grappled them closed, shrinking away from Ada's hands at the same time. Brushing wouldn't help her lost cause of a skirt, anyway. Like the rest of her dress, it was wet, and now a deep border of dirt and who knew what else stained the bottom third.

With her modesty hastily anchored in place, she raised her eyes. To a man. The one with the voice, she guessed, and no longer behind her. He was in front, now, so close and looming that she reflexively took a step backwards. The shed was awful, but she'd felt more or less safe inside. Out in the open, she faced...

She'd never heard of highwaymen in Whitechapel but, if there were any, she reckoned she was looking at one. Relaxed but watchful, he must have been waiting for targets like her to burst out of sheds and faint at his feet – his big feet, shod in working man's boots. Some distant notion of courtesy told her it was wrong to gawp at a person's shoes, so she dragged her gaze up to the man's face.

A flat cap was pulled low over his forehead and she couldn't make out his eyes. Even without the eyes, the man was view enough for a week. He had to be six feet or a bit more in height and was apparently impervious to cold, since he wore no jacket, no waistcoat, not even a neckerchief. His arms, exposed from elbow to wrists by rolled-up sleeves, were corded and sinewy. And lavishly tattooed.

Like her, he was soaked with rain. His plain, worn-thin white shirt clung to his torso, the outline of his undervest so clear Jillian could've picked out the style from a catalogue. It was impossible not to stare at the broad chest pushing aside his braces. Flat dark nipples and undulating tattoos showed even through two layers of cloth.

Because she was rooted to the spot and stunned senseless by – everything – she caught the slight movement when the man pushed up the brim of his cap with a stocky forefinger. A lock of raven hair fell onto his forehead. Just for an instant, the black comma seemed unguarded and tender, like a boy whose hair tumbled after sport.

There was nothing boyish about the quirk of the man's mouth when he smiled. Canny, even insolent, the one-sided smile told her and the world that he had brawn enough to swing a hook but knew sharper ways to earn a living.

The eyes she could now see were startlingly blue. He directed words at her friend, but those eyes never left Jillian. 'You're joking, Ada. She looks like a wet hen.'

'Never you mind about that. Just give us the key, if you're goin' to, and sheer off to the Strand or to hell, whichever you get to first.' Ada stuck out her hand.

The man threw back his head and laughed. Like everything else he showed the world, the laugh was bold, lawless, skirting the edge of arrogance. It took Jillian somewhere else for a delusional instant, somewhere wild and warm where people danced and drank ale and laughed like that. She was whirling in the man's arms, light-headed from–

What in the name of heaven was she thinking? Had her skull struck the pavement when she fainted?

The man reached out, opened a big fist over Ada's palm, and dropped an iron key in it. 'Get her something to eat,' he said, settling his cap and chucking his chin at Jillian, 'or she'll be swooning from here to Stepney and I won't be around to hoick her up.' He gave Jillian a wink to go with his lawless grin.

Whistling, he strode off. Even his gait was an outlaw's, long legs eating ground, his swagger a dare to anyone who disputed his right to every inch of it.

Ada pulled at her elbow, breaking the spell. 'Who– Who–?' Jillian began like a soggy owl, but Ada cut her off.

'Not important. We got us a place to sleep tonight and for, well, a while.'

She glanced in the direction the blue-eyed man had gone. 'Is it his place?'

'He don't need it. Come on, the rain's stopped, thank God and the government. What we need now is some clothes.'

'But,' Jillian tugged her bodice together more tightly, 'we've got clothes.'

Ada slewed a look at Jillian's dress and hissed, 'Some *other* clothes, Jilly.'

Wobbling as she was on the top step to fugitive felonhood, Jillian took Ada's meaning in a queasy second. If the police were issuing bulletins about a murderous maid gang, she and Ada matched the description perfectly.

'Come on, then,' Ada said. 'I know a place you can find a ballgown for a nanny goat, if you give a butcher's hook.'

Jillian scrambled to translate the Cockney. Butcher's – nook, crook, took? *Look,* that must be it.

Ada, ever the optimist, curled her arm through Jillian's and grinned broadly. Her cough had stopped, the sun was out, and coins jingled in her pocket.

'After Petticoat Lane, me girl, we'll go round to another place I know. Markey's got fish and chips for thruppence a plate. A penny more,' she giggled, pulling Jillian closer, 'for beer.'

Kell probably shouldn't have called her a wet hen. Wet she was, from the copper hair that spilled over her frightened green eyes to her falling-apart shoes. The shoes squelched as she lurched out of the shed and made it three paces before she collapsed in the muck.

She'd be wetter now than before. But hen? Wrong bird. Hens were plump and dowdy, while this bird...

'What's that one there, Finn?' He pointed to a cage, one among several wobbly towers of cages stacked against a building fifty yards from where he'd met the woman with his sister. The small black and yellow bird, its eyes shiny like jet beads, cocked its head at Kell's finger.

''That's a goldfinch, that is.' Finn threw out his scrawny chest with pride. '*Carduelis carduelis*. Not singin' so much today on account of the pleasure and pain.' Pleasure and pain, rhyming slang for rain. 'Sun's comin' out, so she'll be a right shantoose in a minute or two.'

Kell nodded, taking Finn's word on the bird lore; he barely knew a crow from a cormorant. The bird seller's withered right hand rested on the cage and seeing it gave Kell a twinge in his gut. He remembered the night Finian lost the use of that hand, in a fight with the Cortellis. Even now, eight years later, the sight of the contorted fingers brought it all back. The sweat, the taunts, the Sicilians milling on one side, red neckerchiefs like battle flags, knives out and gleaming dully. On the other side, the Jacks, cocksure and strong, ranks at their fullest, ready for mayhem.

The Cortellis' plan was to break the Jacks, the gang Kell and Finn called brothers, and muscle into Seven Dials, the place the two men called home. All the Cortellis got was a long night of bloodletting, while Kell got a knife in his shoulder and Finn got one through his hand. The shoulder healed, the hand didn't. Fifty pounds was Finn's recompense, enough to start the bird stall and keep it running for a while. The Jacks took care of their own.

Kell had no opinions on whether the green-eyed girl was a chanteuse like the goldfinch, but he'd heard her speak. Before he knocked, he stood outside the shed, eavesdropping on her conversation with Ada. The girl had a soft voice, soft but not thin, not the thready, wheedling sound some soft-voiced women made. Velvety, that's how he'd describe it. Pitched low. A whiskey voice, some might say, though she didn't look like she'd got it from late nights in taverns. When she came out, he expected some big, chesty woman, as that's the sort that usually had that voice. She was a little thing and pretty, despite being soaked and scared. When he caught her as she fainted, she felt pretty all over. Pretty curves, pretty warmth, a pretty smell coming off her.

Kell looked away from the caged bird to a youngster sitting on a barrel next to Finian. 'That your boy?'

'Aye, that's me youngest, Sean. Twelve come November, he'll

be.' To his credit, the boy didn't wait to be prompted, but popped to his feet and snatched off his cap. His eyes were as dark and sharp as the finch's in the cage.

The eyes got sharper when Kell pulled out a coin. 'You'll be knowin' my sister, Seaneen.'

'Oi know 'er. Proper jammy, she is. Black 'air like yerself an' the nicest pair of–' Just in time, the boy caught himself. 'Eyes,' he finished, flushing from the roots of his ginger hair to his shirt neckband.

'It's yor eyes I'm wantin', Seaneen.' Kell's voice slid easily, too easily, into the accents of his youth. 'Keep 'em on 'er an' the filly wif 'er. Both of 'em in maid's dresses, headin' for Spitalfields, Petticoat Lane. Stay on 'em till they goes to ground in Soho.' The boy took in the orders, nodding, but his gaze stayed on the coin in Kell's fingers. 'Report to me then, right? The Flower Garden, Catherine Street next to the Royal. Ask at the back, an' there'll be anuvver o' these for you. Mind 'ow you go, lad.' Kell handed over the coin. The boy pocketed it and streaked like a greyhound into the thronged streets.

Kell passed a second coin to Finian, who took it without comment, but his eyes were no less dark and sharp than his son's and he kept them on Kell. The two men nodded and Kell moved off into the familiar warren of Whitechapel.

Would he see her again, the girl with the scared green eyes and copper hair? Probably wouldn't. Definitely shouldn't. She had enough troubles without him and his murky past, his aimless present. Still, he'd like to see her. He'd like even more to touch her again. His hands fit her slender waist like they were created to span it, and the brush of her hair against his cheek was like silk.

His body didn't calm and his mind didn't settle, all the way to his work in Catherine Street.

CHAPTER TWO

'Are you still not sleepin' nights?'

Jillian shrugged wearily. 'I'm fine, Ada.' She stopped rubbing her eyes so Ada wouldn't keep on and on about it. 'Fine' was a lie but the truth was worse. She was so tired that the stitches she was putting into the corset in her hands looked like rows of ants, marching in ten different directions. She squinted at her needle. *In through the lining, push it through, measure the interval, out through the lining...*

Blast and botheration, the workroom was quiet as a church today. She needed noise to keep her awake because *no, Ada, I'm not sleeping nights.* The room they'd got the key to from the cocky brute in Whitechapel was comfortable enough for a matchbox with a bed, but that wasn't the problem. She'd be lying if she said the brute and his startling blue eyes didn't visit her thoughts at night, uninvited. That wasn't the problem, either.

It was her dreams that destroyed sleep. Ada kept saying, 'It was the old git's fault, not yours,' and seemed to believe it. As did Jillian, mostly. Sometimes. But it kept prodding at her, even after weeks, even while she slept. Her very own *Tell-Tale Heart.*

And it wasn't only the dreams. It was the constant, skin-crawling fear. Fear that any minute she'd be arrested, that police would turn up with shackles and warrants and she'd be dragged away. To keep that spectre away she needed work, hard and absorbing work, all the time.

'Is this right?' Ada held out the corset she was sewing.

Jillian bent over the wobbly edging of silk ribbon. 'Are you asking me if that's a slip stitch or if it's a good slip stitch?'

Ada mumbled something coarse. 'I'll start over.'

'Do a few inches and I'll take a look.' Jillian lifted her hand from her own work and gently patted Ada's wrist. The fine stitchery of bespoke corsets, each made precisely to order, required a sensitive touch. Ada's hands were scarred by years in sculleries and kitchens, by scalding water and scouring grit. She probably could barely feel the needle in her fingers. 'You're getting better every day, Ada. Madame will be pleased. And no one can turn a casing like you.'

Her friend smiled, head down, and toiled on with the ribbon.

Had Madame taken Ada on because she and Jillian were conjoined, like Siamese twins? Because it was take both or neither? Jillian didn't care if she had. They were in the door, now, and had no intention of being put out again, singly or together. Ada would improve. She was a steady worker, and the other girls liked her. Jillian would help her. They all would.

She put down her sewing to look around the workroom, still astounded she and Ada were in it. To be *corsetières*, the staymakers that everyone in the London trade called corset girls, was a very big step up from service. It was all Ada's doing that they were here, and how bold of her, though it came just in the nick of time. They'd used up nearly all the money from the smelted carving knife and had no idea what they would do when their funds were gone. Ada kept saying, *Don't worry, something will turn up*, like Micawber in *David Copperfield*.

Jillian wasn't at all sure anything would turn up, and she certainly didn't know why Ada was dragging her around Mayfair that day. It wasn't as though they could buy anything in the district. They dodged wheeled and foot traffic for hours, hemmed in by tall buildings and bewildered by the maze of streets, all of them leading to the well-ordered foliage of Grosvenor Square. Jillian's stomach was twisting with hunger, but Mayfair wasn't the sort of place where they'd find penny pies for lunch. On teeming South Audley Street, people glowered at their shabby clothes and shopkeepers watched their every move. The cough of a police constable made Jillian almost jump out of her skin. Finally, Ada towed them into a side street, Shepherd. A few doors down, she whooped and grabbed Jillian's arm.

'That's us, then!' She pointed to a placard in the half-glass front door of Number Six.

Jillian backed up a step to take in the whole shop, feeling her mouth go slack. Number Six looked like a Cadbury's chocolates box. It was painted a rich, deep blue, with a bright red door whose brass doorknob shone like a mirror. The façade and the door had gilded accents, and an ivy vine in gold paint trailed around the wide front window. Inside, a gowned dress form stood on a dais, defying onlookers to imagine anything more elegant. Above the ivy-framed window, curling red and gold letters spelled out the shop's name. *Salon Sirena*.

Ada tried the door-handle – locked firm. Before Jillian could read the placard in the window or ask Ada what on God's earth they were doing there, her friend pounded on the door.

Ada hardly lowered her fist when a buxom, middle-aged woman in a loud puce-and-yellow-striped dress threw open the door. The woman's dark-eyed scrutiny lanced and held them, while Jillian quivered like bait on a hook. Under the mass of salt-and-pepper hair piled haphazardly atop the woman's head, she was frowning. The frown grew sterner when she got a good look at their clothes.

Jillian cringed. Their hard-worn woollen skirts and once-white shirtwaists from Petticoat Lane had seemed acceptable in lesser neighbourhoods, but even she would say their moth-eaten shawls, wafting *arôme de mildew*, shouted for the Mayfair Fashion Division to enforce them back to Whitechapel. Certainly, there was no way they could meet the standard of the puce-and-yellow paragon in the shop doorway.

While Ada and the paragon engaged in a silent duel of facial expressions, Jillian peeked past the doorway into a simply but beautifully furnished room. A showroom, she guessed from the shelves of boxes at the back and two gilt chairs.

Ada took her shot. 'Good day, madam,' she began, loud as the paragon's dress, then gestured toward the placard. 'We've come in answer to your notice.'

The notice. Jillian didn't want to look away, but she managed to read the window placard from the corner of her eye. *Corsetières wanted. Experienced only.*

'Oh, you 'ave, 'ave you?' The response was one part Cockney, two parts sarcasm. The woman's one hand curled around the edge of the door, while her other fist found a pillowy spot on her broad hip. A pale pink corset, silk ribbons dangling, was gripped like a lacey prisoner in the hip hand. 'And just wot might you two miseries know 'bout makin' corsets?'

Ada pulled herself up to her full height, one and a half inches taller than Jillian's five feet two, which was just one of the many reasons Jillian let Ada handle sticky social interactions. 'You might ask, madam, what we don't know, as it will take a good deal less time.' At that, she drove a sharp elbow into Jillian's side.

Galvanised by fear and the elbow, Jillian shot a hand toward the captive corset at the paragon's hip. 'With your permission, madam?'

The corset brought relief and familiarity when it landed in Jillian's hands. *Bless you, Sister Agatha.* The nun at St Margaret's School looked like an angel but tailored like a demon, and Jillian was Sister Agatha's star pupil. 'If I may just observe, madam, the seams on this otherwise nicely made set of stays do your establishment no credit. Here, as you see, there is puckering...'

She went on in that vein for a few minutes, feeling almost guilty when at last she offered the heavily criticised corset to its owner, who didn't take it. Instead, she lifted her voice to a volume that made the door glass rattle. 'Evangeline Broussard! Minerva Hawkins! Here, now!'

Two young women plunged through a heavy curtain at the back of the showroom as though they'd been pressed to the other side. One was lushly built with unruly black ringlets escaping the ribbon that held them back from her tea-with-milk face. The other was slight and bespectacled, with porcelain skin and chestnut hair trapped in a single, very long braid lying across one shoulder.

The paragon chucked her chin at Jillian and Ada. 'These two frowsy baggages are the new corset girls. Give 'em aprons and show 'em 'ow to get started. Wot's your names?' she added, jabbing a forefinger toward the frowsy baggages.

'Adaline Gubbins,' Ada said, her face as blank and pure as a nun's.

Jillian blinked. That wasn't the name her friend had gone by at Larches. The paragon's eyes drilled into Jillian. 'Jillian... Phipps.' *Goodbye, Miss Morehouse. Hello, Miss Phipps.* It was her mother's maiden name.

The older woman's eyebrows hiked marginally. 'Right. I'm Mrs Eunice Sapier. You'll call me Madame. Go on, then.' She hooked a thumb over her shoulder at the drape from which the other two girls had emerged and then disappeared again.

Ada sprinted for the drape as though trying to outrun a change of heart by her new employer. The second frowsy baggage was slower off the mark. When Jillian finally moved, Madame stopped her with a heavy hand shoved into her middle.

'You, Jilly girl.' Madame pointed at the pink corset Jillian was still holding. 'Fix that one first.'

Jillian forgot she wasn't a maid anymore and dropped a

curtsey. Then, she pelted toward the back of the shop like devils were on her heels.

<hr>

There wasn't any excuse for Kell to be standing, at half eight in the morning, in the deep shadow of a doorway in the alley behind Shepherd Street. But here he was, as he was most mornings, scratchy-eyed from lack of sleep and hollow from lack of breakfast. His sister, when he prodded her enough, kept him advised of how things were going with her and her friend from Larches, but he needed to see for himself.

As always, Ada discouraged him. 'Wind it in, brother. We're just ducky.' To which assessment, as always, Kell paid no heed. Two weeks ago, Ada and the other woman had got themselves hired at the smart corset shop whose back door he faced now. That was good. He'd not liked it when Ada was in service, where too many women got roughed up by one thing or another.

He hadn't expected to learn Ada's friend took the roughing up done to her in quite the way she had, but what was done was done. Ada was loyal. She'd follow her friend to the steps of the gallows, if it came to that.

Not that it would. For his sister's sake and the sake of that trembling beauty he'd not seen enough of in Whitechapel, Kell would make sure.

The women entered the alley from South Audley, and Kell pressed back into concealing shadows. The two were still wearing the shabby clothes they'd bought off some stall in Petticoat Lane. He'd offered Ada money for better clothes but, being Ada, she'd thrown it back in his face. Kell had never figured out whether she turned down the brass because of its origins or her own stubborn pride, but Ada would rather dress like a Billingsgate fishwife than wear something bought with money the Jacks made.

Kell didn't know how it was possible for the other woman to

still be pretty in a skirt and shirtwaist that looked like they'd been on someone's body since the reign of George III, but pretty she was. While Ada knocked, the pretty one waited below the two steps to the back door of the shop. A sunbeam forced its way through grey clouds and landed on her coppery hair, washing it with gold like the edges of a Bible. Kell forgot to breathe for a few seconds. The sunbeam quickly remembered it was in London and hid its face. The shop door opened and the women entered, exchanging merry words with their workmates. The door shut behind them.

Kell left his blind and headed toward South Audley, reaching into his waistcoat pocket for tobacco pouch and papers. On its way to the pocket, his hand unaccountably paused, pressing flat over the centre of his chest. What he felt there, what he felt every morning in this place and at this hour, was a spark, sudden, hot, and hopeless. It flamed up at the mere sight of the woman his sister told him was named Jillian Morehouse.

It's just a fancy, it'll burn off.

The deuce it would. But he knew a lost cause when he saw one, so he wouldn't come back to the alley.

Yes, you will.

Yes, he would. Tomorrow, and the next day, and the next.

You're a damn fool.

Yes to that, too.

CHAPTER THREE

'Killed by *burglers*?'

It was twenty-eight days since they'd left Larches. Jillian knew exactly, since she'd kept track on a blank page of *My Plan for Life*. Nothing incriminating, just rows of marks with a diagonal slash for every fifth. It was afternoon at Salon Sirena and Madame was out, buying cloth. Evie and Min were making deliveries. That left Jillian and Ada alone to stretch out their tea break at the two-foot-square excuse for a table in the six-foot-square excuse for a kitchen at the back of the workroom.

Jillian pinked seams while Ada read two newspapers, one she filched from Madame and one she bought from the newsagent on the corner.

Ada grunted. 'That's what *The Daily Telegraph* says the coppers say. "Chief Superintendent A. L. Foster suggested that Sir Hubert met his end defending his residence from burglars who entered from an unlocked door to the scullery".'

Jillian's eyes met Ada's over the top of the paper. 'Didn't he have– Isn't there any family?'

'Coupla cousins nine times removed in Yorkshire.' Ada went

back to her reading, licking a finger to turn a page. 'Not so gutted by the loss as to be "helping the police with their enquiries".'

There was the fiancée, of course. The thought seemed to come to Jillian and Ada at the same time, and their eyes locked again over the top of *The Daily Telegraph*. The fiancée. The hapless débutante whose engagement was to be celebrated the evening of the very day Sir Hubert's throat met the sharp edge of a carving knife.

Below-stairs gossips had sniffed out scandal well before the proposed groom's murder. Cook asked Mr Cruikshank, 'Faugh, he's marryin' *who*? What's the matter with the lass? Is she missin' an eye and a leg?' And Mr C answered, 'Family's at the workhouse door. Sir Hubert offered to bail 'em out.'

Jillian swallowed the last of her tea and cleared the table, barely listening to Ada.

Then, Ada snagged her attention again. 'The faster the better.'

'What?'

Ada had dropped *The Daily Telegraph* and was rattling the day's second newspaper, *The Illustrated Police News*. 'I said, the faster the inquiry goes away, the better. Considerin' what come out at the inquest.'

The inquest. *Of course, Jillian, you dolt, there had to be an inquest. He was murdered, wasn't he?* By person or persons unknown. She stared at the open paper in Ada's hands.

DEATH AT DEATH'S DOOR.

That was the attention-grabbing headline on the front page. The artist's illustration, a blood-splashed, half-clothed body lying across a bed, was even more grabby than the headline. And totally inaccurate, but she wasn't about to visit the paper's offices to request a correction.

Ada, deep in the page two article, spoke without raising her eyes. 'This reporter, James "Jimmy" Sullivan. A corker, he is. Gives all the pacifics.'

'Specifics,' Jillian corrected.

'Those, too. Says here, "the surgeon's report revealed that Sir Hubert Alloway was already within months of death before his demise, his body and brain ravaged by the late stages of a wasting condition".' Ada smirked broadly. 'Me and you and the rest of the world know what sorta disease is called "a wasting condition".'

'We do?'

Ada tsked and put down the paper. Her lips moved, silently.

Jillian shook her head. What was Ada trying to tell her?

'French disease,' Ada whispered.

Still nothing.

'Social complaint,' she hissed, louder.

Jillian blinked like a hedgehog.

Ada shouted loud enough the shop next door might have heard her. 'Nuns on toast, Jilly! I'm talkin' about syphilis!'

That word she knew. Revulsion made her stomach flip, sending her tea up her gullet. She forced it down with a hard swallow and tried to think optimistically, like Ada. Murdering Sir Hubert had saved his fiancée from going to a marriage bed crawling with vile contagion, hadn't it? *Every cloud has a silver lining.*

She shook herself. Wiping down the table with a rag, she gathered Ada's teatime reading and took it to the wastebasket. Quickly, before she rolled it up and consigned it to the can, she thumbed through *The Daily Telegraph*.

In a month, Sir Hubert's death had retreated to the paper's interior and had fewer column inches. Bigger news had taken its place at the front. Mineworkers threatened a strike. The Women's Suffrage Movement petitioned Parliament. A scandal brewed about the condition of the ageing Royal Navy fleet, as though Jillian didn't have enough nightmares. Now she had some new ones. Ships running aground, boilers exploding, seamen going to the bottom of the ocean. She wished Pon were back on land.

Another small cloud with no silver lining hovered. 'Ada, do you think anyone's feeding Tige?'

'The dirty white doggie what scrounges around the scullery yard at Larches?' Jillian nodded and Ada shrugged. 'I reckon Cook is. If she's still at the house. She acts like a tartar but she's not so bad.'

Jillian wasn't reassured and Ada noticed. 'Tige's his name for a reason, Jilly. He's a fierce little beastie and he'll do all right.'

Jillian nodded again, glumly, and swept the newspapers into the rubbish. She went back to the worktable and picked up her needle.

A few weeks passed and, despite Jimmy Sullivan's energetic effort in *The Illustrated Police News*, the murder of Sir Hubert Alloway faded out altogether. Jillian continued to watch the papers with the eye of a pirate looking for X in the sand. But no one – at least no one in the press – seemed to care anymore about Sir Hubert Alloway, Larches, the rest.

It was done, finished, over. Forgotten by everyone except her and Ada. And maybe by that good-looking brute from Whitechapel who had picked her up when she fainted. She wondered if he'd forgotten that day. She wondered if he'd forgotten her.

Because she couldn't seem to forget him.

Chapter Four

'They're just too busy to leave their establishments. That's why Madame is kind enough to provide concierge service for them.'

Evie and Min tittered at Jillian's remark, while Ada laughed outright. 'Madame, kind? If she is, Jilly, I'm a lady's maid at the Vatican. And you don't really think *concierge service* is why one of us has to go to them houses for measures and deliveries, do you? Madame don't want any of 'em settin' foot in the shop, and you know it.'

They were – mostly Ada was – talking about *the specials* while they sewed. Jillian wished Ada would shut up about them. In the two months since she'd started working at the salon, Jillian hadn't had any direct dealings with the secret and lucrative twenty per cent of Madame's trade. She'd like to keep it that way.

The specials. Jillian smoothed the casing she'd just sewn into a pale blue silk corset. The specials didn't live on Grosvenor Square, like the baronet's wife who'd ordered the blue Number Eleven. The specials slept in well-used beds at the Crimson Lantern, or Mrs Binghampton's Ruffled Pony, or the Painted Birds. Jillian knew about the houses, all right. How could she not know, when her workmates brought back lurid stories from their visits. Visits like the delivery Evie made last week to the Lantern.

'One of *les femmes*, she is in the foyer with the coffee in hand,' she told the workroom. 'Naked as the *bébé* just come. She stands *comme ça*,' Evie jutted her hip and turned one hand up, 'at noon in the day! I can see all of her...' Evie flapped a hand below her waist and swayed her shapely hips in a way that made further description unnecessary. "Ullo, ducks,' she say to me. I say, "You are not cold?" and she laugh like the hyena.'

Ada piped up. 'Just be thankful some lady parts was all you saw. I dropped off two Number Eights at the Painted Birds last week and one of the birdies was bent over the parlour stair banister.' Ada, who was as far from shy as Houndsditch was from Ascot, still lowered her voice when she added, 'With a bloke behind her goin' at it hammer an' tongs.'

Jillian's jaw went slack from shock. Evie clapped her hand over her mouth, whispering '*Mère de Dieu*,' through her fingers. Min gave a strangled cry and dropped her threaded needle, which the others then had to find for her.

Jillian cut a length of ribbon and started on another casing. Knowing about *the specials* was one thing, but dwelling on them was another. It was just business, just trade. No reason to feel awkward, and no reason to get involved. Madame hadn't sent *her* to any of the whoring establishments. Maybe she never would. Min hadn't made any delivery or measures-taking expeditions to the brothels, either. True, that might be because Min was timid as a mouse. She'd probably go paralytic at the sight of a naked *demimondaine* and have to be carried out on a board. But–

'Evieeeee!' Madame bayed as she wrenched aside the curtain to the workroom. 'Wrap that order for The Flower Garden. Hop to it, girl!' Madame pointed at Jillian. 'Give her a hand, Jillian. Your turn to deliver.'

Jillian halted in mid-stitch. Ada patted her shoulder. 'You'll be fine, Jilly. Just keep your knickers up.' Muffled laughter all round, *ha ha*.

Evie stood on a chair to get a large box from the shelves on the workroom wall. She began spreading the contents on the table, while the other girls moved their work out of the way.

The corsets emerging from the box were lovely. No, more than lovely, they were exquisite, even if the colours were a bit – strident. Evie arranged them on sheets of tissue, each with a yard of Salon Sirena's trademark mauve silk ribbon, stamped at intervals in gold, *S.S.* Each corset bore a small paperboard tag with a neatly printed title. *Camellia, Lilac, Dahlia, Marigold, Iris, Peony.* Works of art, they were, and priced accordingly.

'That's my favourite,' Min murmured, touching *Dahlia*. It was deep rose silk brocade with even deeper rose edging and laces. 'Though this other that Evie made...' Her pale slender finger drifted to *Marigold*, a lime confection with citron-dyed laces.

Evie was her usual humble self. '*Difficile,* to dye the laces. But now it is not bad, I think.'

Not bad? Stunning, is what Jillian thought. Too elegant for, well, that wasn't for her or any of them to decide, was it? Whatever anyone said about *the specials*, Ada's opinion in the end was Madame's. 'The notes they pay with 'as got Bank of England on 'em, just like yours and mine.'

Ada and Madame were surely right. *Just business, just trade.* Jillian and Evie made six neat tissue-wrapped bundles of the corsets and tied each with the mauve ribbon. Madame's corsets usually went out in lavishly imprinted boxes, but she apparently didn't waste those on fallen women.

The ten minutes it took to pack the corsets in a deep carpetbag went by too quickly. Jillian stalled for time, searching for a tape measure, scissors, pins, and thread spools, in case she had to make alterations. The other *corsetières*, suppressing laughter, watched as she ran out of things to pack, then closed and latched the carpetbag with a *snick*. No more stalling. It was time to confront her fate.

She met Madame in the showroom and took money for cab fare. A cautionary lecture came along with the money.

'It's a new 'ouse for us.' Madame wagged her finger at Jillian. 'I'm told it's very 'igh class, but I'll reserve my opinion till I see more of it. Nothin' to be chalked on account, as yet, and that's *firm*. Collect twelve pound nine for the stays and fifteen bob for delivery and alterations on the spot. You're to get the money the second your toes cross the doorsill. Not a single inch of lacin' to be 'anded over till then. Understood, Jilly?'

Jillian nodded numbly. Madame went out the salon door, calling up a hackney with a whistle that could be heard in Croydon. Jillian went into the vehicle, Madame gave the driver the address, the driver slapped the reins, and away they went.

Even though the seat smelled of sweat, humanity, and stale tobacco, a ride in hired transport lifted her spirits. Jillian hugged the carpetbag to her chest and ogled London through the cab window. When she was younger and life was good, her parents took her and Pon to the park on Sundays, in hackney cabs just like this one.

When life was good. Anger and love warred inside her whenever she thought of that. It had been so full and happy, her life. She'd never for a minute thought it would disappear – Jillian craned her neck to see the layer of yellow-grey that replaced blue sky in London – like smoke.

She really must stop letting it bother her. Most people idealised their childhoods, the time when they'd been safe from realities like work, money, struggle, and loss. But she, her brother, and her parents had *all* been happy, hadn't they? Mother singing as she picked out tunes on the piano. Father laughing and calling Mother 'Twinklie', his pet name for her. Jillian and Pon sailing paper boats and hunting tadpoles in the stream at the bottom of the lawn. Plenty of clothing, warmth, food, and time.

Just then, a ragged, dirty child dashed into the street, pursued by a shouting mob of older children. The child nearly ran under the wheels of the hackney, while Jillian gasped and the driver yelled and cursed. Somehow, the child made the pavement safely and disappeared into the crowd.

There but for the grace of God. And St Margaret's, her home for four years after her parents' deaths. The wardens could call it a school until the moon turned to cake, but everyone knew it was an orphanage. That was part of the shame attached to being in it. When the wardens visited, all the inmates were lined up next to their beds, like in a better sort of asylum. Better because they weren't mad and they weren't paupers. The wardens never tired of reminding them how very lucky they were that their parents had left behind just enough to keep their children from the workhouse. Or the streets.

Yes, how *lucky* to be at St Margaret's. No privacy, no pretty clothes, never quite enough food, never quite enough warmth. No singing and hardly any laughter. Lots of time, though. Time to think about how she'd ended up there.

The cab entered Leicester Square, slowing to deal with the clog of omnibuses, carriages, wagons, and pedestrians. To the east, the nearly rebuilt Alhambra Theatre rose, white and exotic, its oriental cupolas obscured by scaffolding. Jillian had seen it once before, years ago, when her family first came to London. Father had pointed it out, still a partial ruin after a fire, and the Turkish Baths next door. Pon and Father had both snickered and Mother shushed them.

Jillian sat back in her seat, letting her thoughts drift back to the orphanage. It had been easier for Pon at St Margaret's, for all the boys over twelve. They were apprenticed to a trade. While she counted the days at the orphanage and then in service, marking them in the back of *My Plan for Life* like a convict ticking off his dwindling sentence, Pon was in a boat builder's shop. For Pon, it had all been a wonderful lark, working at something he loved and then joining the Navy to do more of the same.

When the wardens at St Margaret's reminded her about luck, Jillian guessed Pon got it for them both.

The driver pulled his horse to a walk in Covent Garden and Jillian peered out the window again. She'd always been curious about the Garden. Mother thought it was dangerous, not only the market but the whole district, and wouldn't allow Father to take them there. Just ahead loomed its most famous feature, one Jillian knew though she'd never been inside it, had never even seen it close. People got up to all sorts of wicked things in the surrounding streets, but the Theatre Royal still seemed very dignified. Famous plays were acted in it, famous players acted in them. There'd even been an assassination attempt on George III there, in the early years of the century. Not that attempting the King's life was anything Mother would approve of, but at least it showed the place got visits from royalty.

Passing it now, the theatre looked to Jillian like exactly the sort of grand and scandalous building where all of that would go on. Long, two-storeyed, with ranks of windows and a vaguely classical façade, it filled the entire space between Catherine Street and Drury Lane, built right up to the pavement like it was elbowing pedestrians out of the way. The cab went into Catherine Street, halting in front of a mansion that faced a side door to the theatre.

She directed a long, hard look at the mansion. She'd never seen a whorehouse before, but what she'd imagined was – different. A ramshackle house, maybe, with a red lamp over the door and undressed women hanging half out of the windows. The building in front of her was at least 150 years old and quite serene. Such a shame the dun Cotswold stone was streaked and darkened by sooty rain, but every building in London was the same. It still had a fine presence, solid and well-tended. Two freshly-painted white pillars supported the portico and framed a black-painted door with a fanlight above. She risked examining the windows for signs of debauchery within, but they were all discreetly curtained. Overall, the building was as respectable as any building could look.

So respectable that when the driver came round to help her down from the hack, Jillian hesitantly asked him, 'Is this– are you sure this is The Flower Garden?' She wanted to bite her tongue when she saw the man's expression.

'Oh, yes, miss.' Had he just given her a leer and a wink? 'It's The Flower Garden, all right. Would you like me to wait, miss?' The leer turned into a grin. 'Or will you be stopping a while?'

Heat rose all at once from Jillian's collarbone to her scalp. Dropping her gaze, she pretended to brush city dust off her skirt and said, 'I am making a delivery and should not be long. Please wait.' Without meeting the driver's eyes again, she marched to the door. *I shall be dignified. I shall be authoritative. I know exactly what I'm doing.*

The bronze doorknocker gave her a moment's pause. It was shaped like a rose on a stem. With thorns. Finally, she grabbed it and rapped twice, so hard that her hand stung.

A minute passed, agonizingly long. She was steeling herself to knock again when the door was opened by a neatly dressed maid. Beyond her, Jillian could see a tasteful entrance hall with a checkerboard tile floor. Wall sconces glowed, filling the space with kind light that seemed to spill from the hall and into the street.

She opened her mouth, but the maid spoke before her. 'Good afternoon, miss. Please come in. We're expecting you.'

What a lovely room. The thought popped into Jillian's head almost before her feet crossed the threshold. The walls were tempered a very soft pink. Blush, she would say, if it was a corset colour. At waist height, a cream-painted dado ran the length of the hall on both sides and, below that, paper in a subdued stripe. Gilt-framed paintings hung every few feet along the walls. English landscapes, a piazza in Venice, ruins in Rome.

She looked up. The ceiling was exquisitely decorated. Plaster borders, like icing, frosted the perimeter. In the centre, an elaborate chandelier hung from a plaster medallion of rosettes and leaves.

There wasn't much furniture in the hall, but what there was denoted good taste and high quality. To her right, a *demi-lune* table of cherry-wood was so highly polished that she had to stop herself from checking her reflection in it. Atop it perched a huge Chinese porcelain vase in the shape of a crane. Its wings embraced a crowded floral arrangement, filling the hall with the scents of lilies and roses. Where on earth did people get flowers like that so early in the spring? To her left, the doors to a receiving room were open. A cheery fire beckoned.

It was all just lovely. Perhaps she'd be asked to wait in the receiving room, by the fire. Jillian relaxed. In a lovely house like this, what could possibly go wrong?

Chapter Five

No receiving room for her. The maid set off for the broad staircase at the end of the entrance hall and Jillian assumed she was to follow, so she did. She couldn't help but examine the back of the maid's dress. A fashionable number in black silk satin with ruched trim, the dress was as elegant as the hall décor. Too elegant, perhaps, for a domestic, but who was she to say how those who could afford them dressed their servants? She glanced down at her navy skirt and white shirtwaist. They were new, the first clothes she'd been able to buy from her wages, but they seemed drab by comparison, like a school uniform.

The woman preceding her didn't dress like a maid and didn't walk like one, either. Her silk-swathed hips rolled from side to side, a black-sailed galleon on the waves. Jillian, feeling plain, like a small dory on a rope, followed until the woman gained the first step of the staircase.

Madame's warning suddenly returned like a jabbing hatpin. 'Wait just a moment, please! Before we go any farther, I should say I've been instructed to– that is, it's customary to collect...' She trailed off, wishing Madame had told her how to politely say *hand over the blunt now or I'll turn on my heel and scarper.*

The maid didn't stop walking, just rotated her head a quarter to give Jillian a disdainful profile. 'Why, miss, I'm sure I don't know anything about that. Mrs Arbuthnot is in the drawing room. She'd be the one to handle any... commercial arrangements.' From the maid's lips, the phrase 'commercial arrangements' came out like *sheep's trotters* or *soused pig face. That's rich,* Jillian thought, *coming from a domestic in a house that sells... well, what it sells.*

At any rate, Madame's lecture hadn't included any contingency clauses. The maid mounted the stairs, swaying, and Jillian stayed just behind her, not swaying. After a first grab at the gleaming mahogany railing, she snatched back her hand, remembering Ada's story about the Painted Birds. She'd like to have gloves, but that wasn't likely any time soon. Even the second-hand straw boater she wore today was a gift from Evie.

At the landing, the staircase split in two. The maid turned left, and Jillian, close on her heels, nearly trod on the maid's hem. From the slightly ajar door at the top of the stairs, sounds of laughter wafted. Men's and women's voices in conversation, and a high, happy warble of, 'Pimms! You read my mind, you adorable man!'

Threading through the voices, Jillian heard a piano sonata being executed quite well. Chopin. A sweet, stray memory, very out of place, reminded her of Mother teaching her to play. Mother, who loved Chopin.

The maid pushed open the door to the room and stood aside for Jillian to enter. She did, and happy childhood memories disappeared in a blinding flash.

She was looking directly at the hairy buttocks of a man bending over a chair. Correction. Bending over a woman who was bending over a chair. The man was naked from the waist down, his trousers and drawers puddled around his ankles, his shirttail thrown up to free his haunches.

Jillian wanted to avert her eyes, but they were glued to the clenching arse no more than two yards away. As she stared, mouth open, the man increased his forceful movements. Both he and the woman were making noises, hers like a sportsman urging a horse to the finish line.

'That's it, Bert! Go on, send it home, Bertie!'

His noises – Jillian couldn't call them words. Hoarse and painful groans, maybe, tortured utterances like someone being disembowelled. Suddenly, the man threw back his head and shouted.

'Jesus Mary fucking Christ!' His whole body convulsed, buttocks quivering as though electricity coursed through them.

Jillian dropped her carpetbag. It landed with a thud at the same instant someone stepped between her and the spectacle. The someone, a woman in an aggressively blue taffeta dress, had brassy blonde hair in a complicated corona of braids. Heavy perfume rolled in with her like fog.

Before Jillian could follow her bag to the floor, the woman picked it up. She backed Jillian gently but firmly out the door, turning a hateful glare at the maid and then beaming, all sweetness and light, at Jillian.

'Nothing for you in there, lovey,' cooed the brassy-haired woman, her voice as tooth-hurtingly sweet as treacle. She took Jillian by the elbow and guided her down the stairs and across the landing. 'I'm Mrs Theodora Arbuthnot. Let's just find a quiet place to talk, shall we?'

Jillian, almost as shattered as she'd been after Larches, let herself be led like a puppy up the opposing staircase and into another room at the top.

As The Flower Garden's proprietress – for that's surely who she was – opened that door, she kept talking in her treacly voice. 'Deepest apologies and so on for that, dearie. I should have been downstairs to greet you, but it's been a veritable *crush* today, don't you know, just like Sanger's Circus and Waterloo Station rolled into one. And that maid! She's a fright, I won't argue, but it's such a trial, finding help. Why, I have resigned myself to being grateful if they don't steal the paint off the walls. Now!' Mrs Arbuthnot threw out her arms as though ushering Jillian into a suite at the Savoy. 'Here's a cosy spot for you to receive my ladies and fit their corsets. I'm ever so grateful for your accommodating us, don't you know.'

Jillian looked around the room. It wasn't large, and the big bed in the middle not only shouted its purpose but made the room seem even smaller. A gold satin counterpane, smooth and inviting as the flesh of a harem favourite, stretched across the bed. Jillian couldn't take her eyes off it, until Mrs Arbuthnot put the carpetbag on the bed, making the counterpane ripple. The proprietress pulled a wad of pound notes from her pocket and nudged Jillian in the ribs with it.

'Here you go, duckie. Count it, if you like.'

Jillian's eyes jerked from the bed to Mrs Arbuthnot. What a cloying scent she wore, lily-of-the-valley – a laugh if ever there was one.

Trying not to think about where the money had been, Jillian took the bundled notes with a thumb and forefinger, then shoved them into her pocket without counting them. Madame would be furious if she saw that.

Mrs Arbuthnot also saw it and winked conspiratorially. 'Just between you and me, lamb, I've given you a bit extra for the, ah, exposure, if you get my drift.' She squeezed Jillian's arm. 'See that you tuck that bit away before you're back at your shop, as your higher-ups might not remember to give it to you. Not everyone's as kind as me, don't you know.' A wink, a squeeze, a subtle bribe. *Just us working girls together.*

Brisk and businesslike again, Mrs Arbuthnot told her, 'I'll send my ladies to you one at a time. Try not to keep them too long.' She left the room in a loud rustle of taffeta.

Never fear, I shan't stay a second longer than I must. Jillian sighed, then sniffed. She thought the perfume would leave with

Mrs Arbuthnot, but it didn't. The room had its own heavy fragrance, rose or carnation. Jillian refused to think about why so much scent was necessary.

She emptied her carpetbag, unwrapping and arraying the corsets across the end of the bed since there was nowhere else she could see to put them. Nowhere to put her hat, either, except the bed. Somehow, she didn't want to put anything back on her body that had been there. Finally, she unpinned the dark straw boater and put it in the bag.

The whole time, she tried to forget what she had just seen in the room across the landing. What sort of world was she in now? Granted, she'd been in service, and in service one saw things. The contents of chamber pots, stains on bedsheets, hand towels that had been used for something other than wiping shaving lather off a face. But nothing like *that*. A man and woman rutting like beasts, in full view of others, shouting oaths as they–

Somehow it made it worse that Jillian had missed her tea. She was still thinking of that when the first of the 'ladies' arrived, her yellow silk kimono swishing grandly.

'Ullo, 'ullo! I'm Peony.'

Jillian glanced at the small tags on the corsets. What a complete idiot she was. She'd thought the tags bore the names of the corsets, not the women for whom they were intended. She lifted the purple corset with white lace trim.

Peony in the flesh was a brunette, with a generous mouth and black eyes. She looked more Mediterranean than English, and the deep purple would suit her, the heavy frill of white lace vivid against her olive skin. As soon as Jillian held up the corset, Peony shrugged off her kimono. She was totally nude beneath.

Jillian stilled, then cleared her throat. 'It will fit differently over your camisole and drawers.'

The woman fluttered long dark lashes and smiled coyly, holding out her arms. 'Never wear 'em.'

Well, Jillian couldn't argue against the efficiency of that. She put a few pins in her mouth, then wrapped the corset around Peony and fastened the front busk. 'Turn, please,' she mumbled around the pins and the woman did, so Jillian could tighten the laces. Peony turned again and Jillian assessed the front. Two temporary pleats at the top would have to be unpicked since the woman's breasts, like big, dusky melons, didn't fit into the gored bust without spilling over the edge.

Jillian took the pins out of her mouth. 'I'm just going to take out the stitches in the bosom darts to give a bit more ease. Won't take five minutes.'

The instant Jillian removed the corset, Peony flung herself across the top of the bed, crosswise. She unselfconsciously scratched the oval mound of her belly.

'Fine by me. Nice to be on me back without some punter on top.' Then she laughed, showing good teeth except for a missing canine on one side. She stretched up her shapely arms and rested her head on her crossed forearms. The pose gave Jillian an eyeful of the woman's treble-furred body, a thick patch of chestnut between her legs and two smaller patches under her arms.

Trying to focus on her stitch-picking, Jillian considered her own sparse pelts, which hadn't really come on until she was sixteen. She tried not to look at them when washing, but she was sure they weren't like Peony's. Peony's were wildlife. Dark brown rabbits under each arm and a luxuriant fox between her–

'Say,' Peony asked loudly, 'do you know this one?

'There was a young lady of Harrow
Who complained that her cunt was too narrow,
For time without number
She used a cucumber,
But could not accomplish a marrow!"

Peals of laughter from Peony. Jillian jabbed her middle finger with her seam ripper. She'd forgotten to bring a thimble.

Peony sat up on the edge of the bed, supporting herself on her hands and swinging her legs alternately from the knees. Up and down, up and down. 'Hold on, what about this one? "A young woman got married at Chester–"'

The door flew open, revealing Mrs Arbuthnot. 'Just what're you doing, you lazy slattern?' she barked at Peony. 'You've got Mr Pendergast waiting in Number Four!'

'All right, all right, keep your hair on.' Peony stood with a gusty sigh and snatched up her kimono. She didn't put it on, just draped it over her arm. As she swayed out the door, she said to Jillian, 'You go right on with your sewin', missy. This won't take 'alf a tick. Footie Pendergast's a thirty-second man.' She exited, laughing, ahead of Mrs Arbuthnot, who shut the door as they went out.

Alone with the purple corset in her hands, Jillian savagely unpicked stitches from one of the bosom pleats. This really was too much.

Twenty minutes later, she had both pleats unpicked, but Peony hadn't returned. She didn't know at what sport Mr Pendergast was a 'thirty-second man,' but he'd apparently let the side down. If all the Flowers took this much of her time, she'd be fitting corsets until nightfall. Night in a brothel. It was a horrifying thought, but what could she do?

She hesitantly opened the door. Not a soul around. Muffled sounds drifted from the drawing room at the top of the opposite stair flight, but she wasn't going to venture *there* again. The other doors she could see in the upper hallway were shut.

She called into the landing. 'Hello? Anyone there?'

Where was that wicked maid? Jillian pushed the door shut again. For safety's sake, she'd better stay where she was. She spotted a small, red velvet chair she hadn't noticed earlier, so she sat on it, looking around. Two large paintings hung on the walls, brass labels affixed to their ornate frames. The one opposite her chair was *Nymphs and Satyr* by William-Adolphe Bouguereau. Peter Paul Rubens' *Leda and the Swan* loomed over the bed.

Apart from the paintings, the chair, and the bed, there wasn't a great deal of what she'd call 'décor'. A cheval mirror stood in the corner. Were reflections of what happened in the room trapped in it? She'd read a story like that, once, but the trapped reflections in that mirror were quite a bit tamer than the ones she could imagine trapped in this one. Two gas lamps hissed and rattled on the wall, their flames turned down lower than she would like, but it wasn't her place to raise them. She reached into her skirt pocket, feeling for her notebook. Nothing about this room was in the *Plan*, that was certain.

The room was too warm. *Of course it's warm, you fool. People cavort around here in the nude, like a Roman bacchanal.* She fanned herself with one hand, using the other to unbutton the collar of her shirtwaist.

Min had loaned her a pocket watch and she tugged it from her skirt to confirm the time. Twenty more minutes had passed since she'd finished altering the purple corset. With the time she'd already spent on Peony – and her brief excursion to the Land of Chopin-accompanied Lust – she'd already wasted more than an hour at The Flower Garden. She still had five more corsets to fit.

She started swinging her legs up and down, like Peony. Then she stood and paced for a while. Her scalp itched and she worked her index finger into the coiled braid she'd pinned to the top of her head, trying to loosen the pins. It was one thing for Madame to tell everyone to be neat and tidy in public, but what was the point in a place where Loose was everyone's middle name?

Groaning, she tore out her hairpins and tossed them onto the bed. Then she bent over and shook out her hair, madly scrubbing at her scalp with the fingers of both hands. She straightened, looked in the mirror, and giggled. Heavy reddish-blonde waves massed around her shoulders and midway down the buttons of her shirtwaist. All she needed was a fishtail and she could be the mermaid mascot of Salon Sirena. She snatched up a few pins and made a loose twist of her hair on the crown of her head. She'd make a better job of it before she left.

She checked Min's pocket watch again. Ten more minutes had passed. She started whistling between her teeth with boredom. Whistling wasn't ladylike, but Pon had taught her to do it when she was eight and it did pass the time. She idly walked her fingers over the corsets on the bed, stopping on *Dahlia*. That was the rose one, the one Min liked so much, the only one that didn't look like it belonged on a music hall stage. She picked it up for a closer look. Quite beautiful, really, that shade of pink. Evie's work was excellent, right up to Sister Agatha's standard. And the silk brocade was so rich. Jillian stroked the cloth.

She'd never own a corset like *Dahlia*. Madame let them make their own stays in the workroom in their free time, but only in white cotton coutil, like schoolgirls wore. Even so, they were better than the ones she wore at St Margaret's. All the clothes they'd been given there were painfully dull. Linsey-woolsey undervests and knickers, not warm enough in winter, itchy in summer. Brown wool skirts and laundered-to-death cotton blouses, baggy machine-knitted stockings, shoes worn by another girl until they were outgrown.

And the corsets, ugh. Institutional drab, replaced every year.

Everything was designed to make all of them feel like what they were. No, what St Margaret's made them, made *her*. For four years, unnoticed in dull clothes, a girl whose face was turned toward a dull future.

Jillian pressed *Dahlia* to her torso. Nothing dull about it, just blooming style against her body. The corset made her feel like a woman of means, loved, desired, *noticed*. She turned up the tag. The measurements were nearly the same as hers.

She would wear it. Just for a few minutes, just so she could see herself in a garment that cost two months' wages at Salon Sirena, three at Larches. Didn't she deserve some little treat for waiting all this time while the Flowers did... whatever they did?

Like lightning, she stripped off her shirtwaist, skirt, petticoat, and boring white stays, down to her camisole and drawers. Then she loosened the laces on *Dahlia* and opened the front busk, wrapping the corset around her torso. She hooked the busk from top to bottom, tying the thin silk ribbons at the top edge to secure the join, and tugged the dyed twill laces at the back until there was only a small gap along her spine.

She looked in the cheval mirror. Wide, surprised eyes looked back, eyes in the face of a total stranger. The Jillian in the mirror... Who on earth was *she*? She couldn't be the Jillian who left the orphanage at eighteen, birdlike, undernourished. Cowed and broken, all the fight gone out of her.

Now she was twenty, and the scruffy fledgling had definitely flown away. Her arms and shoulders were creamy, smooth, and unblemished. Her neck was long and well-modelled, like a ballerina's, the oval of her face a cameo above.

She and Pon both had regular features, clear, smooth foreheads, large eyes of the same ocean-green that changed in different lights. But her eyes had somehow grown long dark lashes, and instead of Pon's wide, usually laughing mouth, she had rosy plump lips beneath her mother's slightly tip-turned nose. The shape of her mouth was Mother's too, expressing something between petulance and expectation. It was a mouth that looked – Jillian blushed, but thought it was true – like it had just been kissed and might like to be kissed some more.

Below the fragile yoke of her collarbone, full breasts were lifted by the steel boning, russet aureoles just visible above the top edge of her camisole. Jillian pushed the soft cotton garment down, into the corset, so the upper half of her bosom was exposed, nipples and all. Is that what a man would do? Reaching into her stays, large hands cupping her breasts, large fingers touching her nipples? The thought made something in her, something deep, clench and grow warm.

She let her gaze travel down the length of her body, past the bottom edge of the corset. Her camisole and drawers were ordinary cambric, but if they were laundered many more times the cloth would disappear altogether. She could almost see through the gauze-thin, overlapped placket of her knickers. There was a shadow there, between her thighs. It was hiding and not hiding, as through a veil.

Hang it, she should add another reflection to the cheval mirror, a cracking huge one.

She might not have another chance. There were mirrors at Salon Sirena, but Jillian certainly wouldn't dare disrobe in front of any of them. There was no mirror at all in the small room where she and Ada lived, the room they got the key to from that good-looking brute in Whitechapel.

Him. The deep place that had clenched before clenched again. The man was attractive, all right, but he gave off waves of danger like scent. Jillian wondered if a dangerous man like that would ever see her as she was now, an odalisque posing with a broad bed behind her, flickering gaslight making the room into a Moroccan seraglio. What would a man, *that* man, do if he saw her like this? Would he kiss her, woo her? Ask her permission to touch her? Would she give it?

Him. That's why women wore corsets like this, she knew that much. Older women, women who didn't have or didn't care about husbands, or had been seen by them thousands of times... Corsets like *Dahlia* weren't for those women. Corsets like *Dahlia* were for *men*, for their eyes, their hands, their hard bodies, their hard...

It was suddenly there, the image of the man in the drawing room just across the landing, the man pounding the bent-over woman. Jillian went to the red velvet chair and dragged it in front of the mirror, turned it around. The top of it came just to her waist. She separated her legs a little, then stood on tiptoes. Moved her legs apart a little more. Grasping the chair, she leaned over the top, pushing her hips up and back. She turned her head to look over her shoulder and–

'Oh, Papa's little *sweet cake!* You've been naughty, haven't you, poppet?'

Jillian whirled around and screamed.

Had she left the door unlatched? She must have, because she hadn't heard it open. A man was in the room now, and if The Flower Garden was a business, the man definitely meant business.

He was in his late forties, she guessed, and gone to seed, hair greying, jowls sagging, one arm out of a well-cut suit coat that dangled from his other shoulder, a large belly straining against a silk check-patterned waistcoat.

What riveted Jillian was the very considerable protrusion in the man's trousers, a protrusion he massaged casually while he kept talking. And weaving from side to side, since he was obviously drunk.

'Papa's sweet cake has been *baaad.* Now she must bend over Papa's knee and take her spanking like a brave little soldier.'

'I'm not taking anything from you, you–' Jillian wished she had Ada's street vocabulary. Ada would know what to call the man. He lunged at her and as he did, Jillian remembered the pincushion she still had on her wrist. She yanked out a needle and stabbed the man in his shirt-sleeved arm.

'Bloody hell!' The man rubbed the place where blood spotted the white sleeve. 'Well, now, if it's a pricking my little mopsy wants.' He threw himself at her again.

Jillian leaped onto the bed, scattering corsets, hairpins, and sewing tools. She screamed louder. 'Help! Help meeee!'

The man seized her ankle and grinned up into her face. The smell of liquor came off him like fumes from a gas lamp.

'Come now, poppet! If you let Papa spank you, he'll let you spank *him.*'

'I'd rather be eaten by cannibals!' She screamed a third time, so loud it felt like she'd ruptured something in her throat. She rotated her foot and contorted her ankle, trying to break the man's grip, but his hand was like an iron shackle. Lifting her other foot to kick him, she lost her balance and fell with a cry, bouncing like a tennis ball on the bed.

The man, still clutching her ankle, started to climb onto the counterpane, his free hand busy with his trousers fly. He got one knee anchored, but Jillian managed to drive her heel into the side of his head, and he slithered off the slick satin. The blow stunned him into releasing her ankle but did nothing to stop his mouth.

'Oh, you're spicy today, aren't you, dollymop! Papa will redden your little bottom for that, you minx!' He began crawling onto the bed again.

Jillian almost dived for her scissors but had a horrible vision of Sir Hubert and the carving knife. Frantic, she scrambled to her feet, spun around, and grasped *Leda and the Swan* with both hands. The picture frame was solid wood, so heavy she could barely lift it off the wall. Turning to face her assailant, she heaved the painting overhead and–

The good-looking brute from Whitechapel burst into the room.

Chapter Six

Horror, utter horror. Jillian was standing half naked on a brothel bed with the brute's startled blue eyes more or less level with her thighs. She jerked *Leda and the Swan* downward to cover her body from neck to knees.

Luckily, the man who'd just hurtled into the room was intent on something other than a seamstress with her clothes off. He seized the back of the drunken man's coat, pulling him to his feet and spinning him around. Planting broad hands on the man's shoulders, he tried to quell his struggles with reason.

'Now, now, Your Lordship, let's have none of this. You've gone into the wrong–'

His Lordship threw his fist wildly but with force at the younger man's cheek. The blow produced no effect beyond a slight jerking back of his target's head. Then, the younger man let go of the older one's shoulders, cocked his arm, and drove a massive fist into the other's jaw with an audible smack. His Lordship dropped to the carpet like a felled tree.

The silence was abrupt but not total, the young man's hoarse breathing scoring it. Like the first time she'd seen him, he was in shirtsleeves, though today he wore a plain wool waistcoat. Still no collar, and the top two buttons of his shirt had come undone in the scuffle. A triangle of ruddy chest showed in the gap, and a vein pulsed in his neck.

He shook his head – ruefully, Jillian thought. Then, he raked through his hair with both hands, curling them afterward into fists and lowering them to his sides. Was he readying himself to deal His Lordship another facer? If the old fool on the floor got to his feet, he deserved what he got.

The Whitechapel brute wasn't wearing a cap as he'd been the first time she saw him. His hair was sleek, inky as a crow's wing, and fell to his jaw. It was disordered now and hung partly over the reddening patch where he'd been struck in the face. The hair, the wild look in his eyes, the heaving chest, the balled fists – they made him look like an ancient Celt about to tear off someone's head.

'Excuse me, pardon me, if you don't mind.' Pushing her way through what Jillian was dismayed to see was a small crowd of whores and patrons in the open door, Mrs Arbuthnot stepped daintily into the scene. She might have been apologising for arriving a little late for a tea party. The niceties dissolved when she dropped into a crouch next to her unconscious customer and began rifling his pockets. From her swift and practised style, she'd done it before. Trousers, coat, waistcoat, even the watch pocket: she relieved them all of banknotes and coin.

Without a hitch in her work, she glanced up to catch Jillian staring, big-eyed. 'What are you looking at, peaches? His Lordship paid for relaxation and now he's got it.' To the brute, she ordered, 'His coach will be round the corner, like always. Pour him into it.'

She extended a beringed hand and one of the whores took it, helping the proprietress to her feet. After fluffing her skirts, she pointed to Jillian. 'Get yourself out of that corset straight away, missy,' she said tersely, the all-girls-together gone from her voice. 'I paid for it and it's mine, along with the others. And put that painting of the girl and the goose back on the wall.'

Mrs Arbuthnot swirled out of the room and the crowd of

onlookers dispersed. Everyone ignored Jillian except the blue-eyed pugilist. He spared her one raised eyebrow before he bent to the body on the floor, hauled it up with a grunt, and hefted it over his shoulders. Staggering a little under the weight, he left the room. Jillian heard him moving heavily down the stairs.

She was as wobbly as jelly on a plate, but her mind had never worked faster. *Drop Leda.* She did. *Shut the door.* She did, and for good measure pushed the red velvet chair against it. *Painting up.* Clambering back onto the bed, she somehow wrestled the heavy frame onto the wall. *Get dressed before–*

She wasn't sure before *what*, but just in case it had something to do with the black-haired, fist-throwing Whitechapel brute coming back, she needed to dress. Fast.

In record speed, she flung her sewing tools into the carpetbag and struggled into her clothes. What must he think? First, he'd picked her up from a mucky lane when she'd burst out of a shed and collapsed in a soggy mess at his feet. Now, he'd seen her teetering on a bed, in a whorehouse, in her underclothing. There were as many people in London as sardines in the sea. Why did that particular man have to see her at her worst twice in two months?

She'd barely got her own corset, petticoat, and skirt on, her shirtwaist buttoned halfway to the neck, when the man she feared would return, did. He pushed open the door as though nothing bigger than a bobbin blocked it, toppling the red chair. Without a word, he stepped over the chair, snatched up her carpetbag, and tilted his head toward the stairs.

'Wait, my–!' Jillian began, remembering her hat in the bag, but the man had already plunged out the door and was stamping down the staircase. Jillian trotted after him, leaving the deceptively respectable Georgian mansion with a black door and white pillars behind. Forever, she hoped.

The hackney cab that brought her had disappeared,

unsurprising after her 'delivery' had wasted hours. A two-wheeled pony trap waited at the kerb. The Whitechapel brute, who'd donned a jacket, she was pleased to see, tossed her bag in the trap. Without a by-your-leave, he put his hands on her waist, hoisted her up, and settled her on the seat. It was the second time he'd lifted her with no more effort than if she was an umbrella. His strength made her breathless.

He got in and the trap started moving with his gruff 'Walk on' to the pony.

After a minute or two, Jillian found her breath. Somewhat later, her voice. 'Do– do you do this often?'

He shrugged as though laying out a drunk patron, then shouldering said patron and delivering him to his carriage, was no more than waving away a swarm of gnats. 'Now and then. It's my work, after all.'

That deep, rough voice again, the green hills of Ireland, the gutters of Whitechapel. The voice she'd heard close, too close to her ear when he brought her to her feet after her faint.

'Your work. You're a– I'm sorry, I'm not sure what your correct title is.'

He sidled a glance at her. His eyes really were astonishing, like sunlight on blue ice.

'Doorman,' he answered. 'Some call it a floor man. The proprietress, Mrs A – you met her – she calls me a chucker-out. You know that American writer, Horatio Alger? He calls it a bouncer.' The young man snarled lazily out of one side of his mouth like a cowboy. 'Heave that ornery cuss out and see if he bounces.'

Jillian winced. The people she met in London added to her knowledge of the world every hour. 'You didn't, that gentleman who... did you–'

The door- floor- chucker-out bouncer man shook his head with a chuckle. 'No, course I didn't. Just helped his footman tip him, ever so gentle, into his coach, and told his driver to take him home.'

'They didn't ask any questions?'

'Not the place of servants to ask questions.'

Jillian should have remembered that.

'I'll wager they've seen their master in that condition more times than they can count. He may be a peer, but he can't hold his liquor worth a tinker's damn.'

He pulled the pony up at Leicester Square. A team of dray horses hauling an enormous wagon of beer barrels was making its ponderous way through the cross-street. The man next to her used the halt to take tobacco and papers from a pouch in his jacket and deftly roll a cigarette, putting it between his lips. He didn't light it, just spoke around it. 'Lord Somerset won't remember a thing when he wakes. With any luck he'll think he was rendered senseless by carnal discharge.'

Carnal discharge? Jillian supposed men of the sort that sat next to her said things like that on a regular basis. And what sort of man, exactly, was he? He was focused on the sluggish progress of the beer wagon, allowing her to examine him slantwise, without blatant goggling. What she saw made her want to slew around and goggle anyway.

It wasn't that she hadn't been in close quarters with men before. Her father and brother, naturally, but they didn't count. Menservants at Larches. She brushed against them now and then no matter how she tried to avoid it. Men who did work or sold things in the street. Not that she stared at labourers, and she couldn't remember scrutinising grocers or chestnut sellers. Why would she want to? Even if they attracted her notice in some way, they were men but not really *male*.

The man next to her was male. She hadn't saved enough money to buy Ada a new copy of *Wilmott's*, but she was sure when she did, she'd find the word in it. The entry would read, '*see man adjacent.*'

The man adjacent was incredibly, disturbingly male. She'd figured that much out the first time she saw him, on that rainy day in Whitechapel. His size. His muscularity. His barely harnessed power. His – she didn't know what, but there was something else about him that made him different from every other man she'd seen. Different, and more.

The seat of the trap was too small for such moreness. The two of them were so close together that her knee actually touched his trouser leg. She'd told herself not to goggle, but she couldn't stop staring at the place they touched. *His thigh. My knee.* Only some cloth between them, and so close that when the trap rocked, she could feel the iron thigh under the...

Suddenly flustered, she raised her eyes, blinking. *Oh, God.* He was looking at her. At her looking at him, at his trousers, at his *thigh. Oh, God.* Her brain was a team of runaway horses.

She jerked the team to one side. 'You called me a wet hen.'

The corner of his mouth lifted, but he looked away from her. 'I did.'

I did. Why did the bland, ordinary words sound, in her head, like *I did and I wanted to strip that wet dress off you.* Tamping down panic, Jillian feigned interest in the blocked intersection, willing the beer wagon to move. 'What's the problem with that wagon? Does it have a broken axle? Has one of the horses died?'

She couldn't blame the man for not answering; what sane person would? After a few seconds, though, he turned his head to look at her again. Even though she kept her eyes on the square, she could *feel* him looking, as though his eyes were fingers and they played over her face and body. Boldly, thoroughly, from the half-pinned hair that was falling in strands around her face to every button on her shirtwaist. Drat it all, she hadn't finished doing them up. Her hands flew to the four at the top and she fumbled at them.

He watched her every move like a hawk eyeing a mouse, deciding whether to eat the head or the tail first. Jillian swallowed uncomfortably. There were looks that were frank, direct, forthright – and there was *this*. No one had ever looked at her this way. Blood rose to her face and she cursed herself, but there was no stopping the blush. Without touching her, the man was undoing her buttons as fast as she closed them, along with all the hooks, pins, and ribbons holding her clothes on her body.

The body he'd gotten a whacking great view of when she was standing on a bed in a whorehouse in nothing but her frillies.

And, he'd caught her staring at his trousers. She could hardly shout, 'Forfend, sirrah! You are too bold!' She returned to deep interest in the square, hoping the man wouldn't speak again, but, of course, he did.

'You look better now.'

All that visual undressing, and *that* was what he came up with? Not that she gave a rat's posterior about what he said or didn't. 'Don't go overboard,' she huffed.

At first, he didn't reply. The silence stretched to a minute, wordless but thick. When he finally spoke, the words were so soft Jillian wouldn't have heard them if she hadn't been just inches away.

'Too late.' He slapped the reins and called to the pony, who walked on.

Five minutes passed without further incident, staring, or talking. Finally, the man cleared his throat. 'I'd like to know why you were... that is, what you were doing in– never mind.'

Jillian had no intention of minding. Or replying. Two more minutes passed.

'I just thought I'd ask. I mean, you were standing on the bed in your–'

'That's really none of your business.'

Another minute. He cleared his throat again. 'It's just that I have to wonder–'

'Stop talking now, please.'

Smiling his faint, *infuriating* smile, the man one-handed a match from his waistcoat pocket, flicked it alight with his thumbnail, and put the flame to his cigarette. He smoked quietly for the last part of the trip. When the trap finally halted again, it was at the Shepherd Street kerb in front of Salon Sirena. Chucking the end of his smoke into the street, the man wrapped the pony's reins on the seat rail, dismounted, and came around to help Jillian.

After the innuendo-laced journey in the trap, she should have expected she'd react when he took her hand, but it still caught her off guard. His grip was like the rest of him – smooth and rough, restrained and savage. She looked at the join of their hands and saw, with a pang, that his knuckles were bloody and skinned. All right, she might not like how he'd looked at her buttons and she certainly didn't care for that wet hen remark, but he was hurt. Because of her.

Leaning on his hand, she used the braked wheel to step down. 'Thank you,' she told him as her feet touched the ground. She hoped he knew she meant not just helping her from the trap but saving her from a drink-addled peer and getting damaged in the bargain. As long as he didn't ask again why she was on that bed in her... As long as he didn't ask that, she'd remain grateful for everything and forget all about the wet fowl and the staring and the buttons.

He kept her hand as he lifted her carpetbag out of the trap. 'It's nothing. I had to get you out of there, didn't I? Before you did murder again.'

If he hadn't still been holding onto her, Jillian might have crumpled to the pavement. '*Again?*' she bleated. 'What in the name of– What are you– How did you–'

'Ada told me about Larches.'

'Ada...' What name should she use? 'Kelly?'

'That's the one.'

Jillian yanked away her hand and the carpetbag, and bolted to the salon, thumping the door so violently with her fist that the wood vibrated. Min opened it and Jillian shoved past her, leaving her open-mouthed on the doorsill.

'Is Ada in the back?' Jillian snapped.

'Yes, she's– Why are you at the front door, Jilly? Is something wrong?'

She charged past Min toward the workroom, another kind of murder in her eyes.

Chapter Seven

Even with a blanket over the window, the light squeezed through. Kell usually slept in spite of it, but today it was a bloody persistent nuisance. Not as much of a nuisance as the thoughts that had kept him awake. There was no end to the bad things about his job at The Flower Garden, but the worst was the hours. The place roared until the door was bolted nearly at dawn, then invited new roarers in at five in the afternoon. Nearly always, Kell slept like a stone until half four, when he washed, shaved, dressed, and turned up at his post in a cupboard-like alcove of the ground floor. There, if the place wasn't too much of a madhouse, he could tilt a chair against the wall and nap for a few more hours.

He'd need that nap tonight, because there'd been no sleep for him after The Flower Garden closed this morning. That damned corset girl. How had she taken over his mind and his body so fast? From his first sight of her, shivering in a wet maid's uniform that clung to her breasts and hips, her spun-gold hair darkened by rain and her big green eyes full of fear… He'd laughed and mocked her, not wanting her or, God forbid, Ada, to see the way his tool jumped up and pressed against his trousers.

Then, to watch her comings and goings the way he'd been doing, lurking like a deviate in the alley behind the shop where she and Ada worked. That was folly through and through, and torture besides. But to see her the way he'd just seen her at The Flower Garden...

Kell groaned like a man in pain as he grabbed a washrag from the stand next to his bed. His fisted his cock, driven and ashamed to be pulling himself over a woman he'd seen in her smalls for ten seconds.

But Jesus wept! What a woman. Lord Somerset was drunk as a cockeyed fiddler but, drunk or sober, what man wouldn't have hurled himself at a vision like that? Her sweet little body, ripe as a plum, wrapped like a gift in those pink stays, her round, jiggling breasts pushed over the top edge. Ten seconds of that, while all the blood charged out of his head and into his privates, distracted him long enough to give that titled English weasel a chance to crease his cheek. Ten seconds of not being able to take his eyes off her nipples, her pert, rosy nipples, fully exposed as she stretched up her arms, ready to bring that painting down on Somerset's head.

Holy Christ, the breasts alone would have been enough to reduce him to the wanking eejit he was now, but what he saw below the corset's bottom edge...

He groaned again. Spitting on his hand, he spread the scant moisture on himself, wishing with everything in his soul that it was *her* hand, *her* wetness, the slick leavings of *her* cunny after he'd made her come, that was lubricating him. Working himself faster, he saw her wee muff as he'd seen it when she was standing on the bed. The soft-shadowed triangle between her thighs called to him, pleaded for him. It was just the size of his cupped hand and barely covered by the thin cloth of her knickers. The placket gaped slightly open, a single red-gold curl peeping out to beg for his mouth on her–

His release nearly tore the spine from his body. Every muscle clenched and he thrust forward, jerking and twitching. He usually came keen and fast, but this time it went on and on until he collapsed on the sweat-damp sheets.

Spent and panting, he took a minute to determine if any part of his body was still operational. When he finally opened his eyes, he sighed, not from desire but misery. He was still alone, still in the bare cold room at the back of the whorehouse, still abusing himself in the room that came with the job.

The job. Plenty of blokes thought Kell was uncommon lucky to have it. Mountain ranges of bosom, valleys of quim, heaving and wiggling around him six days in seven. With all that on offer, he never gave the 'flowers' a second look. He didn't blame them, the women, for what they did, what they were. A couple were lewd, a few were lazy, and one was a borderline lunatic. The rest were just desperate, doing what they had to do in order to get by. Who was he to judge, having done what he'd done to survive?

If only he hadn't spent a half hour in the pony trap taking Jillian Morehouse back to that Mayfair shop – but he had. It was both the finest and most frustrating half hour he could remember in his life.

She'd been so close he could smell her. Lavender. That and something else, a faint scent unlike any woman he'd ever been close to, and yet more woman than all of them. How could that scent unleash some rampant sexual animal in him when its source was as fresh as a meadow in spring?

His heart plummeted, bitterness rushing in, as always, to fill the abyss. Just what did he have in mind for him and her? That he could ever touch those perfect curves, those bee-stung lips? That he might ever hear her whisper his name, sob it as she came apart under him? Kell felt a stirring against his thigh.

Sufferin' saints and martyrs. He'd just emptied his brains into a washrag, and he was hard again.

He forced himself to sit up, on the edge of the bed. Time to wash, dress, and go to work. Time to shut out the sights and sounds and smells of vice in a brothel. Maybe some other punter would make trouble tonight, like Lord Somerset had. He wouldn't mind that at all, if it gave him an excuse to put his frustrated desire into his fist and hammer the man's nose or jaw until it broke.

He flexed one mighty hand, looking at the abraded knuckles where they'd pounded Somerset. That had felt good, that had. To knock the peer senseless so his filthy rich hands couldn't touch the woman on the bed, so his filthy rich eyes couldn't rape her with a look.

That thought led to another, the titled monster that Jillian Morehouse had killed with a carving knife. He wished she hadn't killed him. Disabled him, maybe, so Kell could do the killing. He rehearsed that mentally for a while and found it very satisfying, then sank again into despair. That sort of impulse, to say nothing of the skills that came with it, was why Jillian Morehouse wouldn't want anything to do with him. Ever.

He closed his eyes, opened them, and stared at the ugly, familiar walls. Just once he'd like to wake up to something other than his pathetic job and his pathetic room. Not that it was anyone's fault but his. He didn't have to be where he was, doing what he was. He'd got plenty put by, so why was he still wallowing in slime?

Easy answer. *I don't know.*

Real answer. *I belong here.* If he got too far above where he started, it'd be just that much farther to fall. When he did, which he must.

That was the way of people like him, wasn't it? Like foul Thames water, they sought their own level. His was Whitechapel. Lower. Seven Dials. He'd been resigned to that until his meddling sister brought Jillian Morehouse into his life.

Kell rose and went to the window, pulling aside the blanket that screened it from the street below. People coming and going, in wagons, hackneys, carriages, on foot. A woman with a market basket over her arm walked briskly up the pavement, pulling along a little boy with her free hand. The boy was four, five? He had black hair like Kell and his sisters. Like Andy.

What age would his little brother be now, if he'd lived? Fifteen, he'd be fifteen years old. Nearly grown, nearly a man. And Nora, the baby, she'd be twelve. The old pain burned Kell's eyes and he ground his fists roughly against them. Then he poured water from a pitcher into the washbowl and dashed it on his face and neck.

When he looked out the window again, the woman and boy were gone. Others had taken their places, the streets boiling with people, everyone rushing. Did any of them know where, to what, or why? Until he saw Jillian Morehouse standing in an alley with Ada, Kell was one of them.

Now, some strange new roads were appearing on a map in his brain, starting with a short street that led to a place he had to go, soon, or the breath would stop in his lungs.

Other than his brother and sister coming back from the dead, he'd never wanted anything as much as he wanted her.

Chapter Eight

Jillian had steamed into the workroom like a Thames ferry boat with a red-hot boiler.

'That *man!*' She flung the carpetbag onto the worktable. 'The man who gave us the key to his room, if you can call that dent-in-the-wall a room. He said you told him I had–' Ada's face warned Jillian just in time. Min came into the workroom and took her coat and hat from the wall hooks.

Min coughed behind her hand. 'I'm leaving, now.' She looked questioningly at them both, one at a time, but got silence for an answer. 'See you tomorrow,' she conceded, and scurried out the back door into the alley.

The instant the door closed, Jillian went back to her tirade. 'You told him I had done...' Words failed her. Even with Min gone, she couldn't say it out loud.

'He's my brother.'

'Your what?'

'Brother. Same mother. Not always but, in this case, same father. Grew up together. Calls me sister. Pret-ty simple, Jillian.'

'Your brother. What's he doing in– in a–'

'Whorehouse? Even simpler.' Ada held up her hand and ticked

off fingers with the other one. 'Wanted employment. Saw a notice. Had an interview. Bob's your uncle.'

Deflated, Jillian sank into a chair at the worktable. Ada took both their coats off the wall hooks and handed Jillian hers.

She clucked with irritation and took the coat, remembering but not caring that her hat was still in the carpetbag.

Ada kept speaking as she pinned on her own hat. 'For all I know, Jilly, you murder six people a week, Sundays only off for church. But Larches, that was my first. I didn't think... well, I still don't think it's somethin' we can do alone.'

Jillian started to ask why Ada thought her brother was the right person to share murder with, but then she remembered the way he handled the drunk patron at The Flower Garden. And the rest of it, the rest of him. The broad shoulders, the muscle-corded arms, the fist like a piledriver, the dangerous eyes. If she had to interview accessories to murder after the fact, Ada's brother really should vault to the top of the list.

She pulled on her coat. 'What's his name, your brother?'

'Michael Seraphin Kelly.'

'*Seraphin?* You mean like the–'

'Right, yeah. Our mother's got a fixation, like, about angels. Archangels, actually.'

'Really?' Jillian looked sceptically at Ada. 'What's your–'

'I'll say it once, Jilly, and then we won't never mention it again. It's Saraqael.'

Saraqael. Even after years in a Catholic orphanage, Jillian didn't recognise that heavenly being. She retrieved her hat from the carpetbag and followed Ada out the door to the alley.

Outside, Ada fidgeted with the key. 'Here's the thing, Jilly. My brother, he's had some hard times. We all did, when we was younger. He did what he had to– what he needed to. There was some rough years and some rough mates, that's all I'm sayin', know what I mean?'

Jillian wasn't at all sure she knew, but nodded. 'Was he in trouble with the law?'

'Not my tale to tell. Anyway,' she finally got the key to turn in the lock, 'about his name. Everybody calls him Kell.'

———

By the next morning, the storm seemed to have passed, but a charge, like high voltage, hung in the air at Salon Sirena. Ada was still defensive and Jillian was still confused.

The Whitechapel brute, Kell, was Ada's brother. He had bad things in his past, but Jillian hadn't any idea what they were, and Ada didn't seem inclined to tell her. Would he tell Ada what he'd seen in The Flower Garden? Probably. Would Mrs Arbuthnot tell Madame? Probably not. After all, Jillian had seen the proprietress robbing one of her customers, so, of a certainty, she and Mrs A had the goods on each other.

How on earth had her life become so complicated?

She tried to sort it while morning activity swirled around the periphery of her thoughts. A steady parade of clients, all wealthy and some titled, came and went, most of them impelled to the salon by a Royal Choral Society gala in a month. Every woman of means in London seemed to want new clothing from the skin up.

In just over three hours, Madame tacked nine new orders on a corkboard in the workroom. Constant background twitter came from the showroom, women chattering about colour, fabric, and style. The corset girls barely noticed. Then, around noon, a deep male voice carried to the back and paralysed them all with surprise.

Evie nudged Min, who had the lightest footstep. Min tiptoed to the drape and peered around the edge. 'It's a man,' she whispered, and the other three rolled their eyes.

'We already know that!' Ada whispered back.

Min pushed up her spectacles and took a second look. 'Not old, but not young. A gentleman, I'd say, or perhaps not. Dressed very nicely. Doesn't seem to be a commercial traveller. Or, I suppose he could be, of the better class, but...'

'Burnin' bustles, Min!' Ada went to the curtain and pushed her aside. 'With you lookin', we'll die of old age before we know anything.' Ada put her eye to the gap.

A long minute passed, while not a needle moved nor a ribbon furled. Then Ada said just one word, scathingly, and Jillian's skin went all over gooseflesh. '*Copper.*' Ada abruptly flapped her hand behind her and darted back to her place at the worktable.

All four corset girls were industriously sewing, heads down, when Madame jerked aside the drape and barked, 'Min, Evie! Take your lunch.' Madame jabbed her finger toward the back door of the shop. 'Now!'

Min and Evie snatched their coats and hats off the wall and flew from the workroom, darting fearful backward glances at Ada and Jillian.

Madame continued to hold the drape open as a man entered, the gentleman-not-gentleman Min had described. Jillian and Ada both stood, unsure of what else to do. Madame let the drape fall, staying on the showroom side. And listening, no doubt, but Jillian couldn't say if that was good or bad.

Listening or not, Madame had to know already what the man said first. 'My name is Ewan Exeter. I am a detective inspector with the Metropolitan Police.' His voice was cool and smooth, a bit clipped, very cultured. Not a born-to-it upper class accent, but a carefully nurtured one. Not what Jillian expected from a policeman, even a ranking one.

Exeter gestured toward the worktable. 'Please, be seated, ladies.' Ladies? Was he flattering or insulting them? 'I have a few questions for you. About Sir Hubert Alloway.'

Ada sat like a normal person sits. Jillian collapsed into her chair as though dropped from a height. Exeter slid easily into Evie's place. With detached interest, he examined the work in front of him, a pale pink and cream Number Seven that Evie had been stitching. When he looked up, Jillian saw his eyes were disconcertingly fine, grey with black lashes. The eyes were the most handsome feature of a lean, cleanly shaven face under ash-blond, close-cropped hair.

Jillian sneaked a look at Ada. She was holding a seam ripper in a white-knuckled grip and glaring at the inspector like she wanted to stab the pointed little implement into his handsome eye. Not the impression a possible suspect should give to a policeman. Jillian reached under the worktable to pinch her friend's thigh, but before she could, Ada surged to the offence.

'We don't know nothin' about that business. We was just in service.'

Exeter's reply was immediate but wordless. He reached inside his jacket and removed a folded sheet of paper. Unfolding it, he reached a long arm over Evie's Number Seven and placed the paper on the table in front of Ada and Jillian. Jillian stared stupidly at Exeter's jacket sleeve, fine quality tweed in a heather grey that almost matched his eyes. A few inches of brilliant white cuff extended beyond the sleeve.

Ada didn't even blink at the paper. Jillian tore her gaze from Exeter's sleeve and leaned forward to read the crabbed writing in thick pencil.

Deer Mr Cruikshank. My friend Jillian Morehouse and me is handing in our notice effective imediate. We are respektabel young women and cannot remane in a house where murdurs is happening.

Respekfuly, Adaline Kelly

'What– how– when did you...' Jillian sputtered at Ada like a paraffin lamp running out of fuel.

Exeter's fingers anchored the top edge of the note. He deliberately pulled it back, folded it, and returned it to his inside jacket pocket.

'It was quite right to hand in your notice, Miss *Gubbins-Kelly*.' The inspector's comment was ironic but not harsh. Even so, Jillian detected a faint hum of threat. She thought wildly of crocodiles, smiling in the shallows.

'No house, however exalted, can be appropriate for young women like you and Miss Phipps, or is it Morehouse? Not after a violent incident like the one at Larches.'

Exeter's grey eyes drifted from Ada to Jillian. Stayed on Jillian. She spun in a cyclone of emotions: fear, confusion, defiance, doom. She also had the excruciating sensation that Exeter had taken the corset in front of him off her body and was examining the woman he had undressed. Even a complete halfwit would say blushing was a bad idea in the moment, but heat spread like a flash fire into her neck and face.

Ada leaned back in her chair, both casual and truculent. 'We,' she raised her chin toward Jillian, 'left as soon as the ruckus started. Once we heard Mr C say there was a body bleedin' out in the scullery, we didn't need the particulars, if you get my drift.'

Exeter nodded. 'You wrote the note before you left the house?'

Ada scowled. 'No, first we left. Then, we sent the note. What do think we shoulda done? Us bein' decent women as has a right to protect ourselves, the fact bein' a murderin' thug mighta still been hidin' in the linen cupboard. After we left, I wrote the note and got it took round there.'

'To Larches.'

Ada nodded, once.

Jillian tried to piece it together. How long was she alone in that leaky shed in Whitechapel? A long while, long enough for Ada to have done any number of things, one of which was finding paper and pencil, drafting the note, and sending a messenger off with directions to Larches.

Exeter was talking again, to them both. 'You weren't concerned that leaving in such a manner would deprive you of references?'

Ada answered with a shrug. She still had hold of the seam ripper, but now she was flipping it in her fingers, over and around like a baton. 'As you can see, *Inspector Exeter*, we got employment.'

Exeter ignored Ada's ironic inflection. He straightened in his seat and surveyed the room. 'So you did.' His survey came around to Jillian and latched onto her again. 'What about you, Miss Morehouse? Were you in agreement that the note should be sent by messenger to the butler at Larches?'

How was she supposed to answer that? Exeter already knew her real name. Did he also know she hadn't known about the note, still less how and when Ada sent it? Or did he think she knew but wasn't saying, or that maybe it was her idea all along? She'd better stay as close to the truth as possible, in case she needed later to remember what she said.

'I wasn't aware at the time that Ada – Miss Kelly – had sent the note. I was shocked by what had happened. It was horrible. Surely you understand why we couldn't stay at Larches.'

A faint neutral smile crossed Exeter's face. 'And you noticed nothing out of the ordinary when you left the house? No one who should not have been there, no one in the park or in the street?'

Ada's mouth pulled down and she shrugged again. 'We was workin', I told you. And then we left. We didn't see nothin'.'

Exeter barely registered Ada's response. His cool eyes slid to Jillian, watching, waiting, unnerving her, so that his next question took her unawares.

'Why are the two of you working now under assumed names?'

Thank God, Ada was primed with another response, since Jillian had nothing. 'They're our names.' She raised and dropped a shoulder dismissively. 'We can do what we want with 'em, can't we? An' we didn't want to be, you know, connected up with that, uh, with the...'

'Fatal knife wound to the throat of your employer?'

Jillian didn't think the act could sound as bad anywhere as it did in her head, but when a detective inspector from Scotland Yard said it, it sounded worse.

Ada tossed her head. 'I was goin' to say *scandal*.'

'I won't disagree with you there, Miss Kelly. Everything about Sir Hubert Alloway was, I am sorry to say, scandalous.' Exeter pushed back his chair.

Ada and Jillian stood when the inspector did. On his feet, Exeter was imposing. Lean and fit in his tweed suit and crisp linen, he still gave off that hum of threat, like a well-tailored wolf. Jillian had seen wolves at the London Zoo, once. Exeter, with his sharp, slate eyes and grey-blond hair, his watchful way of standing and moving, could easily slip among them.

Suddenly, Jillian realised the inspector's hand was extended. She reached for it, uncomfortably. His was dry, warm, and hard. Hers was cold, limp, and trembling. Still thinking about wolves, she missed the first part of what he said as he pressed her fingers once, firm but brisk, then dropped them. Throughout, he kept talking, and with a shock she realised he was still looking directly at her. Why just her? Did he know something? Did he want her to know he knew?

'...file on this matter will be closed soon, as there is scant interest in prolonging it and other more pressing cases await the force's attention. Sir Hubert had little family and few friends, fewer still in high places.' Jillian wondered how many low places the inspector had gone to find Sir Hubert's friends.

'However, if either of you recalls anything, anything at all, that might help us in our investigation, please do not hesitate to contact me.' Exeter extracted a card from his jacket breast pocket and handed it to Jillian.

Again, something just for her. She took the card. Not knowing what to do with it, she slipped it into her skirt pocket, under her apron. After the handshake and the card, her fingers tingled like she'd grazed a pressing iron.

Exeter nodded curtly to them both and left the workroom through the drape. They heard a few words in his baritone to Madame, and her indistinct reply. Then the salon front door opened and closed.

Madame didn't come back to the workroom. Ada didn't comment on the inspector's pointed and particular attention to Jillian, but her narrowed eyes and pursed mouth said it hadn't escaped her. Just as Ada's jaundiced expression and goading manner toward Exeter hadn't escaped Jillian.

'Do you know him?' Jillian whispered, 'The inspector?'

Ada didn't answer and Jillian didn't press her. Neither of them commented again on what had just happened; how could they? For all they knew, Madame or Ewan Exeter or the Prime Minister still had ears to the drape. They sat, picked up their work, and sewed. Not a word passed between them until Min and Evie came back.

Chapter Nine

Kell wasn't building a wardrobe for Jillian Morehouse. He was building it for Ada. God knows, his sister had pestered him enough times for it. The fact that Jillian Morehouse was sharing the room with Ada was pure coincidence.

Giving them the room in the first place – that was intentional. He knew he had to give them the room the second he saw the look in Jillian's eyes that day in Whitechapel. He'd just met the woman, but the look–? He'd known the look too well and too long, from the years he'd spent one step ahead of the law. Those years taught him he always needed a bolt-hole, a cranny, a squirrel's nest. It was why he still hung on to this miserable hide in Soho, even though he didn't have to, since he had living quarters at The Flower Garden. But the Soho room was cheap, and no one had a key to it.

Until now. Now, three people had a key and, just like before, one of them was a lawbreaker. Two of them, if he counted his sister and what she had done to cover up the lawbreaking. The Jacks take care of their own.

He'd nicked the planks for the wardrobe from a building site a few streets away. The builders wouldn't notice the loss or, if they did, they wouldn't say anything about it. Kell knew their game.

Buy more than you need for the job, chalk it up to the client, sell the excess or use it for another job. Write up an invoice for the other job, charging for materials someone else had already paid for and were at the ready for nought. Do the whole thing again. Kell just dropped a link of his own into that rotating chain of thefts.

A half mile. That's how far he figured he'd carried the planks on his shoulders. People shouted and cursed as he blocked the pavement. A few horses shied at him going around corners, and one cab driver threatened to take out Kell's eye with his whip. Somehow, he and the planks got to the tenement and went up four flights of stairs.

He'd buckled a leather belt over his trousers and had a hammer, a handsaw, and a sack of nails hanging from the belt. Getting himself, the tools, and the planks through the door of the room was awkward and noisy. Luckily, either no one besides him was in the building or no one felt inclined to beat Kell's brains out for making a racket.

Inside the room, he dropped everything on the floor and stood breathing heavily for a minute. Carrying the planks had made deep red creases in his arms and shoulders. He stretched and flexed them before getting to work.

With a wardrobe, the women could at least hang their clothes properly. They shouldn't have to stack them on the one chair or quadruple hang them on the single wire hook on the back of the door. Kell would get some clothes hangers later and drop them off. Whatever he knocked together today wouldn't be much of a wardrobe, but then, it wasn't much of a room.

Even 'room' might be dignifying an eight-by-ten box with a bed and an ancient chair, one window, and a single gas lamp on the wall. A wash bowl and pitcher occupied a table the size of a tea tray. The wood floorboards were as stained as a pawnbroker's conscience. A sordid hutch of a room, but at the time he'd furnished it, he hadn't planned on inviting any cabinet ministers to visit with him.

It did sport a bookcase, a rickety item he'd dragged out of a tip and wedged between the bed and the table. Most of his books had gone with him to The Flower Garden, but a few were still in the bookcase. *The Count of Monte Cristo. Ivanhoe.* A battered collection of Shakespeare's plays. Kell edged around the bed to run his hand over the familiar spines. His fondness for them went far beyond their contents, since their authors had raised him from the slum of his birth. Donne and Dryden and Dumas. Swift and Smollett and Scott.

In the past, he'd done without new collars and resoled his shoes again and again, just so he could buy books. Just to stand on the shoulders of those authors to see the world, to move within it as a literate man. He'd chosen this very tenement for a room because it was close to the jumbled shops on Wardour Street, where second-hand books were as plentiful as raindrops.

He still read nearly every night, and had plenty of money for books, now. Someday, in his own home, he'd build bookcases in every room.

Did Jillian Morehouse like to read? Did she read the books he'd left at night before sleeping, the way Kell read between chucking patrons out of the whorehouse? Did her beautiful hands hold volumes he had held, turning the same pages? Did she smile or feel moved by words that had made him smile and feel? Maybe he'd ask her if she'd like more books.

Fucking hell, he could barely summon the nerve to speak to her, much less question her reading habits. Now he stood in a room that used to be his but would never be his again. Everything in it would have some latent trace of her. He'd never again be able to rest here. He'd have to give it up, no great loss.

Kell turned away, assessing the subtle changes in the room. It looked better with two women living in it than one untidy man, that was clear. Ada and Jillian... Their clothes might not be properly hanging, but everything was neat. Over the worst of the plaster cracks in the walls, an inch wide and two feet long, they'd tacked a Pears Soap calendar with a print of two tykes bathing a pup. The attempt to make something only a little better than a prison cell look homey was both absurd and touching. They'd given the room's sole window a good clean from the inside and, for the first time, Kell could see something besides London grime through it.

The women's undergarments were folded on the one chair, its ruptured seat covered with a piece of tissue paper from the salon so the delicate items wouldn't get soiled or torn. Kell refused to linger on the lawn drawers, the simple but lace-edged petticoats; some of them were his sister's, for God's sake.

He went back to the pile of planks, picked one up, and started building.

Two hours later, he'd done enough to justify a rest. He rolled a cigarette and opened the creaking window to let the reek of tobacco escape.

Sitting on the sill and smoking, he thought with a mix of disgust and wonder about what in his mind he was calling his 'condition'. He'd never been overthrown by his attractions or even by lust. But this, this *anarchy* of emotion... To have seen so little of Jillian Morehouse and yet so much, to have barely touched her and yet think of nothing but touching her... It was madness, like a sailor sighting a mermaid in the distance and flinging himself into the sea with desire.

The way they'd sat close in the pony trap haunted him. He kept reimagining it, and every version got more licentious. Why was it that every time he saw her and himself in his mind, she was naked, or he was? Lately, it had been both. Stripped bare, together, embracing. Wrapped around each other and straining, arching, screaming their release into each other's mouths.

Christ, it was hot in the room. Kell flicked what was left of his cigarette out the window.

For days, he'd thought about the touch of her knee against his thigh when they'd sat in the trap. He'd been desperate for her not to realise they were touching and move away, as though she had a choice of places, as in a railway coach. She stared at the spot where they touched, and he saw her staring. She didn't even try to move. He sat there, his cock thickening, the whole world telescoping down to the few inches where their bodies pressed together. In the whorehouse, he'd seen what she wore under her skirt, the skirt that was touching him on the seat. The soft, nearly transparent cloth of her drawers, the round flesh of her thighs under them. Right there, next to him, on the pony trap seat.

And then, unable to stand it anymore, he'd lifted his gaze, only to see the open buttons of her shirtwaist. If he tried, he could remember how many buttons, could count them in memory. Now, he shut his eyes and saw her fingers rush to close the top ones when she realised she'd not finished dressing before he hurried her out of the brothel and into the trap.

He had to hurry. He had to get her out of there. She didn't belong in that house of filth. She belonged somewhere clean and private. Clean, private, and with him, where he could do filthy private things to her.

Back to the buttons. She was closing them one by one as she sat next to him in the trap. Her little hands so near, inches away. Closing the buttons but, in his fantasy, she was opening them. Three, four, how many would it take before he could slide his hand into the opening, fingers brushing the lace edge of her camisole, the satiny curve of her bosom. He would take over her unclothing, stripping the shirtwaist from her body. Then, he'd unhook the top of her corset busk, opening it wide so he could reach in and cup her breast, capture her nipple, ease it over the top of the stays...

Kell shook his head, futilely trying to clear it. His 'condition' was stamping and snorting like a bull. He was stiff as a sailor on shore leave, his balls aching. It wasn't just the woman's clothing that starved his brain of blood, it was her hand, too. He wanted to go back in time, to the moment he moved to help her down from the trap, when she gave her hand to him. It was small, white, and smooth. She was a seamstress, she had strong hands. He wanted to see them wrapped around his shaft, wanted those sleek, expert hands to tug and stroke until he lost himself on her fingers.

Open your eyes, you madman. Breathe. Kell forced himself to stare out the window and read the signs on the shops across the street. Meecham's Sundries. Griswold & Son, Boots and Shoes. D. Farnsworth, Butcher.

Taking deep breaths like a yogi and reading shop signs with the fervour of ten Hail Marys... *Mother of God, you're a sorry mess, Michael Kelly.* Nothing worked to quell his arousal, anyway; he was still engorged. The last thing he needed to do was look at the bed, so–

He pivoted on the windowsill to look at the bed. Just looking at it made him throb, but he was determined to ignore it. *Only a bed, you moron.* Iron head and foot rails, slathered in chipped white paint. Dark blue wool blanket, just the one. Plain linens, turned down over the blanket at the top. Size... Neither woman was big, so he guessed they managed it all right. When he'd slept there, he barely fit and his feet stuck out through the foot rail. If he pulled up his feet and bent his knees, he nearly fell off every time he rolled over in his sleep.

The women had made the bed before they went to work. There didn't seem to be much point to his making the bed in the room where he slept now. Tried to sleep. Tried not to think of how empty the room and his life were.

The women hadn't plumped their pillows, though. There were still depressions where their heads lay during the night. Kell thought he should stay exactly where he was and roll another cigarette, so–

He left the windowsill and went to the bed, a matter of two

strides. Which pillow was Jillian's? It would be convenient if there were a red-blonde hair... Ah, there it was. Just where he hoped he might find it. Because picking up the wrong pillow and pressing his face into it when it was his sister's... Saints in heaven, it was bad enough to be what he was without being an incestuous bastard as well.

The pillow on the right was Jillian's. Even without the single hair, he would have known the second he picked it up, for the same scent of lavender water the pillow and she gave off. Not strong, just enough. He knew where she got it, where all the shop assistants and maids and factory girls got it. Canny blokes bought the down-to-the-dregs bottles of rose and lavender *eau de cologne* from barbers, then filled the bottles with water and let them sit for a day. Decanted into whatever containers the girls brought, the reconstituted cologne was sold for thruppence a pint.

He'd like to buy her a fresh bottle from a chemist, one that wasn't the leavings from a barbershop. He couldn't, of course, she'd take offence, but he could think about it.

He brought the pillow to his face and shut his eyes, inhaling. Blood charged into his prick and it nudged against his trouser placket. Every perverse thought a man could have about a woman filled his mind. It made him sick with shame but at the same time he couldn't stop himself.

He wanted her under him. He wanted her sweet and open, her mouth whispering his name, her hair spread over the bedsheets like a Viking hoard of gold. The pillow in his hands... He'd put it under her hips, raising her up so that when he lay down on her, went into her, the length of him would go all the way to her womb.

His mouth parched and he fought to swallow. For a terrible instant, he had an urge to unbutton his trousers and rub the pillow against himself. He could come that way, he knew it. He could purge his balls into the soft mound of feathers and cloth, imagining it was a peach-furred cunny between smooth, creamy thighs.

A strangled low cry came from his throat as he savagely pitched the pillow, bouncing it off the wall. He stood, shocked at himself, his lungs working like bellows. *You sick fuck. Stop this. Stop it now.* He let his head fall back and focused on a stained patch of ceiling plaster while he counted backwards from a hundred.

Jillian Morehouse wasn't for him. She was a tidy parcel of pretty and polite. From Hertfordshire, Ada said. She smelled of flowers. Kell was a bruiser from Whitechapel. He smelled of sawdust and laundry soap.

He didn't deserve her. He'd told himself that over and over, from the first moment he saw her. With all the repetition, the words should have gotten louder, more convincing, a speech shouted by a Hyde Park orator. Instead, they weakened. Saying them more often wasn't making them stronger.

What would it take to deserve her? Those were the loud words now. Loud and followed by a vow that whatever it was, whatever it took, he would do it. He had to. Because on the other side of the Jillian Morehouse who didn't want him, there was nothing at all.

Twenty-nine, twenty-eight, twenty-seven. The spasm passed. He crossed the room and picked up the pillow, then returned with it to Jillian's side of the bed, where he dusted it carefully. Just as carefully, he put it in place, using the back of his hand to make a depression like the one the sleeper's head had made the night before.

When he'd first snatched up the pillow, the single amber hair that had lain on it was jostled off. It lay now on the blanket, a barely visible *S* against the dark blue wool. He wouldn't have noticed, except the light from the window struck the hair and it glittered like a new penny.

He took it up delicately and began winding it around the tip of his thumb. He'd never seen Jillian's hair loose but, judging from the many turns he made with the one strand, it was long, to her waist, at least. Long, short, thick, thin, light, dark – Kell hadn't thought much about women's hair before now. He decided he only liked it long. Long and the colour of the hair in his hand.

He finished the coil around his thumb. The trifling, gentle act somehow collared his rampant desire. Still potent but calm, the need of Jillian Morehouse wasn't a bull, anymore, but a plough horse, subdued and bending its neck for the halter. For today, for now.

He worked the coil off his thumb and held it up so the sun from the window shone on and through it. It looked to him like a gold ring, a wedding ring. Before Jillian Morehouse, he would have mocked the notion, mocked any man who had it as a love-addled pillock, then laughed for a week.

Not laughing now. Kell took his pocket diary out of his trousers pocket and slipped the hair inside, carefully folding over a page to protect it. He picked up his tools and went back to hammering on the wardrobe.

As he put in the last nail and tested the clothes bar, his thoughts were all about love at first sight and if it was real. He decided it was, it had to be.

If not, he was going insane.

Chapter Ten

'Oh!' It was no kind of greeting, but Jillian was entirely startled.

She and Ada were halfway down the tenement stairs on their way to the salon. Suddenly, there he was, Ada's brother. On the stairs, boldly walking up like he lived there. Which he had at one time, but that was beside the point. They all halted in mid-passage, Jillian and Ada a few steps above the brother. He stared, only at Jillian, and in the gloomy stairwell his eyes were blue phosphorus.

Ada was nonchalant, as though they hadn't met a large obstacle impeding their egress. 'I'll be outside.' She briskly went around the obstacle, not speaking to it, and headed for the street.

Anxiety rippled under Jillian's breastbone as Ada's feet thudded on the stairs. 'Oh! A-Ada?' Why was she stuttering? She struggled to breathe. Why was she breathless? It was just Ada's brother. But why was he here? And why had Ada left her alone on the stairs with him? It was... inappropriate.

'I thought you could use these.' The brother held out his arm. A dozen wooden clothes hangers hung from it like pretzels on a street vendor's stick. 'I'll get more if you need them.' His voice was low and ragged, he sounded tired.

'Oh!' *Stop saying that, Jillian. You sound like an imbecile.* 'That's very thoughtful of you. Ada and I, we're just going out. To work.' Where else would they be going at half eight in the morning, to the opera?

He didn't react to her imbecility, just pointed out, 'I have a key.'

Of course he had a key. If he hadn't a key, he couldn't have built the... 'Thank you for the wardrobe, Mr Kelly.'

'Kell. My name is Kell.'

'I, uh, well, we scarcely know each other.'

'You've been sleeping in my bed for months.'

Now, that *was* inappropriate. Though technically true.

'I've been sleeping *there*, with your sister.'

He smiled that blasted smile of his. Innocent as a child, lethal as a runaway fire. It infuriated her that even when she warned herself not to react, there was something about his mouth... Whatever it was, it was too close now. If Jillian put her hand out, she could touch the bristle that darkened his upper lip and his chin. What would it feel like, that bristle, if his face grazed hers, if he kissed her? Heat bloomed under her corset busk. This was wrong, all wrong. She shouldn't be thinking about Michael Kelly's bristle, about any of his parts.

'Sleeping with my sister. I see.' His whisper slipped under her shirtwaist to keep her corset busk company. 'If I find my sister somewhere else to sleep, will you consider allowing me...'

Jillian jerked up her chin and looked down her nose. 'You are insufferable, Mr Kelly.' *Also too close, too warm, too male.* She tried to move around him, but he sidled over to prevent her passing. 'Let me get by, please.' It was alarming, the way her voice wobbled. With fear? Anger? Something else?

He stepped aside and she fled down the stairs. She had to get away from him and out of the building while she still could. While she still wanted to.

The air in Soho was the opposite of healthful, but Jillian took a huge, relieved lungful of it as she burst out the street door of the tenement and onto Audley Street. Of all the brass-plated, steam-driven, unmitigated nerve! Ada's brother making sly quips about his bed, standing there with an armful of clothes hangers, blocking her way down the stairs with his tall... his big... his muscular...

Was it Michael Kelly's body that turned her into a blithering idiot whenever she was around him? No. Yes. Not entirely. There was something else about him, something barely held back... Oh, pig feathers, she didn't know what it was.

She deftly swerved around people rushing, like her, to various jobs and shops, meetings and cafés. Soho wasn't a place anyone loitered unless they were up to no good, and she had no intention of lingering in the street for trouble to find her.

It was a blister of inconvenience that Ada had stayed behind to speak with her brother. What on earth could she have to say to him that she couldn't have said on the stairs?

'Just go on,' she'd told Jillian, who was pushing out the street door after her own nonsensical chat on the stairs with the brother. 'I'll catch you up.'

They should have set out together, as always, and they would have, were it not for Michael Kelly.

Who was Michael Kelly, anyway? How had he gone in such a short time from a complete stranger to someone who ratcheted up her heartbeat and made her mouth go dry, while she swung between fever and chills like a malaria victim?

Michael Kelly was someone she need not concern herself with. His name didn't appear in any sentence of any paragraph on any page of the *Plan*. She needed to be more disciplined.

Admittedly, discipline would be easier if she didn't keep encountering those disturbing eyes and those broad shoulders, but she supposed that couldn't be helped. She was bound to run into the man, he was Ada's brother. But to her? Nothing, no one. He was not now, and never could be. She needed to remember that.

Just five more minutes to the salon if she hurried. She'd crossed into Mayfair and the morning foot traffic flowed and eddied around her. Jillian had never noticed before how many people were in the streets in the morning. She'd always been with Ada, chatting about work, what they would do that day, orders to fill, Madame to placate.

A large man passed so near that his shoulder knocked against her. 'I *beg* your pardon!' she snapped at the man's back, then hugged her handbag and umbrella to her chest.

She wasn't the only woman alone in Mayfair at this time of day, but there weren't very many. Even the shop girls seemed to travel in pairs or groups. The better class of women, if not with others of their sort, were all accompanied by husbands, brothers, fathers, in some cases footmen or maids carrying parcels.

Before she'd come to London, she hadn't given much thought to being a woman alone in the city. It wasn't something she'd ever envisioned. There had been home, and then St Margaret's, and then service. Now, the salon and the room she shared with Ada. She was never alone anywhere, really, so why even consider it?

A man was standing in front of the newsagent's stall on the corner nearest the salon, and he was looking directly at her. Something about the way he looked, *leered*, actually, gathered all the unease she felt into one dark knot in her stomach. London's vague but ever-present unknowns, the thousand threats that gathered at the fringe of her awareness like a swarm of wasps... They were all there, in the bold stare of his black eyes and the sneer on his swarthy face. Even the scarlet neckerchief above his shirt collar seemed like a warning, an omen.

She pulled her jacket front together with the same hand that gripped her umbrella. As she neared him, the man pursed his lips and made a low, smacking noise at her, the sound you make when you're calling a dog. Or kissing someone.

It's just a noise. A shiver ran through her body anyway. She hated the tremor she got whenever she came face to face with her aloneness, the metropolis churning around her like a huge and deadly machine. The tremor wasn't like her, and the most alarming thing was that it wasn't fear, not exactly.

It was something inside her struggling to get out. The something wanted to shout at the man, lunge at him, put panic into his too-bold eyes. It wanted to hit him over the head with her umbrella, push him over, and beat him like a carpet.

She straightened her spine and walked briskly past the man. What was happening to her? She'd never, in her past, had such a feeling, had felt that something bestial crouched just behind the gentle manners her parents taught her.

'There is in most tempers a natural ferocity which wants to be softened.' That was from *Decorum, A Practical Treatise on Etiquette and Dress*. Her mother gave her the book when Jillian was thirteen and seemed to be developing more sauce than seemliness. She'd read it and even memorised passages from it. One hundred pages of pithy encomiums on ladylike behaviour and ladylike attitudes. There was more to that dictum about temper in the book, but only the part about 'natural ferocity' seemed to make sense to her now. Jillian felt both queasy and vindicated. Her ferocity didn't want to be softened. It wanted to *roar*.

She glanced to her left, up an alley between two buildings, a dozen yards from the salon. A roughly dressed man was urinating against one of the buildings. He was close enough that Jillian smelled the yellow stream as it fountained against the bricks.

She averted her eyes and dashed for the door of Salon Sirena.

The nearness of her as she passed him on the stairs had almost made Kell drop the blasted hangers and seize her in his arms. She flounced away, head high, feet tapping on the stairs. Every tiny drumbeat of her heels drove something hard and hopeless into his heart. He heard her go out the street door.

No point in dawdling on the stairs. It wasn't as though the dance chorus from The Gaiety was going to pass him on their way to rehearsal. He didn't give a fig if they did. The star of the show had already said her dozen words to him and pranced off.

Kell climbed to the landing and opened the room with his key. The scent of lavender hit him as he crossed the threshold and if some rugger hurled a ball into his face, it wouldn't make him any dizzier. He put the clothes hangers in the new wardrobe, wondering if he could make an excuse to come back and build a shelf near the bottom, for shoes.

Enough torture for today, mate. He left the room, locked the door, and went dispiritedly down the stairs. What a bleeding halfwit he was. Why was it that every time Jillian Morehouse got within arm's reach he turned into a ten-year-old boy, pulling a girl's pigtail or dangling a frog in her face to make her squeal? Like he'd just done, making jokes about his bed. If she never spoke to him again, it would be exactly what he deserved. He was a lout. Had he totally forgotten how to speak to a decent woman? Apparently, he had.

It was that voice of hers, that was the spell she worked on him. Every word she said wrapped another coil of velvet rope around his heart and squeezed until he thought it would burst. All he could think of when she was near was asking her something, telling her something, just to make her respond. Just to keep that voice wrapped around him while he went weak with its sweet promise.

She would speak to him again, wouldn't she?

He left the tenement by the street door. His sister was just outside, her face like thunder, and she didn't waste any time. 'You can't keep doin' this.'

Kell looked up and down the street in both directions. 'Where did she go?'

'To our employment. Where I should be, except I'm here, yammerin' at my eejit brother.'

'You should have gone with her.'

'It's broad daylight and Mayfair is a quarter hour away.'

'There's crime in Mayfair.'

'True, but not like Seven Dials.'

Fast as yanking a drape across a window, memory threw darkness between them. They both took its measure, he from his side and she from hers. Ada, who had the greater hunger for light, made the first cut through, as she usually did. 'You can't keep doin' this,' she repeated.

'Doing what?'

Ada's mouth twisted as though she was trying not to spit on the pavement. 'Don't play innocent with me, Kell. I know you're followin' her around.'

'I'm following you both around. London's not a safe place.'

'Safer now the Jacks ain't operatin'.' Blue eyes fixed on blue ones, sparks of anger in them both. 'Or are they?'

'The Jacks are dead and gone, sister.'

Ada wasn't soft, but her next words weren't as hard as the ones before. 'That bein' so, you got no excuse for not tellin' her. If you feel somethin' for her, Kell, you'd better tell her now. And I know you feel somethin'. Jillian's not just some lightskirt.'

As fraught as the conversation was, Kell gave Ada a fleeting smile. 'I'm not sure that word's been used since the reign of George the fourth, but no, Ada, she's not a lightskirt, and yes, Ada, I feel something for her.'

Habit made Kell pat his jacket pocket, even though the gesture was as empty as the pocket. He wanted a smoke, but he was out of tobacco, damn it all. 'Answer me this, sister. Is Jillian your friend?'

Ada took a second, eyes averted, no doubt gauging whether to answer or tell him to sod off. Even odds, with his sister. She finally nodded.

'Fine, then, she's your friend. The only one you've got, near as I can see. What's *your* excuse for not telling her things? Things like how you know Ewan Exeter, how you've known him for years?'

'I knew him the way he was then, not the way he is now.'

'The same could be said of you, Ada. At least that's what Ex would say.' Kell let that sink into his sister's hard head, which it apparently did, since she went quiet again. He pressed his advantage. 'Take a new way home after work.'

'What?'

'You heard me.'

Kell took off his cap and ran his hand across his forehead. He was sweating like a blacksmith. 'There's a cove loitering around Binney Street. I don't like the look of him.' That wasn't half of what Kell had felt when he'd spotted the cove. Black hair, dark eyes, olive skin. The red kerchief around his neck, like all Cortelli's men wore. He chivvied his sister again, harder. 'Did you forget what I told you or are you just being pig-headed?'

'I remember. But you can't–'

'Say it.'

'Jesus O'Reilly, Kell.'

'Say it, Ada.'

She rolled her eyes and sighed, both dramatically, as though he'd handed her a bucket of pig iron and told her to carry it from London to Plymouth. Kell was used to the drama; it hadn't affected him for years. And it confirmed that his sister knew there'd be no getting around him. Especially now that Jillian Morehouse had landed in their lives.

Ada mumbled into her collar. 'We don't take the same way home every day.'

'Well done, Miss Don't Tell Me What To Do Kelly. But if you know it, why aren't you doing it? You've used the same route *eight times* in a row. You and Jillian, you're marks by now, for sure.'

'I hope the lags in Mayfair have more sense than to think two corset girls have anything worth nimmin'.'

'Robbery isn't the only harm you could come to.' Kell fired a look at his sister, making sure it was loaded with more bad outcomes than Ada knew about, and she knew about plenty.

She relented. 'All right, all right, Nanny Kell.'

Kell took his pocket watch from his waistcoat and noted the time. No matter how he tried, he never succeeded in changing Ada's cross-wired mind in less than thirty minutes. He tucked the watch away and gave himself permission to rub his sister's nose in the rule. 'Different. Route. Every. Day.' Then he turned abruptly and strode toward the Strand, not looking back.

The band of fear around his chest loosened as he walked. In a few minutes, he was able to breathe more normally than when he set out. The whole while he was talking with Ada, he'd been bound in steel wire, holding his nerves together so he didn't grab her and shake her until her teeth rattled, and all because she was careless in the streets.

No, not *just* that. The wind-up was because, after years of worrying about Ada, he now had Jillian Morehouse to worry about, too. He spared some pity for his poor sister, God help her. She was a keg of contrariness, but she'd never given up on him, not even during the years he'd been wicked and wrathful and mad as a box of frogs. She'd seen him in a lot of moods, Ada had.

Never a mood like this one, though. In this mood, he was fused and ready, his hand stretched out for a match, and Ada saw it.

He'd told her the Jacks were dead and gone, but one of them was alive, present, and about to explode.

Chapter Eleven

After Detective Inspector Ewan Exeter visited Salon Sirena, there wasn't even a distant rumour about Larches for three weeks. Then, a single small news item connected to the crime popped up in *The Times*. Madame had it delivered on Sundays and Ada routinely salvaged it on Monday from the wastebasket.

'Dancin' piglets, she's a lucky miss.' They were dawdling on their tea break, alone in the workroom since Min and Evie were with Madame, shopping for notions. Ada read aloud, '*Miss Constance Philippa Forsythe announces her engagement to His Lordship Simon Marcotte DeVere, Viscount St Colstyn.*'

Jillian would never forget the prior engagement of Miss Forsythe, or her fiancé, Sir Hubert Alloway.

Ada grinned over the edge of the newspaper. 'Blimey. Didn't waste any time, that one. Waded right back into the season and it must've been a busy one to trade up to a viscount in that time.' She folded the paper neatly to take to her mother and a younger sibling. Jillian didn't know anything about them except they were Irish and poor.

The notice in *The Times* was the last glimmer of anything even remotely connected with the murder. Why would anyone dredge it up? It would only give the muckraking press months of indulgence in ridicule and censure directed at England's elite. The detective inspector was right all along. No one cared much about Sir Hubert, his life or his death. Jillian should probably be sorry about that, but if ever anyone had made their bed and deserved to lie in it...

Good God. How could she think that? What was she becoming? Jillian tried to drink her tea, but it had gone cold and so had she, her hand trembling around the mug. She shakily returned it to the table, hoping Ada hadn't noticed. She didn't want to explain to Ada or anyone else that she trembled because she feared she was turning into a monster. Maybe killing Sir Hubert wasn't a singular event. Maybe she'd had a monster inside her all along, and it just chose that morning at Larches to show itself.

Get hold of yourself, Jillian. She focused on the folded newspaper on the table, counting the lines of dark grey type. Twelve, thirteen, fourteen.

She wasn't a monster. A monster wouldn't have the *Plan.* The *Plan* hadn't been with her for four years in the orphanage and two in service for her to abandon it because of one mistake.

Murder's rather big as mistakes go, Jilly. Maybe if she vowed never to do it again... *One measly murder, is that it?* It wasn't as though she'd stabbed the Queen. *Maybe it was a practice murder. Maybe you're working your way up.*

No, no, *no!* One mistake, however monstrous, would not define her. She wouldn't listen to any more deranged thoughts. The *Plan* would make up for it, for everything she'd done and lost. All she had to do was follow it. Advancement. Respectability. Husband, hearth, happiness.

Besides, it was water over the dam. Over, as well, were visits from the police, though, if she was totally honest with herself, she'd have to admit Ewan Exeter and his grey eyes visited in memory, now and then. Part of her wanted those eyes to look at her again the way they had when Exeter questioned her. He'd been so attentive. And not unkind, considering she and Ada were being interrogated. It was as though the detective inspector was interested in her as a woman, not just a witness.

Suspect, Jillian, suspect. Grey eyes notwithstanding, he probably still thought she was one.

Jillian hopped to her feet and grabbed her mug. Work was still the only reliable cure for plaguing thoughts. At the tiny sink where the four of them took it in turns to wash up at day's end, she scrubbed first her mug, then the ones belonging to Ada, Min, and Evie, then all the spoons, and finally the sink itself. With nothing left to clean unless she wanted to mop the floor and polish all the doorknobs, she returned to her chair at the worktable, calmer in mind and body.

As she threaded her needle, she admitted she'd have to be barmy to think again about Exeter's eyes. She should never, ever, want to see or be seen by Exeter or any policeman.

From here on out, her life would be all about the *Plan*.

CHAPTER TWELVE

The week after her washing-up revelation was dull as the back of a knife. Her mates weren't jigging with excitement, either, but no one complained about the pace. After the Royal Chorus Society gala came and went, things slowed at Salon Sirena. Just enough new orders arrived that the corset girls kept their heads down and concentrated on stitches and steel splints.

One afternoon, though, when they were all reduced to counting the minutes until shop shutting time, their boredom was shattered by three sharp knocks on the workroom door to the alley. Everyone's head snapped up, but only Jillian and Ada locked gazes. They knew the three-times knock and the man whose knuckles made it.

Jillian put down her sewing and went to the drape but, before she could put her eye to the gap, Ada spoke. 'Madame's still out. He wouldn't have come round if he didn't know she was out.'

'Who's he? Who's come round?' No one answered Min. Ada went to the back door, opened it a crack, then wider. Before she slipped through, she looked sharply at Jillian and tilted her chin toward the alley.

The whiff of cloak and dagger ensured that Jillian and Ada weren't the only ones who went through the door. When the four of them crowded outside, they faced two men. One was Michael Kelly. The other was a stranger, at least to Jillian, and he was a giant of a man.

There were big men aplenty in London; Jillian had seen them. Dockers and draymen. Men clearing slums for the tramway, labourers on the new underground railway tunnels and the Battersea Bridge works. But this man was Atlas among the lesser gods.

At a guess, he was three inches taller than Ada's brother, who cleared six feet. If Michael Kelly was, as he was, heavily muscled, this man was nothing *but* muscle. He was neatly, almost nattily dressed in a muted plaid suit, with a gold watch chain draped across a matching waistcoat that strained at his broad chest. If she got close enough, which she had no intention of doing, she'd probably see herself in the mirror-like shine of his shoes. On the man's glossy, whiskey-coloured hair, a neat derby hat was cocked at an angle, not too rakish, just– sporting. His eyes, the same colour as his hair, sparkled affably.

Uncomfortably for Jillian, she'd seen a hawk up close once, in Hertfordshire, and the hawk's eyes looked just the same before he tore into a squirrel.

In one hand, the plaid-suited man held a paper bag of sweets. The hand was so huge the bag almost disappeared.

Evie and Min were speechless and slack-jawed, ogling like farm girls seeing their first locomotive. Ada seemed unimpressed. She leaned against the workroom door, sending a look toward her brother Michael that was... *Peevish* came to Jillian's mind.

The brother ignored whatever critical barb Ada was flicking at him and addressed all of them in a vague way. 'This is my associate, Étienne Sansecours.'

Sans secours. Without help.

'Is that your real name?' It was out of Jillian's mouth before she knew what she was saying. Even after she wished she could take it back, she'd already delivered what sounded very like an insult to a man at least twice her size, a man with the eyes of an avian predator and a name that suggested it wasn't wise to get on his bad side. And who was she to cast stones, anyway? Was Sansecours any different from the rest of them? From Michael Seraphin Kelly alias Kell, or Ada so-called Gubbins, or Jillian Morehouse AKA Phipps?

Was any of them who they said they were?

Luckily, Sansecours didn't seem offended. A wide grin split his face, showing even, white teeth, a slight gap between the front two. 'If you prefer,' he said in perfect but heavily French-accented English, and in a register so deep it almost vibrated, 'you may call me Le Dague.'

The *Dagger?* Oh, yes, that was *infinitely* better.

Evie promptly began chattering in French to the man, whose replies rumbled warmly. He rattled the paper bag in his hand and held it out to the four women. Ada and Jillian both shook their heads. But Evie reached in and rustled around, giving a little squeak of delight when she extracted *dragées*, pastel sugar-coated almonds. Dague held the bag out to Min. His whiskey eyes seemed to lick over her like she was a sweet herself.

Min dipped her hand into the bag and came out with a single gold almond.

'Ooh-la-la, Minnie!' Evie squealed. 'You get the gold one! Today, you find your true *amoureux*!' Everyone laughed and Min's fair face turned pink.

Jillian caught an intense glance from Ada's brother. He chucked his chin up the alley. Now what? Was he coaxing her somewhere so he could make more rude remarks about his bed?

Jillian scanned the alley up and down, but no one was paying any mind to her or him. Ada was still holding up the workroom door, scowling. Evie was talking and laughing with Dague as though she'd known him for a month, not five minutes. Even

Min's face was aglow, as she uncharacteristically joined the conversation.

Michael Kelly walked up the alley. Jillian followed, not sure why, not sure why not. He stopped about thirty feet from the others and spoke the instant she caught up to him.

'You're all right, now.' His sentence turned up at the end, so it was as much a question as a statement.

'You mean, after the– that thing in the–' Jillian held her breath, hoping he wouldn't make her say the name of the brothel aloud. Why was he even bringing it up? At least he didn't mention any beds. 'Yes,' she finally breathed out, 'I'm well, thank you.'

He didn't say anything else. She didn't say anything else. Minutes passed while they stood there, mute as a couple of pillar boxes. Jillian fixed her eyes on a drainpipe running up the building opposite. Michael Kelly's eyes, she noticed out of the corner of her vision, were never still. They darted toward the outlets of the alley, to the back doors of the buildings on either side, even the roofs. Alert, watchful.

Keeping her own eyes off Ada's brother didn't mean Jillian was unaffected by him. She was disturbingly affected. For one thing, there was his scent. It was a cool day but, as usual, he wore only a shirt and waistcoat over his wool trousers. His shirt was collarless, white and starched, the sleeves not rolled up but fastened at the cuffs. He was closely shaved and a gust of fragrance, sandalwood maybe, came off him, mixed with a faint whiff of laundry soap and something else, a scent she couldn't identify. Unfamiliar but beckoning, subtle, barely there.

Without warning, the scent grabbed and shook her so hard her shoulders jerked. She wanted to strip off Michael Kelly's waistcoat and bury her face in his shirt, his chest. The scent coming from him was man. Not just any man but this man alone, the one inches from her.

She didn't dare meet his eyes. Just to stand so close, pulled by his scent, leaning into it... It was too intimate to bear.

She broke the tension with a blurt. 'You smoke tobacco, don't you?'

No blame to him for the expression he turned on her. Incredulous, as though she'd said, 'You perform on a trapeze, don't you?' Jillian blundered on. 'I saw you roll a cigarette and smoke it, in the pony trap.'

'Yes, I smoke now and then. Does it bother you?'

'No! I mean, it's something men do.' As though she, Jillian Morehouse, would know what men do. A tiny light glimmered. 'My father smoked a pipe.'

No reply from the man next to her. Why would there be? It was a statement of fact, irrelevant and personal. Jillian tried to imagine Michael Kelly with a pipe jutting out of his mouth. When her father smoked his pipe, he looked like what he was, a dignified, ageing Royal Navy officer. The man next to her would look like Captain Kidd.

The pirate coughed behind his fist and said, 'I only smoke when I'm nervous.'

He'd smoked in the pony trap. Did that mean he was nervous then? Jillian was astounded. He'd looked perfectly relaxed, sure of himself. She'd been the one shaking like a leaf, what with his stare and her buttons and his thigh.

'It's just... you never smell of tobacco.'

'It's only habitual smokers who...' He seemed to be searching for a word. 'Who have an odour,' he finished lamely.

Jillian looked back at the others, Min and Evie and the man called Dague. Their laughter bounced and skittered off the buildings flanking the alley. Boon companions, old mates gathered for a chat. Their ease made the pauses between her and Ada's brother that much more uncomfortable. She lurched toward something polite.

'I hope we're not inconveniencing you by keeping your room all this time, Mr Kelly.' She forced herself to look directly into his eyes and was glad she'd spoken before she looked. Something twisted and raged in them, making her throat close.

'Call me Kell. The room, it's no problem.' His voice was tight. 'I've got– I've been given a bed at The Flower Garden.' A small muscle in his cheek twitched. 'A room, I mean. With my position. It's– it's a thing they gave me, with the work. It's at the back, the very back. Almost not in the...'

Den of iniquity. Nugging-house. Knocking-shop. His room might be at the back, but the back was still attached to the front, and the front was full of fallen women. Fallen, available women. *You're as foolish as a peahen, Jillian.* Why should she care if they visited his room, singly or *en masse*?

She feigned insouciance. 'That's convenient.' *Oh, God.* 'I mean, that's a savings for you.' Because he didn't have to pay for female companionship. 'I mean, since you're there so much, you may as well have a room to– a place to...' What in England, Scotland, and Wales was she saying?

Kell clearly thought the conversation wasn't sliding into chaos fast enough, so he added his ha'penny worth. 'It's got nothing to do with the– That is... it's just a room. And not even much of one, really. Just four walls and a bed.'

A bed was all a man needed in a place like that. Jillian got a vivid mental picture of herself standing on a bed in that exact place. Standing all but naked, wearing not much more than a pink corset. Oh, horrors, was he seeing it, too?

Apparently, he was seeing something else. His eyes showed steel in their azure depths. 'Listen, that police officer. Ewan Exeter.'

Laughter and clapping distracted them both and Jillian's head swivelled toward the noise. Min was holding the sweets bag, while Dague juggled coloured almonds. There were five in the air, a real feat. Min was gazing at Dague like she'd never seen hands before. Jillian turned back to Kell.

His unyielding regard was still fixed on her and he hadn't lost his place in the conversation. 'Exeter. You shouldn't- you don't want to have anything more to do with him.'

'I didn't want to have anything to do with him in the first place! But he's a detective inspector. From *Scotland Yard*. He asked me questions and I had to answer them. He kept-'

'I know, I know.' Could his eyes get more steely? They could and did, and Kell added a frown to them. 'Just don't have anything else to do with him.'

That got her back up. 'Are you *angry* with me? Because I assure you, none of us invited the inspector to the salon.'

'I didn't say you invited him, did I? Not that he wouldn't have come running if you had.'

'Just what are you suggesting? And what does a Scotland Yard police officer have to do with you? For that matter, why are you getting worked up?'

'I am not worked up!' It was loud enough that the others stopped what they were doing and stared. With visible effort, Kell lowered his voice. 'I just think it's prudent that, in future, you have as little as possible to do with Ewan Exeter.'

A few laden seconds passed while Jillian connected her thoughts. 'Do you know him? That is, do you have some... history with him?'

Kell went very still, not even an eyelid twitching, for a count of ten. Then, he took a deep breath and let it out raggedly, as though grappling for control. He took one step, closing the distance between them.

Jillian's inner voice, the voice of the *Plan*, warned her to back away. He was too close. Really too close. But she didn't move.

His next words came out softer, quieter. 'Forget I said anything. I apologise if I gave offence. It's difficult not to be concerned.'

Difficult for Jillian not to be concerned that he was so concerned. Equally difficult to admit that she would be more concerned if he wasn't. And now, they were as close as they'd been in the pony cart, as close as in the stairwell, almost touching. It was all wrong, but she wanted to lay her hand on his forearm, to reassure him. She stayed the impulse but not the words, as soft and quiet as his.

'Please don't apologise. I'm not offended. And I don't plan on having anything more to do with... that man.'

She'd ordered her hand to stay at her side, but there it was, resting on Kell's forearm. They both stared at it as though it was an exotic bird, fallen from the sky to land there. The world stopped. Everything in all the continents and oceans vanished except for the tiny points where Jillian's fingertips touched Kell's solid flesh through his shirtsleeve.

Their gazes rose together, joined. The hollow yearning in his went through her like current, like fire.

There was another, louder eruption of laughter from the others, and boisterous applause. Jillian and Kell flew apart, only a few inches but enough. After a self-conscious shudder, Jillian realised the others weren't sending so much as a glance at her and Kell. They were fixated on Dague and Min.

Dague stood very close behind Min. She had two *dragées* in her hands and the big man was apparently teaching her how to juggle them. Min giggled. Her long braid had come undone. Rich brown tresses cascaded over one shoulder and got in the way of her fingers. Dague reached over and took a swath of her hair in one hand, then twisted it deftly and held it away from Min's neck. His other massive hand rested on her shoulder. As Jillian watched, he bent over her, his mouth almost brushing the top of Min's head.

'Back to work!' Ada squawked.

Ada yanked open the workroom door and Evie and Min pelted through it. Ada followed more slowly, leaving the door open and not looking back. Jillian hesitated, not ready to go inside. She wanted to watch Kell and the Frenchman, walking now toward Audley Street. They didn't look back, either.

A faint roll of thunder distracted her. Grey clouds were massing overhead and rain hung in them, an unspoken threat.

Kell should have said goodbye. No, goodbye was the wrong word and maybe that's why he hadn't said it. It was a word someone said when a conversation was finished. *'That's me, then. Goodbye!'*

As disjointed as it was, their conversation had nothing finished about it. She shouldn't want to talk to him again, considering how badly the talking always went. Why, then, if it went so badly, were there twenty more things Jillian wanted to say and another twenty she wanted to hear from Kell?

And why was it every time they talked, she got so muddled? Her pulse raced, she felt flushed and chilled by turns. The words she tried to form in her brain didn't fit together in logical sentences but scattered like frightened chickens. Her nerves went on alert, her muscles tensed as though any second she might need to... what? Run away, run toward, run to the ends of the earth to escape a feeling that rushed to overwhelm her?

She couldn't even say what the feeling was. Closest to hunger, perhaps, but even though she felt flutters in her stomach, the feeling didn't settle there. It was expectant but aching, more like... *Need*, that's what it was. Need of a sort she hadn't known existed. She knew what it was to need food, drink, rest, warmth. The thing she needed when Ada's brother was around was different in degree, different in essence.

That's what gave her such an odd and helpless feeling. Improbable as it seemed, she needed Michael Kelly. She needed him because he was a key, and somewhere deep inside her was a lock he fit. When the key turned, the wards would click. Some secret, sacred place would open.

And then? How could the two of them get the key and the lock to the same place at the same time? They couldn't even manage a conversation. If they ever did, though, if they were ever alone with each other...

Alone with Michael Kelly. Just thinking of it made fires of sensation blaze up and down her body. Under her ribcage. Lower, between her thighs. The place she'd seen in the mirror at The Flower Garden. The place that gathered moisture like a storm cloud before it wept rain.

As though she'd called it, a gust of damp air whooshed into the alley, raising eddies of grit from the bricks and making a discarded paper handbill dance. Raindrops followed the gust. She should join Ada and the others in the workroom but, before she could move, she heard a voice.

Song was coming from an open window somewhere up the alley, far enough away that the voice was indistinct, but near enough she could tell it was a woman's. A high voice, not as high or as sweet as Mother's.

What a lovely singer Mother had been, a voice like a lark or a nightingale. It was one of Jillian's earliest memories, Mother singing to her, to Pon, to Father, to herself.

When they moved to London, there was less singing. Less of everything, but Jillian particularly missed the singing. Well, they hadn't brought the piano and that made a difference.

She shut her eyes, the better to see the old music room in Hertfordshire. The piano, her mother sitting at it. Light streaming through the garden windows, gilding her mother's hands on the keys and painting highlights in her copper-gold hair.

Jillian opened her eyes. She wasn't in a music room, now, nor in a cottage in Hertfordshire. Now she was in an alley in London. Brick paving befouled with dirt. Dull pewter skies above and the smell of drains. People.

So many people in London, so few she knew. Until her parents brought her to the city, she hadn't really understood how many people there were, and how different from her they could be. Everything before London was small, neatly arranged, and familiar. Like the neighbours she'd known for years or the flowers in the garden her mother replanted every spring. Like the music room and the piano.

Now, her life was a picture puzzle that someone had dropped on the floor. She tried to put it back together, but pieces were missing or – odd. Like Michael Kelly. He was a piece from a different puzzle altogether, and he would never, should never, fit into hers. She had the *Plan*. Michael Kelly, she reminded herself, wasn't in it. She shouldn't and *couldn't* have feelings for him. That's why she was uncomfortable around him; that's all it was.

But if that's all it was, then why, when they'd stood so close and her hand was on his arm, did she want to rest her weight there, so she could rise up on her toes and kiss him?

'Oi, Jilly.' Ada, calling from the open workroom door.

Jillian faced her friend. In addition to whatever else had been making Ada scowl for the past hour, she was scowling now at Jillian.

'Shift yourself,' Ada said. 'If Madame comes back and finds any of us out here, we'll never hear the end of it.'

'Don't grouse, Ada. I just wanted some air.' Ada withdrew and Jillian followed. She stopped at the door, one hand on it, and took a last look over her shoulder at the alley. The narrow brick passage would never be the same, never be just the back way to Audley Street. The afternoon had changed all that. Sugared almonds, the smell of laundry soap or sandalwood, a snatch of song from a hidden window... They would always bring Michael Kelly to mind.

Disturbed, excited, and deeply confused, she hurried into the workroom and slammed the door, throwing the bolt.

Everyone was at the worktable, but no one was working. Ada's brow was still creased and her mouth set in a stubborn line. She sat sullenly, arms crossed, not saying anything to anyone. Evie and Min, who was re-braiding her hair, were whispering, heads close together. The half-empty bag of *dragées* lay on the table in front of them. Evie's profusion of black curls had escaped her topknot, spilling over her ears and her smooth, antique ivory forehead, while Min's usually pale cheeks were rosy. They both giggled between whispers.

Jillian didn't know why, but the whole scene annoyed her. She started in on Min before she even got her braid finished. 'Min. About that man.'

'Étienne.' No question which man, then.

'Yes, that one. He's...'

'Impressive.'

'I was going to say dangerous.'

Min shrugged. 'Aren't most men dangerous?' Leave it to Min to say something no one expected from that tender mouth and innocent face.

'Min, he's, well, I can't prove it, but his name... It seems like some sort of alias. He could be a criminal.'

Min gave a delicate snort, like an aggrieved rabbit. 'With a *surnom criminel*? You don't know that.'

'He's called "The Dagger", Min. Doesn't sound like a tobacconist to me.'

Min didn't look up from the remnant of silk ribbon she was tying around the end of her braid, but what she said next convinced Jillian that her shrinking violet workmate was gone forever. Some other bloom, something unexpectedly bold and foreign, was inhabiting Min's body, now.

'A man needs a trade.'

Because he'd not had time to do it earlier, Kell jotted his purchases from the day before in his pocket diary, saying them aloud as he did. 'Bucket trowel, two pound nine. Box of Wilson's Lime, eightpence. Joint knife, two pound two. Penny pack Rizla rolling papers.' He never forgot what he paid for things, but he liked recording them, anyway, a habit from the lean years when he guarded pence like a turnkey. Tucking the diary into his pocket, he picked up his new trowel and got back to work.

He wasn't fixing up the house for Jillian Morehouse. He'd said that to himself, the house, and sometimes to his tools, at least ten times today alone. Why in blazing hell did he need to keep saying it? He said it because, like her, the need had become a dangerous habit.

He dragged the trowel across a plaster patch in the parlour. The room, like the rest of the house, was flooded with light from open windows. There were no drapes nor any furniture; the house was still a shell. Some punter – *neighbour*, Kell corrected, trying to get used to the word – with nothing better to do was standing on the pavement outside, just yards away. As men will do, the neighbour was smoking a pipe and peering critically at another man's work.

There was no way under heaven Kell would talk to him, even though the sash was raised to the stops. Talking to him would just be asking for a lot of time-wasting opinions. *If it was my wall, I'd use Partin's instead of that muck you're slappin' on there. It's tinted-like, so's you won't have to use so much paint later.*

Neighbours. Kell supposed they came with the patch, so he'd better get used to them as well as the word. The estate agent who'd sold him the house said Hackney was up and coming. Kell wasn't sure what that meant. He'd asked around, though, and discovered that a lot of people besides estate agents thought Hackney was where respectable people of respectable means were choosing to live.

The house wasn't new, though it had been built when the district was new, maybe thirty years ago. Nor was it the largest, the grandest, or the most beautiful of the terraced houses on Fassett Square. But it was only a few minutes' walk from the railway stop and was at the end of a row, so it had not just the garden in the back but a narrow side strip that got sun and might do for roses. Eight rooms, the advert said. Everything but an indoor washroom, and he'd already plumbed for that. He'd even installed a tub. With a heater.

The house had come from his portion of the obscenely large profits the Jacks had made from the obscenely wrong things they'd done in Seven Dials. Another portion had gone to Mam and Eileen, the youngest of his siblings and the only one left at home, for decent lodgings. The Hackney house and the rooms for his mother put the shine of decency on the money. Bright enough, maybe, to hide the ugly ways he'd gone about getting it.

At least, that's what he'd thought at the time, though it made a lot less sense to him now than it did then. No matter the good it did, the money would still disgust Jillian Morehouse when she knew where it came from. If she ever found out. If he ever had the stones to tell her, which he'd have to, at some point, if he expected her to–

To what? Kell shook his head, then wiped sweat off his face with his sleeve. What the hell was he doing, expecting anything? He'd bought the house because it was a place to live away from reminders of his past. A place to make a new start. He'd assumed he'd be living in it alone.

That hadn't changed and he was mad to think it could. His past was dyed in the wool; it would be with him, would *be* him, forever. He slapped the trowel harder than necessary on the wall.

As though things weren't black enough, Dague turned up. Why here, why now? And the Frenchman about as inconspicuous as a rhinoceros on Bond Street. What was wrong with France? It was his home, wasn't it? Couldn't he have stayed there, since he wouldn't have gone back in the first place if he hadn't made London too hot to hold him?

Kell even asked him, 'Sure it's safe to be paradin' around the Smoke, you great oaf?'

Dague gave one of those Gallic shrugs that drove Kell round the bend, so he persisted. 'Ex won't take risks to cover for you, you know. He likes his new life too much. Those fine cigars, the Savile Row tailor. The society bints who don't know him as the Scraper.'

'*Cela ne veux rien dire.*' That means nothing, his huge confederate grunted. 'And the society *filles*, they like a bit of the rough, you know? Do not fear, *mon frère*. I am well insured.' Then he put one thick finger alongside his nose and winked.

Another Gallic gesture Kell could do without. But he figured it meant that in addition to the secrets they were both keeping, the ones Kell knew about, there were others. Secrets that only Dague guarded, and those made the big man feel safe.

Kell hoped Dague wasn't overvaluing his secrets. He hoped for his friend's sake, but also for that delicate little *corsetière* who had looked at Dague like the sun shone out his French arse. When Kell thought about the pile of arrest warrants with *Étienne Sansecours* on them, the things that could go wrong, the fact that Exeter could do a lot but wasn't God Almighty...

Christ, when did I turn into such a bloody coward?

In the Jacks, Kell was called Stammer. Rhyming slang for "hammer", since that's what he did to anyone who was in the gang's way, or deserved a beating, or sometimes for no reason at all.

Exeter was Scraper, because if you crossed him, the coppers would be scraping what was left of you off the street.

Étienne was Dague. Deadly accurate with a throwing knife at twenty paces and eyes that could see in the dark, like the big cat he was. If his blade didn't take out the target, his sheer size and power would. He could crush a man's windpipe with one hand.

There were others in the gang. He'd forgotten most of their names. Why remember? They were dead, in prison, or had disappeared. He'd forgotten them because he wanted to forget, not just them but the past, all of it.

He stepped back and surveyed his work. The wall looked good, and he'd done enough for the day. He began slowly putting away his tools, first wiping the trowel with a wet rag.

Seven Dials. The Jacks.

It was long ago as time went, but it would never seem long enough. He'd been young, too young. Between fourteen and nineteen – how can a man be held responsible for what he does in that part of his life, when he's about as formed as a lump of dough?

Unformed, too young, and too poor, as they all were. London was full to the brim with poverty; he couldn't claim that as an excuse. But when his father drowned, there was no one to care for the family he left behind. Mam, Kell's one older sister, three younger – one a baby – and a wee brother just walking. To keep them all alive there was Kell, only Kell.

And Exeter, that snake. Born Ewan MacBride, he'd

rechristened himself after a stint in Tothill Fields, where he got a broad education from other young thugs. He got a new name, too, from a straight razor sign he saw on the day he finally walked out the prison's gates. *Exeter Blades.*

'The closest shave you'll ever get!' He used to say that in the Jacks, drawing his index finger across his throat and laughing like a bloody lunatic. Nineteen. Exeter was nineteen when he scooped up the handful of young turks that included Kell, then fourteen and barely sprouting whiskers, and Dague, just gone sixteen. Exeter was older, meaner, and more ambitious than the others. He guessed, rightly, that made him their leader.

Five years in the gang. For Kell, they'd started with outrage. Outrage at being left to hold together a family with no wage earner except him. At his older sister Con, for running away with some man because she figured nothing could be worse than Whitechapel, then vanishing so completely that she hadn't been heard from since. At foul water and disease that took two of his younger siblings, the boy and the baby girl, and no money for help that might have saved them. At crooked coppers, leaking roofs, putrid air, no coal, and streets so low and squalid that the thieves robbed each other, because no one else had anything to steal.

After the outrage, came straight-out rage. The Jacks fuelled it. Rage that was pure, white-hot, useful after a fashion in his new profession, the profession they all shared. The things they'd done, the things *he'd* done... At what point had the leg-breaking and skull-cracking become a sick sort of normal? A day on the docks. A rota in the factory.

At that point, the Jacks thought they'd earned respect. All they'd earned was fear.

'Fear's good,' Scraper said. 'Good for trade.'

Trade. Vice. One and the same. Of most sorts, but the one that made them the most coin was gambling. By the time the Jacks dispersed, there were twenty hells in the miserable warren of Seven

Dials. That was only two less than in the last year of the century before, when the press and the Bow Street Runners claimed they'd wiped them all out. Of the twenty, Exeter, with his closest mates Kell and Dague, owned three quarters, the other quarter being so low and unprofitable they weren't worth the trouble to manage.

The money poured in, a swollen river of gold, half black with the gobbets of blood from everything they did to make it and keep it. They told themselves they had no choice.

Kell wiped his damp rag over the patches on the wall, smoothing the edges and wondering, with half his mind, if he had enough plaster mix to finish the other rooms that needed patching, or if he should buy more. He'd make a note in his pocket diary.

Maybe it was true the Jacks didn't have a choice. It was certainly true after Aurelio Cortelli decided Birmingham wasn't enough of an empire, and he and his sons thrust greedy fingers into London. Into Seven Dials.

The Jacks cut those fingers off, one by one. Cut them off as they'd cut off the greedy fingers of other gangs. The Fitzroys, the Marylebones, the Prince Arthurs.

Cortelli knew the game. He expected losses from his grab. A cold bastard, he wasn't much bothered by the losses until one of them was his nephew, Federico. The nephew Kell had beaten to a bloody pulp and left for dead in a fight ring. The nephew whose death had generated a vow of vengeance from Aurelio.

It was no real comfort, but Kell hadn't thought, when he left the ring, that he'd killed his opponent. No one thought it, until Fedo died the next morning of a blood clot in the brain. It was also true that Fedo was widely known to be a hothead. He'd entered the ring on his own steam, on a wager he had no business making and that two of his brothers tried but failed to stop.

Exeter brokered a peace deal. The Cortellis took what Exeter offered them, Seven Dials. The Jacks dealt with their own losses. But the price of peace was that the cards didn't go back on the tables and the dice didn't roll again, not for the Jacks, anyway. Their reign as the kings of vice was over. They retired, rich, one step ahead of their rivals and two ahead of the law, as always.

After all that, how the bloody hell did Exeter land on his feet instead of back in the jug, as he so richly deserved? How did he end up on the right side of the law after years on the wrong? How did he manage it?

Same way he managed everything else, Kell figured. Bribery, extortion, blackmail, threats, promises, favours offered, markers pulled in. Most of all, that smooth snake's tongue he kept behind his teeth until he needed to talk his way out of or into something. Dague and Kell weren't around to see the transformation, however it happened. Dague fled to the Continent. Kell hid his gains and himself in the rookeries, in Devil's Acre, Limehouse, Fenian Barracks, the Docks. The three men went their own ways, none of them with much regard for the others.

Until now, when their pasts were rising like shrouded cadavers from the graves in which they'd been hastily buried years ago. Now, when Kell saw a swarthy cove loitering on Binney Street in Mayfair.

Seven Dials. The Jacks.

He pulled down his braces and unbuttoned his spattered shirt, the one he wore to work on the house. He hadn't bothered with an undershirt and had completely forgotten the open window and the punter still standing and smoking on the pavement a few yards outside. It wasn't until Kell stripped off his shirt that he remembered the man, looked up, and saw the man's jaw drop, pipe falling out of it.

Get a good look, then, neighbour.

The man did, gawking at the rippling muscle of Kell's torso and arms, the tattoos that covered them. He didn't have to, but Kell couldn't resist turning his back on the window as he shook out his soiled shirt. As long as the man outside was goggling, he should goggle at them, too, the vivid twin dragons on either side of

Kell's spine. He flexed his back muscles, knowing it made the dragons undulate from his shoulders downward, their tails disappearing below the waistband of his trousers.

When Kell faced the window again, the punter was gone. *Not so clever, Stammer.* News of the dragons would be all over Hackney in a few days.

He had a cock and bull story for the rare occasions when someone not on the game saw his body, though it was even rarer that he cared enough to trot it out. 'In His Majesty's Navy, five years,' rang as false as tin plate to discerning ears, but most people would rather believe the lie than the truth, which was that he was a Jack and they were all inked. Like his room at The Flower Garden, the ink came with the work.

There were times he wished he didn't have so much of it, but there was no way to make it disappear now. He'd seen more heavily tattooed men, by far, and worse tattoos. A skull here, a dancing girl there. Badges, their owners called them, and he supposed each one had some meaning in their thick heads.

Kell's ink covered his shoulders and arms, stopping at the wrists. In front, the figures crawled across his pectorals and down his ribs on either side, flaring out to his hips and upper thighs. In back, the dragons.

There were several scratchers the Jacks favoured, but Kell's man was a Chinese who worked under an awning in Limehouse. It was just around the corner from where Kell got a woman for the first time, a desperate little filly who'd let him take her up against a wall. They were both virgins. He gave her a gold sovereign for his two minutes of pleasure and hers of pain and blood. He never crowed about it after, but that didn't make him a better man. What made him a marginally better man was that he went farther up the dark lane and lost his dinner on the cobblestones, then didn't touch a woman for a year.

Seven Dials. The Jacks.

Kell slammed the window shut and threw the latch. He pulled

on a clean shirt, tucked it in, and hauled his braces over his shoulders. He picked up his jacket and looked around the room once more. Then he left by the door and turned the key, locking his bitter memories and fragile hopes in together where they could fight it out.

Chapter Fourteen

It had been a week since her strange interlude with the man she now called Kell in the alley behind Salon Sirena. Jillian was still trying to untangle the threads of it. She had time to think on this calm Thursday morning, since Madame was at a cloth supplier's, examining new stock. Jillian, Madame's unofficial assistant, was in the showroom, showing polite but distracted deference to a cabinet member's fussy first-season daughter and her dithering mother.

A tap on the locked salon door alerted her to look through the half-glass. She was just in time to spot a small, scruffy boy shoving an envelope through the mail slot, then scampering away. Jillian assumed it was something for Madame, so she left the clients bickering over presentation corsets while she retrieved the envelope from the floor and examined it. *Ah-hah.* Not for Madame, then.

Miss Jillian Morehouse? was inked on the front.

Very amusing. The question mark after her name should have been her clue to the sender, but she didn't tumble to it until she opened the note inside.

Dear Miss Morehouse,

If you would do me the very great honour of answering just one more question about the unfortunate event at Larches some time past, I should be deeply appreciative and wholly in your debt.

Do not be alarmed, the question is purely procedural, but your discretion in the matter will be something on which I will, as I know I can, rely.

So that we are spared the rude surroundings of my office, let us meet in Hyde Park, Sunday forthcoming, one o'clock in the afternoon, at the Statue of Achilles.

With abject gratitude and apologies for taking more of your valuable time than I have already consumed,

Ewan Exeter, D.I.

Evading Ada was easier than Jillian thought it might be, though it added to her qualms about meeting Exeter at all, much less alone and with no one the wiser. The two women had slept in a bit on Sunday morning and, when Jillian woke, Ada was gone. She'd left a note on the washstand:

Visiting my muther.

Jillian wondered if she'd ever be asked to go along. Ada's visits with her mother, wherever she lived, usually lasted the better part of the day.

Jillian dressed with almost painful care. Since she and Ada now had regular wages – and no rent, she reminded herself guiltily – they'd bought a few more clothes. Nothing remotely extravagant, just a couple of decent dresses and skirts, one good pair of shoes apiece. Jillian pulled a teal walking dress off its hanger and held it up to the light. It was trimmed in narrow bands of dark teal velvet and made her eyes look even more richly green than they were.

She put on the dress, smoothing the skirt with satisfaction. What a blessing that Ada seemed to know all the best second-hand clothing emporiums. The teal dress had a dozen imperfections when she bought it, but Jillian fixed every one and was sure the repairs didn't show.

She wished she had a better hat than her plain dark straw boater, but she did have a yellow silk ribbon. She could tie it around the crown to smarten it up.

There was no mirror in the dent-in-the-wall but if the light was just right, which it was today, she could see her reflection in the room's one window. She thought she looked nice.

Maybe she should add a touch of something festive. She rummaged around in the hatbox under the bed where she and Ada kept their bits of ornament. Paste brooches. A strand of false pearls. A few silk and paper flowers. She was sure there'd been... There it was. A bitty corsage of yellow silk orchids.

Pinning the corsage to her bodice, she reflected that she didn't have any real experience using what novels called 'feminine wiles'. But whatever Ewan Exeter wanted with her, Jillian thought it couldn't hurt to look her best. Even if the detective inspector wanted to ask her some questions about – that thing – he was at least posing his questions in a park, which would be pleasant. And she hadn't been out in so long, not out in the sense of a pleasure outing. She could barely remember the last time. Six and a half years ago?

Yes, a summer day. Her father was struggling and failing to make a go of things in London, but she and Pon were blissfully ignorant of that. The house in Hertfordshire was lost, true, but the flat in Chelsea wasn't too bad. They'd brought quite a lot of their furniture. Not the piano.

Almost seven years ago, a whole day in St James's Park. They'd thrilled to the parade of the horse guards in the morning, then watched the ducks and swans on the canal until it was time for a band concert. She and Pon laughed and applauded when Father took Mother, squealing in protest, for a turn during a polka, scandalising onlookers. They'd brought a basket meal with them, cheese and bread, and Father bought them all fizzy lemonade in bottles. Mother clucked over the lemonade as it was costly. They ate standing, as Mother refused to let Father rent chairs.

Before they went home, they visited the Turkish cannon. All of them, even Mother, said it was extraordinary. Father made them dizzy with admiration when he told them, with broad gestures and snippets of foreign languages, the story of how it came from Alexandria in Egypt to London.

Near seven years ago, St James's Park. She should have been more attentive. She would have been, if she'd known it was her last outing with her parents, her last outing of any sort. Wasn't that what people said? 'Oh, if only I'd known, I would have...'

Changed the future? Pulled the switch on some machine that would make everything happen differently? Put her feet on a path that didn't lead to becoming a nameless drudge in one of the great houses that bordered the same park where she and her parents had such a fine day?

But she hadn't been more attentive, hadn't known, even though the unravelling of her family's future had started long before they came to London. First, Father telling Pon he wouldn't be going to Eton. Next, giving up the cottage in Hertfordshire.

Then Father, tall and laughing and lovable, his sea-roughened hand covering hers as he said, 'Jillybaby, the sweetest of the sweets.'

He'd been lost in an afternoon. And Mother, so beautiful and kind, so accomplished. Her song filling every room, her fingers magicking embroidery thread into masses of flowers on tablecloths, curtains, and tea towels, until the inside of the house blossomed like a garden. Mother, Father, the house, their lives – all left behind.

Not left behind, ripped away. The years Pon should have had, playing cricket and rugby, going to university, then into law or medicine. The years Jillian should have had, the pretty frocks, the dances, the promising young men who came calling with offers of security, wealth, a future without want.

But Pon became a common sailor who, despite his enthusiasm for the sea, was probably slaving away on some ship in some dangerous place. While Jillian sank into toil, servitude, despair. A shapeless black dress, a starched apron, a bloodied knife.

Her hands shook so much she had to stop dressing and rest for a few minutes, eyes brimming, against the wall of the shabby little room the last seven years of her life had led her to.

A half hour later she was standing at – under, actually – the bronze figure of Achilles in Hyde Park. She would *not* look up. The statue was lavishly and anatomically correct. Within a month of its installation, all London was saying there was no better arse in a hundred-mile radius than the one on the giant nude statue. Of all the spots to pick for a meeting.

Jillian touched the silk orchids on her dress front. She was much calmer now. She had dabbed cold water on her eyes and was fairly sure they didn't show the effects of her memories, the ones that always brought tears. *Silly girl.*

'Good afternoon, Miss Morehouse.'

Jillian started, biting her tongue to keep from saying 'Oh!' Ewan Exeter had come round the other side of the statue and was suddenly in front of her, all height and tailored clothing and cool grey eyes. He reached for her hand, and she extended it without thinking. He brought her gloved fingers to his lips, not touching, just bending over them, closely. She could feel the warmth of his breath through her gloves.

'Shall we walk?' he asked, tucking her hand under his elbow. 'It's a lovely day.'

Jillian's arm fit snugly in the crook of Exeter's, and he placed his other hand atop hers, pulling her gently to his side. The familiarity did not escape her. It was not quite indecorous, but it neared the border.

They walked, unhurriedly. It was indeed a lovely day. The acrid daily smoke of London seemed to have blown away, and summer scented the air. As they chatted about everything and nothing, Exeter let his grey eyes dance lightly over Jillian's face and figure. He didn't comment, but neither did any detail escape his inspection. His smile telegraphed admiration. Not too bold, but, like his hand atop hers, skirting the border.

Strolling around the Serpentine with a man who cast admiring glances at her – it wasn't at all what she'd expected. Not that she'd thought the detective inspector would question her at pistol point and then clap her in irons. If he'd wanted to do that, he could have done it any time in the past few months. Jillian relaxed, watching the breeze tease ripples from the lake, the water reflecting a bluer sky than usual. A few couples in small, rented boats rowed inexpertly, laughing. Children in smocks toddled by on the path, holding their nursemaids' hands. Some off-duty bandsmen stood in a group, smiling at the nursemaids. All perfectly ordinary, perfectly pleasant.

It was time to believe what Exeter had said, that the file on Sir Hubert Alloway was closed. It must be, since she was here on

Exeter's arm and hadn't read a word in the papers about the case since... She couldn't remember. Still, something fluttered in Jillian's breast. Confusion? Nerves? Relief? The flutter was no sparrow; it had black wings and Kell's voice. '...*you shouldn't have anything more to do with him.*'

'Detective inspector.' She looked up at him, so very tall. 'You said you wished to ask me something about–' About the thing she wanted to avoid mentioning more than anything in the world. 'Something procedural?'

'Oh, yes.' Had he just stroked her hand? 'I do. But it's a trivial thing and it's such a very fine day.' He glanced down at her. His smile was broad, warm, and open.

What a fine smile he had, and such a good-looking face, so smoothly shaven. And his cologne, bergamot and citrus, that he must have splashed on his cheeks after shaving. Attractive.

'The truth is,' he said, halting their progress so he could look directly at her, 'I so seldom get away from the Yard, from my work. It follows me nearly everywhere, at every hour of the day.' He formed a rueful smile. 'I can't say when I last took a turn around the Serpentine on my own, much less with a charming companion. Would you oblige me? Only if you care to, of course. Do you? Dare I hope you wouldn't mind?' There was a diffident charm in the way he asked.

She smiled. How could she not? 'Of course, I don't mind. But no boats.'

He laughed, the sound as warm as his eyes and his smile. 'No boats, I do hereby vow.'

They did their longer promenade around the lake and Jillian lost herself in the simple pleasure of it. Exeter had a string of amusing stories about boats and rowing and unscheduled tumbles into the drink. Jillian laughed as she hadn't laughed in months. After they made the circuit, Exeter suddenly said, 'I've just realised, I'm famished! What about you, Miss Morehouse? Shall we lunch?'

Jillian thought if she didn't say yes, the inspector might insist – was insisting, rather – with slate eyes fixed on hers, a soft smile playing on his lips. 'Yes, that would be delightful, detective inspector. If you have the time.'

'I will make the time. And please, call me Ewan.' Then, he did kiss her hand. The flutter in Jillian's chest became the wings of a lark.

The afternoon was delightful. They lunched at the Trocadero Restaurant on Leicester Square. Jillian had heard of it, all London had, but she'd never been. Exeter was known there and they were immediately shown to a quiet table, even though the rest of the place was as noisy and crowded as a railway station.

Exeter insisted on ordering for her, and she let him. Over lobster bisque, then lamb, asparagus salad, and a sorbet, Exeter made her laugh again, dozens of times. His impressions of men who worked for him were so comical. One was a Scotsman named McCabe, whose Glaswegian accent was so thick that even the other Scots on the force couldn't understand him. There was Dufford, a wizened sergeant from the Peeler era fifty years ago. Duff was kept on for sentiment's sake, though he'd quite forgotten where he was or how to get home every day, so the constables took it in turns to escort him. Exeter's portraits were terrifically funny but not mean-spirited. By the time they were enjoying kirsch-flavoured mousse and coffee, Jillian felt entirely at ease.

Then, Exeter asked her about her family and her childhood, and Jillian lost some of her *joie de vivre*. She told Exeter about Pon, about his joining the Navy. Exeter congratulated both of them warmly. It was conventional and patriotic to say that, but she appreciated it anyway. He asked about her parents, and Jillian's narrative ground to a halt. For a while, there was nothing but the muted clatter of the restaurant, diners talking, china and glassware clinking, the swish of waiters moving past.

Exeter ended the pause. 'Please forgive me. I've pried and I didn't mean to. I'm a bounder.' His hand, warm, hard, and dry as it had been the day he shook hers at Salon Sirena, rested on hers for a moment. She had taken off her gloves to dine, and the shock of his flesh made the fluttering in her chest start again.

'It's quite all right,' she told him. 'It's just that I try not to think of them. They died within a few weeks of each other, my father quite suddenly and then Mother – well, her decline was rapid and unexpected.'

Wasn't death always unexpected? People said it wasn't. *Oh, yes, he was quite old, we expected it.* Or, *she had been ill for some time. It was only to be expected.* But no one ever expects someone they love to die, not really, not ever.

Her body jerked slightly when Exeter offered his handkerchief, since she didn't know she was weeping. And she wasn't, really, just a filling of her eyes. He was being gallant, so she dabbed at their corners.

Smiling, she gave back his handkerchief. 'Detective Inspector, as you mentioned in your note, would you care to ask me questions about–' *Say it, Jillian.* 'Larches?'

'Absolutely not.' Exeter rose, then moved behind her chair. He bent over, his mouth next to her ear – because of the noise in the restaurant, of course – and said, 'I am having far too pleasant a day, with far too pleasant a young lady, to ruin it with that or any other police matter.

'We,' he added as he hooked his arm in hers again and led her away from the table, 'are going to a variety show.'

The matinée at The Gaiety was called *Tuppence Thruppence*. It was nearly dusk when she and Exeter left the theatre. He hailed a hackney cab and insisted on accompanying her home. Jillian was too embarrassed to let him see where she lived, the single room in a sad-looking building a fifteen-minute walk from Salon Sirena, so she asked him to leave her at the shop, giving a flimsy excuse that Exeter probably didn't believe but didn't contest. He helped her down at the kerb, then watched while she opened the salon door with the key Madame had given her. Jillian waved goodbye and he gave her an elaborate bow, which made her giggle.

Inside, she waited in the workroom for a few minutes, then let herself out by the alley door. She walked briskly back to her – to Kell's – room, where Ada had returned and was surprised to see her out so late on a Sunday. Jillian didn't precisely lie to Ada, but she didn't tell the truth, either. She gave her a tale that went round Robin Hood's barn and came back to the dent-in-the-wall. It was probably, no, *certainly* wrong, but she left the detective inspector out of it altogether. She was sorry about lying to Ada, or at least lying by omission. But telling Ada anything meant telling Kell, so a vague fiction was safer than the truth.

Ada's chatter occupied part of Jillian's mind as she put away her clothes, washed her face in the bowl, and pulled on her nightdress. The chatter was about Ada's day, about her younger sister and how useless at cookery she was, even though their mother tried and tried to teach her. Eileen had turned a loaf of bread into a doorstop that afternoon, and Jillian managed to laugh at the right parts of the story.

The larger part of her mind was at war. She truly had enjoyed herself with Ewan. He hadn't inserted police business into the day and, when she tried, he brushed it away. Twice. Surely, he had no serious suspicions about her part in the Larches affair, or he would have said something by now.

She turned down the gas lamp and they settled into bed, Ada falling asleep almost instantly, as she usually did. Jillian lay awake, but it wasn't Larches that pushed sleep away.

It was Kell. He'd told her to avoid Ewan Exeter, and she'd defied him. Defied him? Who was Michael Kelly to order her to do anything? Jillian rolled onto her side and stared at the wardrobe that, in the dark, was just a darker shape. Doing a spot of carpentry and delivering some clothes hangers – what did that make Kell to her, that he could tell her what to do?

It wasn't as though she'd done anything wrong. On the contrary, that afternoon she'd felt right about herself, about the world, for the first time in years. The hours Ewan Exeter gave her were everything right about her life before St Margaret's. Grace and refinement, crystal and silver, easy conversation. She refused to feel guilty about them. The only troubling thing was...

The only troubling thing was that, lying in the dark, all she could think of was her hand on Kell's forearm in the alley behind Salon Sirena. What if she'd been in Hyde Park with Ada's brother, her arm hooked not in Exeter's but in Kell's magnificently strong one, his hard, calloused hand heavy on hers as they took a turn around the lake?

She imagined Kell asking her to lunch. Not at the Trocadero. A packed lunch, perhaps, like the one she and her parents had shared in St James's Park. She would sit on a cloth on the ground while Kell reclined, his body stretched like a big cat's next to her.

The theatre... Every time she laughed at one of the actors' silly lines, it would be Kell laughing next to her, white teeth flashing, voice deep and rough as he said, 'That's a good one!' And then he would stretch an arm across the back of her seat, and she would curl into him, into his warmth and power and sandalwood. There, in the curve of his arm, she might turn her face up to his and he might bend to kiss her, the kiss hidden in the dark of the theatre.

Jillian sighed into the night. She'd been looking forward to a few private minutes before sleep to remember the fine afternoon she'd had. The real one, not the one haunted by a ghost named Michael Kelly. She forced her thoughts back to the light-hearted hours with a man who made her remember good things, not a man who tempted her to bad ones.

She shut her eyes and began counting sheep. After fifty, the sheep became dancers in *Tuppence Thruppence*, capering on the stage in the footlights. After fifty more dancing woollies, sleep smothered her guilt about everything.

Chapter Fifteen

Kell and Dague came from the darkness to catch Exeter walking up the steps to his own door. Kell snarled as he seized both the policeman's arms from behind. 'You think you're sharp, Scraper, sharp as a needle. Let's see how quick you can learn something new.'

While the Frenchman stood sentry at the mouth of the mews alongside Exeter's residence, Kell frog-marched the policeman twenty paces up the passage. The closely gathered shadows there were barely kept at bay by the streetlamp on the corner behind them. Exeter went without protest, though his lean body was a tight coil of resistance.

In the alley, Kell slammed his captive cheek first into a brick wall, then gripped and twisted Exeter's left wrist hard enough to sprain it. He used his other hand to yank Exeter's right wrist so high up the policeman's back that the shoulder bulged. Under his body, Kell could feel the joint on the edge of popping from its socket.

'Took her to The Gaiety, didn't you?' he snarled into Exeter's ear. 'Took her there so Reenie Storme could see you over the footlights, see you sitting with a younger version of herself, as young as she was when you made London's sweetheart of the stage your mistress. Give you a stiffy, did it? Watching the one you been ridin' for years while you sit next to the one you plan to ride next?

'I know you're not getting bored with Reenie. Is she getting bored with you, Scraper? Getting restless? Is that why you took Jillian Morehouse there? Thinking it would shake Reenie up, remind her what side her bread's buttered on?'

Kell levered the policeman's arm up another inch, and Exeter bit his lip not to groan, showing blood. 'Or are you buying Jillian's company by not pressing her harder about what you *think* happened to Sir Hubert Alloway? Using what you *think* you know to get in her knickers?'

He laced threats into the pain. 'You fucking bastard, I should cut your prick off. Touch Jillian Morehouse one more time and I will.'

Kell knew Exeter well. Knew what he was thinking through the haze of agony spreading from his shoulder. Thinking that if he could just break the iron grip Kell had on his left wrist, he could reach his *sgian-dubh*, the short, wicked-sharp Scottish knife he kept strapped to his ankle. Thinking two seconds was all it would take.

Too long, Scraper. Kell could spin him around in one second and deliver a drop-hammer fist to Exeter's face. He didn't need to remind his old gang leader what that fist did to the faces of men. Exeter had seen it. The first blow would be just that, the first. There would be more, many more. It would be hard for Exeter to maintain his suave image looking like something the butcher had put through a grinder.

Even if by some improbable chance Exeter got to his knife, and if by an even more improbable chance he disabled Kell, there would still be Dague. Dague, whose size belied his stealth, had spied on Exeter's whole afternoon with Jillian Morehouse and had his see-in-dark eyes on the detective inspector now. Whether Kell or Dague did the deed, Exeter would be just as dead. Kell knew the detective inspector, in the space of five laboured breaths, realised all of that.

Kell sensed the instant of slack in Exeter's resistance when he decided to concede, at least for the moment. He did it in the voice that had been his when they were both in the Jacks.

'Fuckin' hell, mate! Just taking the mickey out ya. The bint don't look like nothin' special to me, but if you fancy her, say no more. She's cut and carried from here on out.'

Cut and carried. Rhyming slang for married.

Kell loosed his hold at the same time he shoved his captive away from him, up the passage. Exeter stumbled with the force of the shove but caught himself before he fell. Kell was gratified by the alarm on his former chieftain's face as he skirted the ultimate indignity. Scraper, leader of the Jacks, falling to his knees in front of Michael Kelly.

Straightening, Exeter rubbed his shoulder, then rotated it to make sure it wasn't dislocated or, as it probably felt, broken. It wasn't, but Kell knew it would be a week before Exeter could shave himself with that arm. He'd be giving Mayfair barbers daily trade until then.

'As far as that Larches business goes,' Exeter began, 'I don't give a monkey's dick what happened. And I've never once needed to threaten any skirt to get her to open her legs. So put that right out of your head, Stammer.'

'Stay away from her, Ex.' Time to drop the gang names and the games that went with them. 'Stay away or I'll...' Kell let the ultimatum hang, unfinished. Even in the near black of the alley, he was sure Exeter could see the threat, hear it in every syllable, feel it in the parts of his body Kell had already treated to pain.

A muscle twitched in Kell's jaw; his hands were flexing and tightening at his sides. Exeter's eyes flickered, an acknowledgement that he saw the signs and knew he needed to tread lightly. He had, after all, seen Kell like that before, in the seconds before bad things happened. Usually to bad people, but no one had ever called Exeter good.

The detective inspector held his hands in front of him, palms outward. 'Kell, mate, let's not do this. Let's not be at each other's throats like pit dogs. I may be an old cynic, but even I can see you don't just want to poke the bint. You're fallin' in love with her. However much I doubt the wisdom of that, it is entirely your affair.' Exeter bowed deeply, rising with a mocking smile. 'Or your funeral. But whatever it is, it's not worth making it mine.' He extended his hand, carefully. 'Mates again?'

Keeping blade-sharp eyes on the policeman, Kell nodded once. No handshake, for which Exeter's shoulder should be grateful.

The detective moved closer, cautiously, like approaching a lion. 'Say now, Kell, I've got an offer for you.'

'You've never offered me anything that ended well, Ex.'

'Brother, you wound me! And the fifty thousand pounds or so you've made off things I've offered you in the past? They say you're a liar.'

Silence from Kell, followed by a barking laugh from Exeter. 'You haven't told her, have you?'

Kell growled a reply. 'When were you going to tell her about *your* past, Ex? Cause it's the same as mine, *brother*, only longer and dirtier.'

'Kell, Kell... I thought we'd just established that there's no need for me to tell the bint about my past, since she and I aren't going to have a future. I'll grieve a bit for the delightful present we were having...'

Kell's growl deepened, and he took a step toward the detective.

'Easy, Kell! One turn around the park, a meal, and a show. No harm done and there'll never be another, per your eloquent instructions.'

Exeter reached slowly and gingerly into the breast pocket of his jacket and removed a cigar case. Opening it, he offered it to Kell, who didn't respond except to keep his eyes trained on the policeman's hands, noting their faint tremor.

Exeter removed a cigar, returning the case to his jacket. He bit off the end of the smoke and spat it out. As slowly as extracting the case, he took a silver vesta box out of his trouser pocket and used it to light up. After a few aromatic puffs, he spoke again.

'As to what you've told or not told the filly, we both have secrets. I've always kept yours. You keep mine.

'No more talk about the past, all right? And no more idle palaver about women. I know you're inclined to throw my offers back in my face but, since we're mates again, I've something for you and you should at least consider it. I need a captain.'

Captain. A chucker-out for a gambling den, but in Exeter's dens Kell had been the enforcer, too. The debt collector, the leg breaker, the ruiner of men already half ruined by the gaming tables. Captain. The half-joking, half-admiring name he wore in the fight ring, when Exeter realised Kell's fists weren't only useful, they were profitable. Captain. The title Kell had left off the list when Jillian asked him what his job was called.

Kell hadn't thought there was much about Exeter that would confound him, but his head rocked back. 'I thought we left that muck behind in Seven Dials.'

'We left Seven Dials behind. But gambling – I'm not talking about some backwater hell. Sneaking, draughty cellars with barrel-top tables and no chairs. That was shillings and pence, mate, hard graft and small beer. Now it's a stately gaming house, posh and discreet. Do you get the picture? Patrons who wear evening dress and bring their jewelled ladies. And better games, Kell. Roulette, chemin de fer, baccarat. A separate room for the ladies to play faro and mahjong.'

Exeter leaned forward, looking like he might try to put a hand on Kell's shoulder. The detective inspector obviously thought better of it and kept talking. 'That American game, poker. *High stakes* poker. Thoroughbred horses, country houses, gemstones, all on the table, mate. And here's the best part.' Exeter looked to the left, then right, before he spoke again, his words hushed like he was sharing some sort of state secret. 'It's in St John's Wood.'

St John's Wood. Another hell, one for toffs. 'And what about the deal you made with the Cortellis, Ex? You're really looking to get a stiletto in the eye, aren't you?'

'It's your eye you'd better have a care for, mate. I'm not the one who took out Fedo Cortelli.'

'It was a fair fight.'

'And things happen. You know that, and I know that. But those Sicilians...' Exeter pulled back and smoked his cigar for a few seconds. 'Vengeance is a long game, Kell.'

'We gave 'em Seven Dials.'

Just for a second, Exeter's eyes turned hard, granite grey and lethal. '*I* gave 'em Seven Dials. Because of you.'

And there it was. The debt Kell would always owe Exeter. For the ten thousandth time, Kell wished it had been Exeter who had dealt the murderous punch, the one that took out Aurelio Cortelli's nephew. The punch that left the nineteen-year-old as good as dead in a fight ring in a warehouse in Wapping. The punch that killed the Jacks.

Exeter rocked back on his heels, the cold stone in his eyes disappearing and his sardonic humour returning. 'Didn't much matter. The law was closin' in anyway. All the Cortellis got when they got Seven Dials was a few months of profit and two years of arrests.'

True. Exeter, with his uncanny ability to stay just ahead of the game, had known he was handing the Cortellis the worst kind of gift. A slum district set square in the sights of a heavily muscled Metropolitan Police Force. The force itching to prove they deserved their expensive new headquarters being raised on the Embankment. All fired up, the force was, to publicly scrub clean the crime-darkened rookeries of London. By the time the bricks were mortared into New Scotland Yard, the Cortellis, what was left of them, had slouched back to Birmingham.

Done with guilt, Exeter went back to flattery. 'Come now, Kell. You were the best captain there ever was, you know that.'

The flattery didn't work on Kell any better than the guilt had. 'I was a captain, and I was a partner. Then it was finished, and I walked away. Why in steaming godforsaken hell would I go back and do it again?'

Exeter turned up his hands. The cigar in his right sent fragrant shreds of smoke into the air. 'Same reason as before. Tevisses, long-tails, gens, thick'uns. *Money*. Just more of it. And you could still be a partner, Kell.'

'You're a detective inspector with the Metropolitan Police.'

Exeter faked a public school accent. 'Dashed fine of you to remember, old chum.' Back in his usual silky voice, he reasoned as only Exeter would, 'What's the good of having a position like mine if I can't use it to get a leg up? Or did you think I'd become a social reformer?'

'Let me guess, mate.' Exeter looked at his cigar like it no longer tasted good, rubbed it out on the wall, and kept talking. 'Between what you gave Mam Kelly and the one whelp still at home – what's her name? Ellen? Eileen? – and what you've sunk into a neat little property in Hackney, you're nearly skint, aren't you?'

Kell wasn't about to answer. It didn't surprise him that the detective inspector had found out about the house in Hackney. Always with his ear to the ground and his nose up other people's jacksies, that was Exeter. There wasn't much he didn't know or couldn't find out.

As to Kell's financial condition, though... A few years ago, he'd found a spirited young banker who wasn't put off by where money came from. Judicious investments had turned his ill-gotten gains into a staggering sum, healthily earning interest from where it was tucked far away from prying noses like Exeter's. His former chieftain didn't know about any of that, as his next remark proved.

'You move the bint into that house, Kell, and you'll want for things. *She'll* want for things. Chairs and tables and sideboards and what-nots. All that costs, mate, all that adds up.'

Still, Kell said nothing. Even if he hadn't had all the money he needed, he'd be damned if he'd let Exeter talk him into being a Jack again for the sake of a sofa. Or the keys to Buckingham Palace or to heaven itself.

Exeter clearly misread his silence as halfway to acquiescence, because that was his style. He always thought he was irresistible. To those who didn't know him, he was.

Kell played his last card. 'And the Cortellis, Ex? You just reminded me they haven't forgotten. Or are you thinkin' different, now?'

'I think Birmingham is a long way from St John's Wood. Aurelio's dead. Son Raffaello's running the show now, and he was in short pants when that other business happened. He's making so much from the racehorses and the docks up north he can't spend it fast enough. We're nothin' to him anymore.'

Bollocks. The Jacks might be nothing to Raff Cortelli but he, Kell, would always be something, if not to Raff than to somebody else. A thorn needing to be pulled. A black mark needing to be scrubbed off. A body waiting for the knife of vendetta.

The detective put his hand into his trouser pocket again, and again Kell watched alertly.

Exeter saw him watching and withdrew the hand slowly, a satyr's smile on his handsome face. 'Just a coin, mate.' He flipped it high, a flash of bright metal in the streetlamp's glow. Kell caught it mid-flight. 'Take your girl out. Show her a good time. Give her a kiss from the detective inspector.'

Exeter sauntered back up the alley toward his house. Dague looked back at Kell, who nodded, and the big man stepped aside to let Exeter pass, which the policeman did with a jaunty salute.

Kell looked at the coin in his hand. A gold sovereign. He strode to the street end of the mews and made a hand sign toward Dague.

Dague responded with the same signal and the two separated, Dague heading one way and Kell the other. Night stalkers. Lawbreakers. They were used to prowling London in the dark.

At the first sewer grate Kell saw, he dropped in the coin.

Threatening Exeter had appeased one dark animal tearing at his gut. Now there was another, and no way to ignore it. Before Exeter forgot the threats and made a run at her again, Kell would have to ask Jillian out. She would reject him, and it would kill him for a while. But nothing would kill him as slowly or painfully as not asking her and then despising himself for it. He'd go by his old Soho room in the morning and slip a note under the door for her to find when she got back from work.

He'd just have to be ready to deal with the reply.

Chapter Sixteen

The next morning, Jillian would have liked to tell everyone in the workroom how she spent her Sunday afternoon. Not Ada, though, because Ada would tell her brother. She wasn't sure Evie and Min needed to hear about it, either. Min would probably fall off her chair if she knew Jillian had swanned off to a restaurant and the theatre with a man – a *policeman* – she barely knew. Or maybe the new Min would take it in her stride. Her workmate wasn't quite the tongue-tied wallflower she'd been before a man named Dagger taught her to juggle almonds in the alley. As for Evie, she had everyone's attention because she was putting finishing touches on the ugliest corset any of them had ever seen.

Evie noticed the three pairs of eyes glued to her work, so she held it up. 'What colour, *précisement*, you would say is this?'

Ada rose and went to the corkboard. She squinted at the order form. 'Says here it's camel.'

Evie rolled her big, brown eyes. '*D'accord*, I agree it is something animal.'

Ada reached over Evie's shoulder to pick up a scrap of the fabric. 'More like somethin' that comes *out* of an animal.'

'And stiff as the board, too!' Evie flexed the corset in her hands. It barely curved. 'Not only fourteen steel bones, but she demand four layers of buckram inside. Four! It is a suit of armour for a *chevalier.*'

Jillian asked, 'Who's the lucky woman whose husband will see her in that thing?'

Ada went back to the order form. 'No husband. It was ordered by a Miss Eugenia Lyttle.'

'Bloody hell!' Min's outburst made the others freeze, open-mouthed, and Evie dropped her scissors. Min's most violent oaths to date had been *good heavens!* and, when really vexed, *bamfoozle!*

'Min,' whispered Evie, 'you should not use such language.'

Even Ada was taken aback. 'Murderin' magpies, Min. What's got into you?'

Min ignored them both. 'If that's *the* Eugenia Lyttle, she's the most– Well, I never met her, of course, but the papers all say... I mean, she's always in the press. And if she's not marching and waving signs in front of Parliament, then she's saying the most *inflammatory* things at– I can hardly believe it's her, she's an Amazon! She's been to *prison*! And she doesn't even *believe* in corsets!'

'Miss Jillian,' fluted Ada, 'you will find smelling salts in the cupboard over the teakettle. I do believe our Minerva is having a seizure.'

Jillian stayed in her seat. 'It's not a seizure, it's news. Miss Eugenia Lyttle is famous in the Women's Suffrage Movement. She supports rational dress, too.'

Ada harrumphed. 'What the blazes is national dress?'

'Rational, not national. You know, bicycling skirts. And no corsets, like Min said.'

Min nodded fiercely. 'She's a *New Woman.*'

Ada took her chair again and picked up her own order, a Number Seven in the palest shade of ecru, with apricot topstitching and matching ribbon trim. 'If this new woman don't believe in stays, why'd she pay in advance for–' she pointed her shears at Evie's work, 'that dog's breakfast?'

Jillian thought she knew. 'Some men have threatened the Women's Suffrage with pistols. *The Daily Telegraph* printed a note Miss Lyttle got in the post. It said she'd get a bullet in the heart if she didn't stop leading the women of Britain to damnation with her blankety-blank mouth.'

Everyone stopped working again. Ada asked, 'Did *The Telegraph* print the blankety-blank?'

'No, they just used underlined spaces, the way the papers do.'

Evie gestured at Jillian with her needle. 'The man who make the threat – do you think he would do it? Shoot Mademoiselle Lyttle?'

Jillian didn't have an answer. She shook her head and went back to her sewing, along with the others. For a stomach-dropping moment, she thought about Larches and Sir Hubert Alloway. About what would have happened to her, what happened to women all the time, if she hadn't had the carving knife in her hand when she was attacked. If only women had better ways to defend themselves from the Sir Huberts of the world...

No one mentioned Eugenia Lyttle, armour-plated corsets, or pistols again, but Jillian was pretty sure they were all thinking about them.

The workroom had just settled when Madame thrust her head through the drape and called, 'Jilly!' in a low, urgent voice. Something in her voice propelled Jillian to her feet. She started for the drape, but Madame gestured frantically at Jillian's apron. While the other corset girls blinked, wide-eyed as a trio of lemurs, Jillian whipped off the apron and dropped it on her chair, then rushed after Madame into the showroom.

<hr>

'Oh, thank God, Ada! You've brought me food!' Jillian shut her eyes and inhaled the steam from the pastry-covered crock Ada plonked on the kitchen table at the back of the workroom.

Ada handed over a fork. 'Steak an' kidney pie from The Crown an' Sceptre. Still warm?'

Sliding into a chair at the table, Jillian dug into the pie and brought a forkful to her mouth. She nodded, making happy sounds around the mouthful.

Min pulled over a chair. 'You were in the showroom with Madame for *hours*, Jilly! What happened?'

Jillian gulped tea from the mug Evie gave her. 'Two clients. New to us, but definitely *not* New Women. The opposite of New Women, I'd say.'

Ada chortled. 'Starchy, were they? As starchy as old Cruikshank?'

'Starchier. A marchioness and her daughter.'

'The Marchioness Melton and her daughter Lady Rosaline!' Min's exclamation brought everything to a screeching halt. The other three watched pink flood Min's face. 'I peeked around the drape and saw Madame introduce Jillian.'

Evie wagged a finger. 'Minerva, you know Madame does not like the peeking.'

Ada liked it well enough. 'Bowlin' bishops, Jilly! You're movin' up in the world.'

'Not me, but the daughter's going up like a gasbag. She's engaged to a duke.'

All at the same time, Ada gave a low whistle, Min gasped, and Evie said, '*Mon Dieu!*'

Ada's face promptly went smug. 'Madame went out right after the la-di-dahs did. She's probably gettin' squiffed somewhere.' She and Evie pulled their chairs over, too, crowding the tiny kitchen. 'Spill it, Jilly. Tell. Us. All.'

Jillian began with the moment she was pushed forward as 'Miss Morehouse, my principal assistant and an expert *corsetière*' to the mother – wife of Rodney Saverin Grenoille, Marquess Melton – and the daughter. After the frightening introductions, Jillian took the daughter, Lady Rosaline, behind a screen to take her measures and listen to her prattle, while Madame showed the Marchioness every costly roll of cloth, card of trim, and style sketch for a trousseau of *sous-vêtements* befitting a noble bride.

'The order will tot up to two hundred pounds,' Jillian said between bites, 'maybe more.'

Ada was less interested in profits than personages. 'Who's the bloke?'

'The Duke of–'

Min's awed voice interjected. 'I didn't think there were any dukes left.'

Jillian swallowed a forkful of pie. 'Must be a few, since Lady Rosaline got her teeth into one. In her second season, no less. Alford Framington Locke, Duke of Fells and St Andrews.'

Ada smirked. 'Some old geezer, is he?'

'Wouldn't say he was decrepit. Thirty-seven, Lady Rosaline said, and she's twenty-two.' Jillian finished the last of the pie and pushed the dish away. 'They met at Lord Melton's hunting lodge in Scotland. Duke's off somewhere now, and the Marquess's Kensington house is being done over, so the whole Melton clan, except for a son who's making the Grand Tour, are camping at the duke's townhouse. In Belgravia.'

'Rich as Croesus,' Ada clucked disgustedly, 'all of 'em.' Ada had just learned about Croesus from her new *Wilmott's*, and the Lydian king regularly worked his way into conversation.

Jillian sighed. 'I imagine so. Isn't everybody, except us?'

That observation took the fizz off the story. Everyone moved back to the worktable, picked up their sewing, and looked for threaded needles and shears.

Everybody's rich except us. Jillian didn't know what the others were thinking as they worked, but she was having a hard time getting that particular thought out of her head. She tried concentrating on her work for the day, a truly delicious Number Seven in sage with blue-green trim, but she kept returning to the spectre she'd raised, the spectre of want. What she'd said wasn't entirely true, but it wasn't false, either.

She and the others were ants, worker bees, the mine ponies of Britain. Jillian didn't consider herself a socialist, but she couldn't help thinking about the injustice of it all. She and Ada, Min and Evie – they might be *corsetières* all their lives, or at least until their eyes gave out and their fingers got so arthritic they couldn't wield needles anymore. That didn't depress Jillian so much as the prospect of plodding into that future alone. *Needle in the casing, measure the interval, pull the thread taut, needle in the casing...*

In the grand machine of British labour, they were just four corset girls. Though there wasn't much that was girlish about them, less and less each day. Listening to the happy gabble of Lady Rosaline made it clear what a sorority of spinsters she and her workmates were, lonely, unattached, and rudderless. Drifting through life like boats broken free of their moorings.

Min, orphaned so young she didn't remember her parents at all, then reared by an ancient couple in the country to be a maiden more of the eighteenth than nineteenth century. Evie, tossed by a Caribbean storm of secrets onto England's shores, sharing little about home and family and nothing about what drove her to abandon them. Ada, child of an East London slum, clawing her way out and up with a sort of fatalistic drive.

And Jillian, who clutched the *Plan* to her breast like armour, like Miss Lyttle's buckram-plated corset. *Needle out, pull the thread taut, tie a knot...*

'*Il est beau.*'

'What?' She looked up from her work to find Evie holding the cabinet photograph of Pon, the one Jillian had just retrieved from the Bakirtsis Bake Shop in Chelsea. The bakery was below her family's old flat and every few weeks she went there to get mail, though two letters and the photograph from Pon were the only mail she'd had since he went to sea. She'd brought the photograph to the salon to look at while she sewed. It made Pon seem closer.

'He is handsome,' Evie repeated in English, pronouncing it *'and-sohme*. She still had the photograph in her hand. Jillian felt a prickle of possessiveness, then quashed it. Why shouldn't Evie admire the lanky mariner with the cocky stance and Royal Navy uniform, his ribboned cap at a dashing slant?

Evie read aloud from the strip at the photograph's bottom. 'Atelier Stephanos. Salamis. Your brother's ship is in the Mediterranean, *oui*?'

'For now, it is. Or was, at the time he got his picture taken.'

'And he will return to England...?'

'I can't say. Some months, I should think. A year.'

Ada's mouth curled. 'There now, Evie. Plenty of time for you to make somethin' nice like that for him.' She jutted her chin toward a white-on-white Number Eight that Min was sewing.

Min tittered behind her hand, then said, 'Oh, no, this one's entirely too tame. I should think a man who's sailed the seven seas would want something bolder. Wouldn't you say so, Jilly?'

What Jillian would say was that Min had been getting more unpredictable every day since she'd met Étienne Sansecours. She'd also say she didn't want to dwell on Pon's taste in corsets, nor the vision of Evangeline Broussard's generous curves wrapped in one while Pon–

Ada stuck her oar back in. 'I've got it! Marine blue silk. It's only natural a broad-shouldered, seafarin' man would like a–'

Min squealed, 'Red brocade! I'm sure Evie wouldn't mind a pair of strong sailor hands tugging on the laces of–'

'I'm right here, you know,' Jillian huffed, 'and it's my brother you're slavering over.'

Ada laughed maniacally and Min giggled, then the two

shushed each other, looking over their shoulders for signs of Madame. Grumbling, Jillian returned to her work, though she kept watching Evie from the corner of her eye. They might be a sorority of spinsters now, but at least one of them was looking to the future.

The future. Where was Jillian's going? She wondered if Detective Inspector Ewan Exeter had remembered the procedural question he was supposed to have asked her but didn't, and if he might call upon her again to discuss it. In a park. Or a restaurant. Or the theatre.

Mr Michael Seraphin Kelly wouldn't like it, Jillian was sure of that. What exactly was his problem with the detective inspector? And who was Michael Kelly to say with whom she might talk, take a walk of a Sunday, or dine?

The detective inspector was polished, charming, and worldly. Also and evidently, well-to-do. His clothes were tailored and costly. He went to fine eateries, to stage shows. And he hung on her every word. Jillian suspected that if she sneezed, Ewan Exeter would smile at her as though it was the most entrancing sound he'd ever heard.

Michael Kelly was... what he was. In the alley, he'd spent as much time looking at the rooftops as he'd spent looking at her. And when it came to charm, he didn't seem to know what it was.

He charmed you into putting your hand on his arm.

That was a mistake. And even if, in that moment, he'd somehow charmed her like a fakir tootling a cobra out of a basket, was that what she wanted, to spend her life answering the call of a flute? As to his clothes, he probably didn't even own a suit. He always looked as though he'd come directly from sawing and hammering something.

Like a wardrobe?

She hadn't asked for that. As to his expression, it was a chronic scowl. Had he ever smiled at her? Oh, yes, he'd laughed at her the first time he met her, that day in Whitechapel.

When he knew you'd just killed a man with a carving knife. And he didn't immediately hand you over to be hauled off to Brixton or an asylum for the criminally insane.

Michael Kelly hadn't to her knowledge ever asked, not even once, what *she* wanted, where *she* wanted to go, whether *she'd* like to take a turn around the Serpentine.

Whether she was all right after she'd had the wits scared out of her by a drunken peer in a whorehouse, a peer Michael Kelly laid out before the man could do something worse to her than grabbing her ankle.

Jillian's chair scraped jarringly as she pushed it back. 'I need more tea,' she told Ada as she stood, 'I've just got the most terrible headache.'

Chapter Seventeen

aybe if Michael Kelly had asked for more, Jillian would have refused him. To accept any sort of social engagement with a man like him just wasn't in the *Plan*. But all he'd asked in his note was for her to meet with him the next Sunday. He wrote that he would like to take her to Hackney to see a house. Harmless enough.

When Sunday came around, Ada went to her mother's again. Jillian was relieved, since she hadn't told Ada about Kell's note and she wasn't sure what her friend might think about it. Jillian wasn't sure what she thought, either. She wasn't even sure where or what Hackney was. A newer part of London, she knew that much. Her work didn't leave her time for exploring the city and she certainly wasn't shopping for a house. She knew there were neighbourhoods springing up all over, barely ahead of the ever-expanding underground stops and rail lines. She'd go to Hackney with Kell to satisfy her curiosity.

What she couldn't decide was whether she was curious about London suburbs or the man who'd invited her. Either way, she also needed to decide what to wear.

After an hour in front of the wardrobe, taking things off hangers, trying them on, and putting them back, Jillian still hadn't decided, any more than she could say why she was so undecided. Finally, she committed to a white pleated shirtwaist and a dark grey walking skirt. She put a tailored red wool jacket on top for warmth, the weather being so unpredictable. The jacket was puffed in the shoulders and very tightly nipped in at the waist. Flattering, but not flash.

She bickered with herself for five more minutes about pinning the yellow orchid corsage to the jacket breast front. It seemed affected, as though she was trying to flirt. Somehow, it seemed fine to flirt with Ewan Exeter, but not with Kell. She stood with the corsage in her hand while *wear it!* and *never!* shouted back and forth in her head like a debate in Parliament. Galloping geese, as Ada would say, it was just a bunch of flowers. Why devote five minutes to it? She put the corsage back in the hatbox and shoved the box under the bed.

The corsage debate was ridiculous, and so was the trouble she was taking with her dress. Every time she'd seen Kell, he was in workman's clothing. Did he own anything apart from coarse trousers and patched shirts?

Bring back the galloping geese and add cartwheeling cats to them. She opened the dent-in-the-wall's door to Kell after the three knocks that always announced him and went utterly still, stunned by the spectacle on the landing. Perhaps she was a cobra, after all. Then, her mouth fell open and a little gasp escaped, a gasp she was pretty sure the spectacle heard. And that was unnerving not only because it was gauche but because the gasp said loud and clear that Kell was the handsomest man she had ever seen.

For a few seconds, it was all she could do – stand there in a trance and gape at the handsome man. The man in the exquisitely tailored dark blue suit, the gunmetal waistcoat, the brilliant white shirt and yellow silk tie.

And the raven hair. Kell was hatless, and if she hadn't already been trembling like a blancmange she would have shivered with pleasure at that. It would have been criminal to cover the smooth, rippling waves of black, neatly brushed back from a shapely hairline and gleaming naturally, not with the oily pomade so many men used. The hair framed the clean-shaven jut of his jaw, the smooth forehead, and the brooding dark brows above his extraordinary eyes.

If Kell noticed she'd fallen into a catatonic state, he didn't say anything about it. It was perfectly possible, now that she'd seen him turned out like a plate in *Men's Wear Review*, that he was inured to women becoming mute, pop-eyed ninnies around him. No wonder he dressed roughly so much of the time. Jillian was sure that if his everyday dress was what he was wearing today, women would follow him up the street in flocks, like ewes.

Without a word, Kell held out his elbow. Jillian took it as they left the room and started down the stairs, the same stairs where – impossible as it seemed – they'd had a fractious conversation a few weeks earlier. His body brushed against hers as they descended, which probably should have alarmed her, but didn't at all. He was warm, close, and solid everywhere they touched, and he smelled so good that she wanted, alarmingly, to brush against him more than was strictly necessary.

Her stomach filled with nervous goldfish, flipping and flopping all the way to the bottom of the stairs.

They took the train to Hackney. Jillian hadn't been in a train since the one that had brought her back to London from St Margaret's and, at first, the view from the window was exhilarating. Tenements and churches, offices and hospitals, an occasional patch of green, all flying past. But not long after they boarded, she realised Kell, who sat opposite, was looking down at his feet, not at her nor even at the scenery.

The goldfish in her stomach sank slowly and died. Was their day out going to consist of her sitting mutely and staring at her attractive companion? Were they not going to talk? Or, if they did, would their talk be as awkward and confused as it had been so far?

That simply wouldn't do. If he wasn't going to start some discourse, she would. Safely. The weather was very agreeable, didn't he think so? He grunted, which she took to be assent, and that dispatched the topic of weather.

After a few minutes, and with a clipped economy of words, he pointed out the train was emptier than on a weekday. 'Usually crowded,' he said, staring at the seat to her right which was, indeed, empty, and adding, 'Not today.'

Jillian offered a foolish and breathless explanation that the vast numbers of people who worked in the City were home with their families enjoying an afternoon of rest or perhaps a concert in a park after their Sunday luncheon so they wouldn't be taking trains or at least that was what she assumed didn't he agree?

Not having a specialist tool to unsnarl her babble, Kell just pleated his brow.

She must. Not. Ramble. Squaring her shoulders, Jillian suggested that their seats seemed new and were quite comfortable. He looked at her like she'd said there were badgers sitting in them, then resumed his fixed regard of his shoes.

Panic rose in her chest and came out as a little screech. 'Is that Bethnal *Greeeen*?' She pointed out the window. 'There was silk weaving there once, wasn't there?'

Kell aimed an inscrutable scowl at the view.

Had her remark about weaving somehow depressed him? She

thought he was from Ireland, not Lancashire, but perhaps he'd worked in a factory. Was he recalling child labour on looms?

She hadn't been completely unprepared for small talk. Before she started quarrelling with herself over an orchid corsage, she'd rehearsed a half-dozen topics, all of which she hoped would spark witty dialogue. Now she ticked them off one by one, each one sounding more ill-advised than the one before.

Had he heard Vincent van Gogh was dead and what did Kell think of his art? No, that made her sound like one of those dilettantes who lived in Bloomsbury and posed naked for dissolute painters.

How did he feel about the Irish Nationalists rejecting Parnell on account of his divorce? Really, if she wanted to pick a fight with the man, why not just throw a shoe at him?

Did he know Spain had adopted universal suffrage? Oh, no, no, no. What had she been thinking, that she could start with vote-casting *señoritas* and go on to Eugenia Lyttle's buckram-plated corset?

There was no point, anyway, if his side of the exchange was going to be made up of black looks, grunts, growls, and monosyllabic comments, leaving her wondering what he'd just said. Maybe she should buy one of those books explorers published, decoding the language of remote tribes.

There would be no sparkling dialogue on the train; on that, they seemed to wordlessly agree. Quiet filled the car like pillow stuffing. The few other passengers aboard also weren't chatting or were speaking too softly for Jillian to distinguish words. The wheels of the train clacked, the scenery passed by, and Jillian worked on pretending a man who smelled like desire itself wasn't sitting a few feet away.

Kell finally took a small paper bag out of his jacket pocket and offered it to her. She reached in and pulled out a lemon drop. Was it her reward for keeping quiet? Kell took a drop for himself, then tucked the bag back into his pocket.

Jillian rolled the sweet on her tongue until it dissolved, all the while thinking that, if she dared talk again, what she really wanted to say was how fine Kell looked. Perhaps she shouldn't. He might think she was being fast. Or she might forget herself and go back to rambling. She imagined with horror what that would sound like. *You know, Kell, your looks and your smell have the most amazing effect on me. I just melt in some places and heat up in others, and would you mind terribly if I rip open your shirt and lick your chest?*

He rescued her from the fatal fantasy by coughing into his fist, then speaking. 'Your ensemble is very...' His mouth worked and his brow furrowed. 'Fashionable,' he finally got out, then looked surprised, as though the word had crept up on him and sprung from his mouth. At least it gave Jillian a chance to mention his suit.

'Thank you. Your attire today is...' *Not your usual grimy togs.* 'The suit is very smart.' Excellent. Neutral but complimentary. There was hope for them. Which Jillian immediately shattered. 'You should wear a suit more often. It becomes you.'

His eyes sharpened into shards of blue ice. 'Not very practical in my line of work.'

No, it wasn't, but why did Kell have to bring *that* up again? Now they were both seeing The Flower Garden in their minds. That room, the gold-covered bed, her standing on it in a pink corset.

An ear-splitting squeal of braking locomotive sounded outside the window. Kell spoke to a spot over her head. 'We're here.'

Here? Kell had told her they were going to look at a house, but all Jillian saw outside the train was a cloud of steam from the idling engine and, through it, a tall, square building, its yellow brick exterior splotched with rain. It bore a painted sign. *Hackney.*

She took a moment to straighten her skirt and her mind. Beauty had been non-existent in her life for years, unless she counted the corsets she now made. Which she could not, because they belonged to others. When she'd thrown open the door of her room and Beauty with an uppercase B stood there, it had been like taking a lungful of opium smoke or a shot of hard liquor. She'd gone all giddy and forgotten the *Plan*. She was sober, now.

Across from her, Kell rose, offered his elbow, and Jillian took it with a resigned sigh. Curtain up on *A Disastrous Encounter*, Act Two.

Chapter Eighteen

As houses went, the one she and Kell arrived at, after a short walk from the railway station, was neat and in good condition. Two storeys, red brick, with nice window surrounds and two chimneys, one at each gable end. Three steps led up to the front door, painted an unremarkable dark green. The last house in a row, it had a gated walk at the side. Leading to a back garden, she supposed.

Not a gentleman's residence, but not a tenement, either. She tried to see Ewan Exeter opening the door to a house like this, and couldn't. Was it Kell's? She had a hard time seeing him coming home to it, either, but his was certainly the hand on the doorknob when he turned it and gestured for her to enter. She stepped over the threshold.

The house was empty of furniture but full of the quiet expectation a house has when it waits for someone to live in it. Cans of paint were stacked in the front room, even in the empty hearth. Tools and a few large folded canvas pieces rested against one wall, next to an open wooden ladder. Kell raised a window, and the pungent odour of turpentine lessened.

He took off his suit jacket, folded it, and hung it neatly over an upper step of the ladder. Jillian let one eyebrow rise. It was polite to ask a lady before doffing one's jacket. Of course, she'd seen him in shirtsleeves, more than once. And he'd seen her in her...

Can we please not think about that now, Jilly?

Kell hooked his thumbs in his trouser pockets and stood next to the ladder. Since they didn't appear to be leaving any time soon, Jillian unpinned her hat and looked for somewhere to put it. Kell crossed to her and took it, placing it on top of his jacket. Then he went back to silently standing, thumbs in his pockets. He wasn't scowling anymore, but his mouth was set. His eyes were cold, deep blue, and still, like the waters of a millpond.

A minute as empty as the house passed. She sighed again. This was hard going. Harder than the ride in the pony trap back from the brothel. Harder than the clothes hanger exchange in the stairwell, or the disjointed conversation in the alley behind Salon Sirena, or the doomed banter in the train. She'd rather sew through a plank.

But they were here, apparently to look at the house, so she would look. After, she'd make some excuse and Kell would escort her back to the dent-in-the-wall. Good thing she hadn't bothered with the corsage.

She strolled around the two front rooms, feigning interest in the ceilings, the chair rails, the fresh paint. The oak floors were rather fine for a modest house. Ending at the stairs, she paused at the newel post. Oak, like the stairs and floors. Her gloved fingers slid over the globe finial and rested there. The wood was smooth, the workmanship on it and the rails excellent. A nice touch, and the house appeared to have many. Not ostentatious but handsome, like Kell. She chided herself for turning into a soppy romantic; she should move to Bloomsbury.

Jillian let her gaze climb the stairs toward the upper floor and linger on the landing.

'Two bedrooms and a washroom,' Kell said.

She nodded, her hand still on the finial, feeling a bit like she was on a Thames boat tour of London. *To your right, the Palace of Westminster, where are located the Houses of Parliament. To your left, Lambeth Palace.* But Kell was obviously proud of the house from parlour to attic. Politeness demanded she see it all. She started up the stairs.

The bedroom at one end of the upper floor was empty. A single window was shut tight and the room was dry and a bit musty with disuse. Jillian went back along the landing, passing a narrow closed door she assumed was the washroom, to the second bedroom. That door was open, so she entered.

It was a good-sized room. The sash of the undraped window was up, admitting light as well as cool air, along with intermittent birdsong. Against one wall stood a bookcase, nearly filled with volumes. Next to it, a padded armchair. A small fireplace, with blue-tiled hearth and surrounds, was centred in the opposite wall.

And there was a bed, of sorts. Just a thick mattress, shoved into the corner. Jillian stared at it. At the pillow, the dark wool blanket, the linen sheet turned neatly over the top edge. Heat raced from her chest to her face, and her emotions churned uncomfortably. The man who'd brought her here slept on that mattress, on those linens, under that blanket, with his raven-haired head on that pillow.

What was she doing here? Just weeks ago, she'd been unnerved by being alone with Kell in a tenement stairwell in the middle of London. Now, she was in his bedroom.

Was he *seducing* her? Facing the fact of her inexperience, she wouldn't know a seduction if it waltzed up and grabbed her by the corset strings. In the workroom one day, she'd heard Min and Evie talking about a play they'd seen, a revival of something called *The Vampire, or The Bride of the Isles.* Since her workmates could only afford cheap seats in the highest gallery, she wouldn't count on the accuracy of what they reported, but there seemed to be a lot of seduction in it. She should have gone to the play with them, to learn how it was done.

She did know that clothing was central to seduction. Even the *Plan* warned about that. Point Eleven, copied from *Miss Dean's Behaviour Book*: 'Showy dress leads to moral decline.'

From the way she'd nearly fallen to her knees at her first sight of Michael Kelly dressed to the nines, she'd say that if moral decline was his plan for her, it was working. To be fair, she'd spent half an hour dithering over a silk corsage and was wearing the most winsome – and scarlet – jacket she owned.

Were she and Michael Kelly seducing each other? If so, they seemed overdressed. While she wasn't learned on the subject, seduction seemed to involve fewer clothes or, at least, more accommodating ones. Conveniently lost buttons, dressing gowns that had misplaced their belts, garters that melted away like snow.

'I have a bedstead.' It wasn't until he spoke that she realised Kell had followed her and was standing just inside the bedroom door, watching. As though he'd entered with a pistol, she took a hasty step back, which put her shoulders against the wall by the window.

What a little fool she was being. She was a grown woman, not an orphan with sagging stockings and second-hand shoes. She tried to sound blasé, as though she toured men's bedrooms all the time. 'Have you been working on the house?'

He ignored her question, just jutted his chin toward some brass railings and posts leaning against the wall near him. It was obviously a bedstead in pieces, the head and footrail beautifully turned, solid and gleaming. 'I haven't put it together yet. I don't usually sleep here, but sometimes I need a few hours' rest before I go to Catherine Street.'

Catherine Street meant The Flower Garden, where he also had a bed. As well, there was the dent-in-the-wall, with the bed she and Ada currently occupied but which belonged to him. And the mattress a few feet from her now, the one Jillian was trying to pretend wasn't there. For one man, Kell seemed to have a lot of places to... sleep.

Jillian rephrased her question as a statement. 'Then you *do* work here.'

There it was again, the glower from the train. 'Do you mean, has someone been paying me to work here?'

Is that what she meant? She opened her mouth, shutting it as he answered his own question. 'It's my house. I own it.'

'Is that so?' Her voice was bright as an uncirculated coin. 'It's very nice.'

Nothing from Kell. How long was she supposed to be polite, standing in a bedroom with a man who was too uncommunicative and too, too near? The room suddenly felt small and crowded, despite the open window and door, reminding her of the shed in Whitechapel with a great many boxes and one knife-wielding maid. She turned her back on Kell and looked out the window.

She'd give Hackney high marks for beauty. After the unrelieved grey of the city centre, the green treetops and graceful roofs, the latter so much more uniform than the hodgepodge of London, looked almost like a village. A wind sprang up from the east. Where chimney tops were visible, the wisps rising from them all leaned obediently in the same direction. Jillian smelled rain, mixed with the faint odour of calcimine from the walls. She ran her hand over the windowsill, then looked at her glove. Dust, plaster dust. Kid leather was so hard to clean. She began pulling off her gloves, finger by finger. It was senseless, but she needed something to do.

'What happened to your family?' Kell's question jarred her.

She spoke without turning. 'Pon, that's my brother Philip, he's in the Navy.'

'I know that.'

'Ah, yes, Ada tells you things.' She shouldn't have let acid etch the words. It was childish.

He rephrased his question as she'd rephrased hers. 'What happened to your parents?'

Something in Jillian arched like a wary cat. No danger, not yet, but... 'Why on earth would you ask that?'

'It's made you what you are. I want to know.'

'Want to know what happened? Or what I am?'

'Both.'

Piqued, she tugged so hard on a glove finger she heard stitches give way. He'd brought her all the way out here for Twenty Questions in an empty house? She didn't have to answer, of course. What he was asking went beyond what Ewan Exeter had asked at the Trocadero. That was just conversation; this was *probing*. She had every reason not to respond.

But Kell affected her. He'd done it at the start, done it later, and was doing it now. He looked deeply and peeled away layers. For some reason, she let him. The wary cat hissed softly. *You want answers? I'll give you answers.*

She'd gotten both gloves off. Not wanting to put them on the dusty windowsill, she kept them in her hands, folded primly in front of her. She remained where she was, though, facing Hackney beyond the window, not Kell. Rude, perhaps, giving him her back, but no more so than his question. Outside, the clouds broke and emergent sunshine warmed her face. She gave her story to the light.

'We had a very pleasant life. We lived in a thatched cottage in Hertfordshire, with a garden that was my mother's great joy. My father had been an officer in the Navy, twenty-one years and a long service medal. Later, he did think of going back to sea, but he was too old by then and Mother feared for him. His pension wasn't sufficient for us to maintain the house and Pon's schooling and, well, looking back, we probably should have made do with a smaller house, but Father put great store in being respectable.

'The house wasn't ours, in any case. It was let. Father had a small inheritance, so we moved to London, where he thought he might make a go of something. I wasn't quite thirteen.'

She stopped. The story was making her restless. No one had ever asked her to tell it, not really, not the whole thing. All the girls at St Margaret's had stories and some were no doubt worse than hers, but they weren't shared. The girls had all been somewhere else and then *poof!* they were at the orphanage, dropped from some Ministry of Abandoned Offspring in the clouds.

Her mouth was dry. It seemed a long time since she'd had her morning tea or even the lemon drop in the train. She turned to face Kell. 'Might I have a glass of water?'

He left the room without a word. She heard him going down the stairs and toward the back of the house, to the kitchen, she supposed. How long would he be? Long enough for her to flee the house and Hackney? She could take the train or even a cab back to her room. Because if she stayed where she was...

At the very least, she should stop telling the story. She could just say her parents died, she and Pon were in an orphanage, she went into service, and the rest he knew. Ta-da! Show over, curtain dropped, all the ugly puppets stuffed back in their boxes.

Too late to flee. Kell ascended the stairs, footsteps louder and nearer, and finally entered the bedroom. He held not a glass but a chipped cup toward her. She took it and drained it in one long swallow, then looked into the cup as though it might magically refill, as in a fairy tale. If she'd brought along a fairy godmother, she'd ask her to refill it with whiskey. That would certainly further the bad impression she'd given Kell with her crackbrained babble on the train. He'd simply assume she was a drunkard.

Because she was standing there holding the empty cup but not surrendering it, Kell took it from her, his fingers barely brushing hers. For a second, Jillian let her hand hang in the air while she stared at it.

Nonplussed, she dropped her hand and watched Kell set the cup on the top of the bookcase. Before he did, he looked inside to make sure the cup was empty. Ah, he treasured his books and didn't want to risk them being spoiled.

If she was going to talk, she should talk about Mother. Mother was still, to her, the best thing about her past. Also the worst, but...

'My mother was the only daughter of a widowed country vicar. She was, oh, protected, as a child, kept in soft wrappings like a

Dresden figurine. Then she met Father, and he wanted to do the same. She married him on the day she turned eighteen.' Younger than Jillian was now, and a mother at twenty.

She looked down at her hands, oddly surprised to see both her gloves in one of them. She toyed with them, shifting them from hand to hand, wondering if the salon had the right colour glove silk to repair the stitches she'd burst. The gloves were her only pair.

'It was difficult for Mother when we came to London, because even though we still had funds for a while, we couldn't really afford servants. We had a little day help, that's all.

'She wasn't used to managing a household, you see. Mother had been brought up to be–' *Why hesitate to use the word?* 'Genteel.'

'Did she bring you up to be the same?'

She tilted her head, thinking of how to answer. 'I suppose so. I don't remember ever considering things like money and where it came from. It was never important. For so long, you see, we'd been doing well. In Hertfordshire.'

She was sorry she'd worn her red wool jacket. It might be smart, but it was far too warm for such a close room, with the sun pouring through the window behind her. Would it hurt the man to hang a few drapes? She examined the lone chair in the room and wondered if she should just walk over and sit in it. Kell could have offered it to her but hadn't, and she didn't like to ask now. She patted the wall next to the window. It was dry and not shedding plaster dust, so she leaned back against it and faced Kell. Perhaps not exactly faced him but looked and spoke to a spot just over his head. As *he* did on the train, she reminded herself.

Why was he pressing her, anyway, why did he want to know all this? Even worse, why was she telling him? Telling and telling and not able to stop if a loaded wagon should pull into her path.

'We took a flat in Chelsea. Five rooms on Hoop Lane.'

Kell nodded. 'I know the street. Not bad, but not– genteel.'

Ah, but the 'not genteel' part hadn't happened yet, ha ha.

Behind her, somewhere in Hackney, the sun finally hid behind a cloud and the room dimmed. For the second time since they'd arrived, she looked, really looked, into Kell's eyes. They had darkened to the colour of twilight. How and why those eyes beckoned her to go on, Jillian couldn't explain, but they did. If she stopped her story now, he wouldn't let it go, wouldn't let *her* go, until he and those eyes pulled every single painful word out of her.

She gripped her gloves tighter, trying to keep her hands still. Her knuckles had gone white, her fingers rigid. 'My parents never really explained what happened. I suppose Pon and I suspected it was something terrible, but all we knew was that things got less and less. Clothes, food, coal, everything. Mother cried but wouldn't say why. Father hardly spoke at all. If only Pon and I had *understood*, you see, but no one told us how bad it really was, and...'

Stop talking, stop talking, stop. But she couldn't. The past – *her* past – was like a horse that shied at something and now was thundering down the street, eyes wild, mane flying.

Her next words came out flat and mechanical. 'It was a Tuesday. I remember, because in Hertfordshire Mother always gave me a piano lesson on Tuesday. We'd been working on a Chopin nocturne before we left for London. Opus nine, Number two.'

She paused, bowled over by something she hadn't, until this moment, realised. She despised Chopin. All those well-mannered nocturnes, smooth and controlled, as though life could be that way instead of the knacker's yard it was. She swallowed hard and forced out the next part, the worst part.

'In Chelsea, we had the floor below the attic. Father went up there and hanged himself from the rafters. Mother found him.' What was wrong with her voice? Shouldn't it express the devastation of that day? Instead, it was appallingly calm, like she was reading a grocery list. Eggs. Bread. Father hanging from a rope. Jillian tried to take a deep breath, couldn't.

'Afterward, Mother was like a ghost in the house. She hardly ate, she barely spoke. Then, she took a very bad chill and just got sicker and sicker. That's when Pon, my brother, he–'

Kell took a step toward her. 'What about your brother? Say it, Jillian.'

Say it? How could she? Her father was a failure. Her mother was the next thing to useless. Her parents lied about how bad things were so she and Pon had no chance to prepare for the truth. Her brother ran away, leaving her to find her mother's lifeless body tangled in the bedsheets she had clutched in her final, breath-starved minutes. Jillian – alone, unconscious from exhaustion – was slumped in a chair three feet away. She had slept through her own mother's death. By the time she woke, the body in the bed was cold and stiff.

'My brother was very close to both our parents. I suppose he left when Mother got sick because he couldn't bear to... Oh, I don't know, we never discussed it. He was gone for– a while.' When had she last taken a deep breath? She silently screamed at her lungs to make them operate. Air in, air out. 'He came back in time to bury Mother. Just. Father left some insurance. That was all. So Pon and I went into an orphanage, a place called–'

'St Margaret's. I know that place, too. Wasn't ever in it. I'm sure you didn't like it, but it was a palace compared to Whitechapel.'

Whitechapel. Jillian knew something about Whitechapel from Ada, just as Kell must have learned from his sister about St Margaret's. There was a lot Kell didn't know about the orphanage and Jillian was sure she'd never know the whole truth about Whitechapel. It was immaterial. She didn't want to talk about his past, her past. All so ugly. Ugly and useless and humiliating, and he was making her relive it. Just who did he think he was? Time to put a stop to his ugly and immaterial interrogation.

'I think we're both a long way from where we started, Kell.' Her voice was like cheap tin, her smile metallic. 'Look at you! Look at this house! It's perfectly charming. Thank you for showing it to me.' Her hands shook and she didn't want Kell to see, so she didn't even try to put her gloves back on. She waved them airily at the room, at the blank walls and the bookcase, the too-near man and the too-near mattress. 'This is just the beginning, I'm sure. You'll advance–'

'Advance. You mean work in a better whorehouse?' He moved closer, one catlike step at a time. A yard, two feet, a foot away. Close enough that she could smell his sandalwood soap, the starch of his shirt, the maleness that underlay his clothes. Like it always did, it made every cell of her body fear and crave him, while her brain stopped working altogether.

He wasn't touching her. The door was unlocked. She could leave any time. So why did she feel as though she was shackled to him? How could she feel the heat of him through his clothes, through hers?

His deep, dark voice lowered almost to a whisper. It seeped under her clothes like his heat. 'What do you want, Jillian?'

Her own voice quavered, and she hated that it did. 'What do I want? You mean, what do I want, in life?'

He nodded, his gaze never leaving her, and she unable to look away.

'I– I want...' What *did* she want? She remembered the Trocadero again, the white linens and crystal glasses, the potted palms. 'I want an orderly life.'

'*Orderly?*'

Why in God's name did he have to make it sound like a curse? The wary cat inside her yowled without warning, claws out. 'Yes, orderly! Is that so hard to understand? I want my life back, the one I had in Hertfordshire! Where the only surprises were good ones. Life was a garden and I was a flower in it. All I had to do was bloom.'

Her voice rose and coarsened, a dull razor cutting through

cloth. 'When everything went to blazes, it wasn't my fault, it wasn't *fair!* Everyone went away and left me to deal with it.

'It's different for you! You're a man. You're *equipped* to deal with hard things. I'm not like that. I'm not even sure *what* I am, now that everything is gone that I... I'm not strong, I can't do the things you do! I'm just a woman and women aren't– we shouldn't have to–' She pushed stiffly away from the wall. Her gloves slid out of her fingers to the floor.

'Whatever you're playing at, Kell, I'm done with it. Done!' He didn't move, just blocked her escape as he had on the stairwell of the tenement. A hot wave, fury and fear together, surged up Jillian's spine. She screamed, inches from Kell's face. 'Let me *go!*'

The palms of his hands landed on the wall, either side of her head, with such force the wall shuddered. 'You're not going anywhere.'

Chapter Nineteen

'What do you want from *me*, Jillian Morehouse of Hertfordshire?' Kell's voice was husky and strained. His mouth was so close that his breath struck her face with every word.

Jillian flinched, pressing into the wall. 'I don't want anything from you.'

'Yes, you do, Jillian. But for the life of me, I don't know what it is. I don't think you do, either. Do you want me to call you a blossom, a china doll, the weaker sex? Is that what you want? Forget it. Those names come out of the mouths of men like Ewan Exeter. Men who use pretty words to dull the instincts of their prey before they rip the very life out of it.

'I don't know what you think you were just telling me, but I'll tell you what I *heard*. Your parents were weak and they tried to make you weak, too. Your father took the coward's way out of his troubles and your mother abandoned her children to follow him. Your brother behaved like a whipped cur, running off when you needed him most. You can dwell on their weakness or be glad you survived it. You're not them. You're not weak, not in yourself and not because you're a woman. Women are strong, stronger than any man.

'You told me a story. Now, I'll tell you one. My mother birthed six children, no money, no midwife, no help. Then she put two of them in the ground. She stood through it all, a house of iron. My father, the drunken, punch-throwin' shite, got himself pitched off a barge and drowned in the Thames, leaving sod-all for his children and wife. And still, my mother stood. Once I watched her put her fist, not a pitcher or a pail but her *fist*–' Kell shook his in front of Jillian's shocked and smarting eyes, '–in the face of a cheating rent collector, a hulking bastard of sixteen stone with a jaw like an anvil, and lay him out senseless on the ground.

'After that, she gathered up her brood and took us to some wretched squat where she kept us alive until the oldest of us could get enough brass for us to move out, move on. She stood, that woman of iron, and she's standing still.

'Listen to me, Jillian. You're every bit as strong as her, little scrap that you are. You're strong and perfect and beautiful. You have the power to break *me*, woman, and I've never been broken by anyone or anything until you.' Kell's voice shook and rasped. 'What you do to me, what I feel when I'm around you, it's like– it's like–'

He pulled her hands up, brought them to his mouth and kissed her palms, her fingers. 'These little hands, they sliced the throat of a filthy pervert who tried to take you against your will. And if I hadn't come into that room in the whorehouse when I did, you'd have splattered the brains of a gin-soaked peer against the wall.'

He gripped her wrists so hard it hurt, while his eyes poured blue fire into hers. 'But hear me now, strong, beautiful Jillian, there are mightier arms in the world. If they ever test their strength on you, so help me God, I'll rip them off the man they're attached to. I will end that man, Jillian, I will end him then and there. I'll smash him into so many pieces there won't be enough left to stain the pavement. I swear I'll do that or anything else I must to protect you, if it's the thing I do with the last breath in my lungs, with the last beat of the heart inside me. Do you hear me?'

Dropping her hands, he seized her shoulders and shook her once, brusquely, the motion wild, his eyes wild. 'I'll not call you a daisy or a violet or a rosebud, not now, not ever. I'll call you by your name, your perfect *name.* Jillian, my Jilly, my– oh, Christ, *Jillian...*'

The impact of his mouth and body emptied her of everything but shock. She couldn't move, couldn't breathe, under the weight and hunger of him. He took all of her; he was rough, feral, and desperate past any point of reason. Then, she heard it. The long, hurting groan he made into her mouth.

The sound spoke to her, schooled her, taught her what to do. Lifting her hands, she brought them to his hips and pulled him tight against her.

Kell drew back his head and looked at her with surprise, then possession. The mouth he had taken – he took it again, harder. His hands cupped her head, holding it while his lips broke from hers only to drag across her forehead, her cheeks, her neck, her ears. His jaw burned against her skin, his teeth raked her throat as he nipped and sucked at it.

They were both groaning then, harsh breaths mingling with unintelligible words. Tears – his or hers, she couldn't tell – slicked their cheeks and ran into their kiss. Their savage kiss, on and on, nothing held back, nothing between them but the revelation that if the seas ran dry and the sky fell, nothing could stop them from taking each other here, now.

Jillian was sure the wall behind her was the only thing keeping her upright. *My first kiss, my first kiss.* Her hands hung on Kell's hips until he went at her mouth again. He did it slower the second time, but his tongue parted her lips and thrust deep and hot between them. She brought her hands to his front, pushing them through the circle of his arms and locking them around his neck.

All her stupid, stupid talk about her past. Gone. The loss and the anger. Gone. The only thing left was Kell, the fire of him, his taste, his body. He demanded, she gave. Then, she took. More, more, she needed *more*.

She melted into him, wanted to *become* him, to open his skin and pour into him so they were one instead of two. He was aroused, she felt the length of it, so hard it almost hurt when he pushed against her. He was a man and he was hard, she had made him hard, for *her*.

The deepest parts of her contracted and oh, such pleasure! She went up on her toes, then pressed her soft sex against and down him, just once.

Kell threw back his head, gulping air, and looked to the side, to the mattress. As he had on the muddy lane in Whitechapel and the pony cart in Covent Garden, he picked Jillian up as though she weighed nothing at all.

For an endless moment she was aloft, suspended between all she had known and all she was about to become. Then Kell tumbled with her onto the mattress, a muddle of limbs and petticoats and shirtsleeves, their mouths seeking each other and their hands frantically working. Kell got his tie, his collar, and waistcoat off, then his boots, cursing at the laces. Jillian wrenched at the buttons of her jacket, dragged it down her arms, and flung it to one side.

Suddenly, panic clawed at her and she stilled, Kell with her. 'Stop! I– we–'

Kell's voice was strained. 'Is that what you want, Jillian? To stop?'

Ten seconds passed, each one a slam of Jillian's pulse. Her answer was barely audible, as low and strained as his. 'No.'

Without looking away from her face, he rolled atop her. The weight of him sent a shock down Jillian's legs. Lust came to her all at once, alien and overmastering. She pushed her body up and against his, pushed with mouth, breasts, hips.

He growled a single word next to her ear, '*Fuck.*'

She wasn't sure she'd ever heard it said aloud. And it wasn't really aloud now, or public, or for others to hear. It was a filthy whisper for her alone. A promise, and a warning. Her heart beat so fast she was light-headed.

Her mind raced like her heartbeat, no two thoughts in sequence, everything out of control. But if she wasn't in control, who was? Was it still Jillian Morehouse of Hertfordshire, matriculate of St Margaret's School? Or was it a different Jillian? A wanting, starving Jillian, one that had been inside her all along, just waiting for this particular man to feed her.

She wanted to press against Kell's hardness again, so she did. He pressed back. Then he nudged her legs apart with his knees and settled into her cleft, his weight on his elbows. He rocked against her and Jillian cried out.

That *place*, the place she'd glimpsed in the mirror at The Flower Garden. It tightened like a fist and pleasure pierced her again. Her eyelids fluttered and her mouth parted on a shallow, eager, intake of breath, while her whole body shuddered and moisture flooded the part Kell was rubbing. Should she be ashamed? Kell knew what was happening to her, inside her, he had to. He'd been with women before, while she was untried. Craving and fear took turns in her brain.

'Kell, I– I've never–'

He slipped his hands under her head, cradling it gently, and murmured into a kiss. 'Don't be frightened, Jilly. Everything will feel...' He kissed her forehead, then the tip of her nose, lightly. 'Perfect.'

He went back to kissing her mouth, even deeper than before. She hadn't imagined kisses could be like that. Before, she thought that when men and women kissed, their mouths touched, maybe stayed touching for a few seconds, lips pursed, like a kiss on the cheek.

Kell's kisses weren't like that. He took each of her lips

separately, pulling them into his mouth with little sucking sounds as though they were delicate treats. His warm tongue outlined her lips, exploring, then insistently probing, until she opened and he entered, just as he had done before. Jillian didn't know what to do when he kissed her like that. She kept her tongue back, out of the way, but he quested for it until some answering need drove it to dance with his. Their tastes mingled – tobacco, cloves, and lemon drops. He had another taste, a barely present musk like fur or a warm animal. It drove her wild. She lifted her head and clutched at his shoulders.

Without breaking their kiss, Kell's fingers got busy in her hair. Jillian felt hairpins coming away and heard them clink faintly as he tossed them onto the floor. It mattered not at all to her if they fell through cracks in the floorboards, if they fell all the way to China and she and Kell followed them. In Hackney or in China, she would spend the rest of the day with her hair unbound and uncombed, a forest fairy that Kell had discovered and ravished.

Her hands drifted across his upper body, delighting in the swell of his biceps, the breadth of his back. She found the edge of his undergarment beneath his shirt and traced it with her nails. Her fingers went to his neck, then into his hair, smooth and slick as water spilling over her hands. She combed it through to the ends, over and over.

Taking hold of his braces, she pulled them down until she freed his arms. Using her nails again, she lightly clawed the back of his shirt and the solid, sleek muscles that ran under it, thrilling at the soft rustle of starched linen and the Michael Kelly smell that rose from it. His differences were joy, they were wonder. Jillian was on fire with curiosity at the same time she wasn't sure what to do next. All she knew was that she wanted to please him as he was pleasing her. She pushed her hand between them, down to where his trousers fly bulged, and wrestled with the buttons. She got one open, then another.

'No!' The word stopped everything as Kell reared up and off

her. He got to his knees and gulped air while his broad chest heaved. Mussed hair fell over his forehead, and he ran a shaky hand through it.

Fear made a grab for Jillian again. 'I've done something wrong! I'm sorry, I–'

Kell's chest expanded as he took a deep breath, then let it out on a low chuckle. 'My precious girl, you've done nothing wrong. It's too right, what you're doing. If you touch me there, I'll– it'll end this too soon.' He took her hand and kissed each finger separately, humming around them. 'We have hours of pleasure ahead. I intend to linger over each... and... every... second.'

To her everlasting shame, her voice came out as a squeak. 'I don't know if I can stand it.'

'You can.' He edged backward until he knelt between her ankles. 'You will. I'll show you how.'

In one smooth movement – had he done this before? – he lifted her skirt and petticoat and slipped his hands below the hems. Grasping her knees from underneath, he pulled them up. Then he pressed them apart, gently but firmly.

She fell back on the mattress, trembling like a snared rabbit. What was he– his hands were–

Speculation stopped as he grasped her skirts again and shoved them quite deliberately up her body. All the way to her waist.

Jillian gave a little scream. Nothing but her thin muslin drawers covered her. With her knees bent and spread, the placket in her drawers would be wide open. She would be *exposed*.

She was dying of shock. Or shame. Or excitement. All of them at once. She hazarded a look down her body as Kell stretched out to lie on his stomach.

With his head between her legs.

What was he *doing* down there? Her understanding was that when men and women coupled, the man was on top, but not like this, not– Was this some Irish thing?

Another startled cry escaped her as she felt his fingers probing lightly between her thighs. He spread her, delving but just barely. 'So wet,' he crooned into her drawers. 'My beautiful Jillian is wet for me.'

In the next instant, a white-hot flare of sensation rippled upward from Kell's mouth, from her under it. Jillian squirmed on the blanket and yelped. Twice.

She squeezed shut her eyes, trying to say Kell's name, to stop him or encourage him, she didn't know which. In under a minute, she wasn't sure she remembered his name, her own, the name of Britain's monarch. She lay helpless and shaking while Kell's mouth and fingers worked all around her centre, as though seeking something–

His tongue claimed it with a single strong swipe and a tigerish growl. Jillian's whole body ignited and her eyes snapped open. Open but seeing nothing, thinking nothing, feeling only lightning course between her legs as Kell's tongue retreated from his first obliterating thrust. He went to her again but carefully, flicking and circling a rising, yearning spot.

He should stop, she should make him stop. No, he should never stop... She gasped, arched her pelvis, curled and uncurled her fists, struggling and failing to form words. A force as relentless as the tide was dragging her away. Faster, faster, there was no time, no time, no–

Her body held for one agonised moment at the crest of a towering wave. Then she crashed onto a shore of sensation so sweet and painful that she felt ripped in two, her halves held together by one thing alone, the man between her legs. Innocence left her as a sea of pleasure rushed in and filled her. She overflowed, finally sobbing his name.

Chapter Twenty

Kell kept his mouth on her, lightly, until the strong spasms of her undoing faded to subtle tremors. Then he wiped his face with a fold of the petticoat still trapped beneath her, using the same fold to cleanse the salt-sweet flood on her outer sex, her thighs. She lay senseless and boneless under him. With a sigh of regret, he carefully straightened her legs. If he could, he'd stay between them all day, all week, forever, staring into her rosy quim. At the drenched and tender pink petals, the tempting opening, so shy, so vulnerable.

He groaned as he pulled himself back up to his knees. When she climaxed, his tool had throbbed so intensely he thought he might finish along with her, pressing against the floor. He couldn't answer for what would happen if he stayed where he was between her legs, the inlet of her body calling to the demon that howled in his loins. In his wildest fantasies, he hadn't imagined that, when unleashed, she would be this beautiful, this wanton. She turned him into a ravaging barbarian. He wanted to hurl himself at her, into her, to drive his whole length into that beckoning snug cavity and fuck her into the mattress, fuck her into the earth, the stars.

Because that wasn't on, he straightened her legs and pressed them together, then edged forward and bracketed her hips with his knees. Taking his weight in his thighs, he sank slowly onto her. His balls rested, tight and full to bursting, just below her pubic mound.

Jillian, his prize, his virgin, his vixen. She opened her eyes and Kell almost lost what perilous control he had over himself. He'd never seen those eyes like this, verdant and luminous. A dappled afternoon light came through the window of the bedroom. It flickered and shifted across her face, a face soft with repletion and framed by the disordered beauty of her hair, the colours of every precious metal in its strands – bronze, copper, silver, gold.

Under him, she made a single sinuous movement and smiled, her lips barely parting. She was a molten lake of seduction and all Kell wanted was to stroke in it until he sank from exhaustion and drowned. If she managed to resuscitate him, he would do it again the next day. And the day after. All the days after, until the end of time.

Dread pricked him with a poison-tipped fang. What had he set free? He suddenly felt a lot younger than his twenty-six years, and a lot more fearful than his violent past warranted.

He'd had women, more than a few in the last days of the Jacks when he was a swaggering young animal and the lovelies stuck to him like snowflakes on a frosty morn. No whores. He'd seen enough of the venom that lurked in their offered bodies to warn him away, no matter how randy he was. There'd been a widow of a certain age, kind and experienced. Artists, bohemians – they thumbed their noses at society as vigorously as the Jacks did. Chelsea was a quarter for unconventional types when Jillian was a child there. Had he ever seen her, a winsome girl with amber-coloured hair and a sweet mouth?

She reached for him. He took her hands, putting a kiss in each palm. Right one, left one, then bending to kiss her forehead. His mother used to do that to her children. *St Brigid on your right,* she'd say, *St Michael on your left. May you always be safe, by Father, Son, and Holy Ghost.*

She brought his hands to the placket of her shirtwaist, setting his fingers on the buttons as delicately as she might set them on a row of pearls. In a flash they were on the pony cart, and he was driving her back to the salon after that donnybrook at the whorehouse. She'd buttoned her blouse and he'd watched, stiffening. Now he was doing what he longed to do then, unbuttoning the garment one mother-of-pearl disc at a time.

His mouth so parched he wondered if he'd ever tasted water, Kell undid the last button. Then he bent over her, grasped her open shirtwaist by the tails, and pulled it upward and off. She was stripped above the waist except for corset and camisole.

Arms free, Jillian wriggled one hand between his right knee and her body, unhooking the vents at the sides of her skirt and petticoat. He helped her wriggle out of them, feeling her tug and push them away with her feet.

Having her squirm and strain under him made him urgent with lust at the same time he wanted to stop everything and assemble the bed. If only he had the damned bed assembled, he could tie her naked to the head and foot rails, legs apart, so he could watch her writhe and gasp as he made her come again and again.

The last of her outer garments came off. Underneath, she was all in white. White drawers, white camisole, white corset, a captive bride pinned under his thighs.

He made a low harsh sound as Jillian ran her hands over the front of her corset. Her nimble fingers flew down the row of hooks and the thing opened like the shell of an oyster, displaying the delicacy beneath. Trying to show some control and not rip it to pieces, Kell tugged it carefully out from under her and dropped it on the floor.

Holy Mother Mary, he must've done something good in his otherwise sin-scorched life. Because here was he, Michael Kelly, straddling a woman whose body could coax an erection from a hayrick. Her beauty was Nature's own, a fawn in the forest, a kitten at play. It softened some things in him and hardened others, and not just his cock. That couldn't be any harder if it was an iron ingot. The thing she made hardest in him was resolve, not just to hold her and possess her, but to shield her from the evil he knew was rampant in the world. Was he man enough to do it?

He'd have to be, because without her he would die. And without him, she would be alone, unprotected, in the world that was more brutal than ever she knew, than ever he would allow her to know.

She laughed, no doubt at the gobsmacked expression on his face. The girlish, innocent sound from her mouth was at complete odds with the monster throbbing so painfully and visibly in his trousers. She noticed them both, the monster and the trousers.

'It's a credit to our ingenuity that we've come this far with so many clothes,' she teased. 'Do you think we're going any farther while I'm nearly naked and you're dressed?'

Kell rolled off her thighs and sat next to her on the mattress, thinking as clearly as he could with a roaring cockstand and the woman who gave it to him just inches away. Could he persuade her to keep doing what they were doing without his getting undressed? Probably not. Sooner or later, she'd see everything hiding under his clothes, so it might as well be sooner. He unbuttoned his sleeve cuffs and started on his shirt buttons. When he reached the last one, he pulled the shirt open and, in one motion, shed it.

He was wearing a combination, a one-piece knit cotton undergarment, knee-length and sleeveless. As soon as losing his shirt exposed his upper arms and shoulders, Jillian's eyes widened. Before Kell could change his mind, he loosed the buttons of his trousers. He unbuttoned the neck of the undergarment, too, and worked his arms out. Roughly, he pushed it, trousers with it, down and off.

He was naked. Naked, heavily tattooed, and scarred. Here a

knife slash, there a ridged star where a bullet had gone in. He sat with his back against the wall, knees bent, waiting...

With eyes shut, he couldn't look at her when the questions came, as they always did. He was well accustomed to the ones about the ink–

An anchor or a mermaid, those a person could understand, but... What's all that on your skin, wallpaper? Were you held captive by Pacific Islanders? Did you work in a circus?

And the scars. Those questions would force him into either a damnable lie or the damning truth. *How did you get all of those? Did you go to war?*

Yes, in a manner of speaking.

When he opened his eyes, he realised she'd gotten quietly to her knees and was sitting on her heels. She'd had time enough to take in the front of him; it was time to meet the dragons. He turned round so he faced the wall.

'I've seen the tattoos before,' she began. From the motion of the mattress and her breath on his shoulder, he knew she'd shimmied forward to kneel just behind him. For a horrible instant, Kell thought she meant she'd been intimate with another illustrated man. There were two he knew of, Dague and Exeter. If she'd seen either one in the altogether, Kell would have to kill them both, just to be on the safe side.

'That rainy day in Whitechapel, your sleeves were rolled up to here,' she pressed against his back, cupping her hands under his elbows, 'and your shirt was so wet I could see everything. Well,' she propped her chin on his shoulder and peeked down at his groin, giving a little giggle, 'almost everything.' She dragged her fingers lightly up and down his arms, making him shiver like a horse shedding flies. 'I thought then that you were the most extraordinary man I'd ever seen.'

His vanity wanted to believe that put him at the top of a regiment, but his common sense told him there probably hadn't been too many men.

'Now that I've seen all of you...' She dropped to a murmur, preceding it with a kiss on the side of his neck, 'Kell, of all the men on earth, you are the most beautiful.'

Kell's eyes filled and stung. Him, a Jack, on the verge of weeping. He released the breath he'd been holding and pivoted to face her again.

Jillian's glowing cat's eyes flicked over his body as she inched forward between his knees. Her hands followed her gaze, touching the hard discs of his chest, the sectioned muscles of his stomach. The tiger, the goldfish, the blooming chrysanthemum.

Wrapping her legs around him so her feet met behind his waist, she wreathed her arms around his neck and they kissed. He could feel her hard nipples though her camisole as her breasts rubbed against his chest. He clasped her buttocks and pulled her tight against him. To settle his length in her cleft, to have her soft, wet curls against it... With control he didn't think he owned, he settled for stroking the downy length of her calves. He reached behind for her slim ankles and found he could encircle them with his hands.

Her breath warmed his jaw as she asked, 'Did they hurt?'

'The tattoos? Or the scars?'

'Both, I guess.'

He wanted to keep feeling her breasts against his chest, but he wanted to look into her eyes and do things to her that he could do only if she was looking up at the ceiling or, preferably, into his face over her. He tilted her carefully to the side and unfurled both their legs so they were face to face. Pressing down her shoulders just enough that she was on her back, he lay on his flank. Even through her drawers, the rub of his cock against her hip was so distracting he struggled to remember what she'd asked.

Ah, did they hurt. 'Aye, they both hurt when they went in. Once they healed, they were fine. I wanted to have tattoos over the scars, but Xu Wei said the skin wouldn't take the ink properly.'

'Xu Wei?'

'The old man who tattooed me.'

'Um, hmmn.' A happy sound, he hoped. 'He was an artist, Mr Xu Wei.'

Kell was glad he'd let Xu Wei decide what to ink and where. The old man put a bony brown finger on a patch of Kell's skin. 'Here,' he croaked, *Júhuā*. Chrysanthemum.' The needle bit, the blood and ink flowed. And on another patch. 'Carp. For long life.' Kell got two of them from Xu Wei, each one rounded over a shoulder, lifelike and fluid as though they'd swum up his arms.

Kell pushed up on one elbow so he could kiss Jillian's eyelids, kiss the eyes that had seen him and thought him beautiful. Then he kissed her mouth and felt her smile through it, her knuckles brushing his chest as she fiddled with the buttons of her camisole.

He almost swooned like a girl when she worked it off and tossed it aside. Satan's wee handmaid that she was, she smiled and reached under her full, bobbing breasts, cupping and lifting them slightly, so the nipples rose. His mouth flooded. Even though he thought all the blood in his body was already in his cock, it felt like it gained another inch, while the weight between his thighs drew up, aching.

He carefully took one of her hands away and substituted his. He'd never felt anything so perfect in his hand as Jillian's breast, the silken surface of it, the way her nipple rose and hardened to his touch. He doubted God listened to him anymore, but he could easily be persuaded to say prayers, rosaries, novenas, even, for what he was holding. He lowered his head and suckled the breast nearest while fondling the other.

Gasping, Jillian reached one hand behind his head to hold him where he was. She stretched her other hand toward his groin and began fumbling at his length.

Kell moaned. Her touch was virginal and inexpert, and thank God for that. A single practised stroke would bring him off before he got her knickers down. He pulled away from her and got to his knees. She lay there smiling, and deftly flicked open the hook at the side of her drawers. He tugged them down her legs and off. To have Jillian entirely naked beneath him – if there was a point of no return, they had crossed it. Or would cross it, when he taught her what to do.

He bracketed her hips with his knees. His manhood bobbed above her stomach, and she blinked once, slowly. As well she might, since he was as full and upstanding as he'd ever been, ruddy, thick. He fisted himself, working his foreskin back. The head glistened with spend that had escaped before the flood that screamed to follow.

'Don't be afraid.' He could see from her expression that a hoarse *don't be afraid* gave her about as much reassurance as handing her a butter knife to brandish at a charging bull elephant. His voice wasn't helping; it was gravel caught in his throat. He tried lowering it. 'Please, just touch me, darling. It won't take long, I – *ahhh, Jilly...*' His begging dissolved as her hand replaced his.

She held him lightly, one hand centred, then making room for the other. A little mewl of delight escaped her when she saw she could span him with both hands, end to end. Then she removed one hand and took his balls, cupping and tugging them carefully, while her other hand stayed wrapped around him, stroking, bringing him so close to the precipice he thought he might die, a happy man, in that moment. Except he had no plans for dying, not yet.

Still fondling him, she said the thing that every man in his basest fantasy longs to hear. 'Show me. Show me how to please you.'

He settled onto her. Taking her hand, he brought it to his mouth and licked it from heel to fingertips as she watched. He wished he could be where he was and between her legs at the same time, lapping the wetness he knew was flooding her.

She didn't have to be told to grip him. He covered her hand with his and began, slowly, to move her fist. Hard down, then up. Hard down again.

It was excruciating, soaring, maddening, good beyond belief.

Kell couldn't stop his hips from moving, from thrusting as though her hand was the rosy slit he'd seen when he lay between her legs, the place he'd greedily probed with his finger, his tongue. If only he could be inside her, spreading her, impaling her.

She got his rhythm, and he took his hand away. He fell forward, catching his weight in his hands alongside her head, trying with the last shred of his reason not to tangle his fingers in her hair.

His breath sawed hoarse and heavy as he looked down, watching her work him. The sight tore restraint away and he snarled like an animal. Her hot, strong little hand moved faster, passing over the crown with every stroke, her thumb sliding against the glans. Dragons gathered in his groin, dragons real and rising, charged with liquid heat that climbed from the base of his spine, poised to explode in fire and fury.

A string of oaths straight from Seven Dials blued the air as his body suddenly locked and his hand flew to Jillian's wrist, stilling it while months of desperate need tore through his loins and spilled onto the bare, sweet breasts beneath. Pleasure seared him, the powerful surges lasting and lasting until he thought he truly *was* dying.

Aftershocks made him twitch for – a minute? An hour? His brain was as hazy as if he'd taken a copper's truncheon to the head, and his body... His body warned him that if he attempted a graceful dismount, it would go very wrong and he'd tumble arse over teakettle onto the floor.

When he could move at all, he fell in a heap next to Jillian like a sack of malted barley. Blood shrilled in his ears; surely Jillian and even the blasted neighbours could hear it.

He should say something. Mother of God, he *wanted* to say something, but his mouth wouldn't move, and his lips were cold and numb. He had died, what did he expect?

His sight still worked. It was joined to the moss-green eyes that were joined to his, and so he poured everything he felt into them. Tenderness, gratitude, longing, possession, hope.

Terror.

How could he tell her what he was? How could he not? Ada would never betray his dismal past, but she goaded him constantly. *'If you feel somethin' for her, Kell, you'd better tell her now.'*

Ada wouldn't give up his secrets. Others might, others like Ewan Exeter. Not that Exeter should throw stones from the glass house where he lived.

Jillian, I'm a killer.

They all were, the Jacks. They weren't cold-blooded assassins. They hadn't taken contracts to end lives, but they had ended them. Defending themselves, defending their gains, defending the hellish patch of ground they held. In dust-ups, one on one, threats answered, revenge gone too far, in street brawls, in gang wars.

In fight rings. He saw it again, as he saw it more nights than he could count. Federico Cortelli, slender, dark, the same age as Kell then, nineteen. Strong but all bluster, no skill. The ring, the jeering faces and coarse cheers, the wagers and the blows. The stiletto, the one Fedo had hidden in his boot. The one Kell wrestled out of Fedo's hand and threw to the ground before sending the man down after it. The blood that poured from Fedo's face and head, as Kell punched him and punched him and punched him...

'Kell?'

He caught the note of worry in her voice. Had his ghosts shown themselves to her, as they did to him? Since his mouth seemed to be operational again, he smiled at her, then shifted so he could free a corner of the bed-sheet to wipe his spend from her breasts.

In the end, there could be only one right decision for him and Jillian Morehouse – no secrets. His rusted, unworthy heart was hers. If she wanted it, once she knew what was in it.

Jillian, I have to tell you about my past. Kell heard himself say the words in his mind. But they were sealed inside his fear of the consequences as in a jam jar, and that shamed him nearly as much as the truth he couldn't bring out.

Jillian rolled onto her side, facing him inches away. 'Kell, my Kell.' She stroked his cheek, her fingers like silk ribbons on his skin.

He pressed a kiss on her shoulder, breathing the scent she gave off, that they gave off together after what they'd done. Her come, his come, lavender and soap and clean sweat and something else, some scent compounded of desire and dreams. He took it into his lungs and willed it to stay there, filling him to his smallest cell.

She spoke tenderly, quietly, almost into his mouth. 'Please, Kell, kiss me again.'

He kissed her, his body responding and reaching for everything Jillian's body promised but warning him of his limits. He'd never allowed himself to believe that he'd find himself in bed with Jillian Morehouse, but some part of him had known all along that he'd leave her intact if he did. No matter how she might spurn him later and leave him keening in despair, if the moment came, she would leave it as she arrived, a virgin.

Kell would shatter like a bottle thrown at a wall when some other man, some better one, took her, kept her. He'd want to shatter that man, too, and dump the pieces in a quarry. But he would make sure she went to the man whole. There was no other choice. It wasn't as though he had any real conviction he could offer Jillian what she deserved.

She was a girl from a rose-vined cottage in Hertfordshire. He was a bully boy from Whitechapel. For someone like him to take the most precious thing her body offered would be worse than his career in the Jacks.

Even so, he wouldn't balk at giving her so much bliss that he ruined her for any other man. That, Kell could do. She'd wonder why he didn't complete the act, and he'd explain. He'd tell her about his past, so she'd understand why he couldn't love her the way a husband someday would. He'd tell her everything, just... not today.

Explanations deferred, they kissed again and again and again. Touched and enfolded, entwined and fondled, peaked and cried out, for magnificent hours, until the sun began to sink and the bedroom gathered dusk into its walls.

'I should go,' she finally sighed. 'If I'm not home by dark, Ada will get the police.'

Kell doubted that. Somehow, Ada always knew where he was, which meant she knew where Jillian was. Besides, there was only one policeman he was worried about, and he'd dealt with him.

They both sat up on the mattress and surveyed the shipwreck of the room. Clothes flung everywhere, a scatter of buttons and hairpins on the floor. Was that her camisole, hanging by one armhole from the back of the chair? And his trousers, where had they gone?

Jillian held out a long rope of spun-gold hair so she could assess it, and moaned, 'I'm a complete shambles.'

Kell put his feet on the floor and levered to standing. 'There's not a woman in England can hold a candle to you, Jillian. They should take all those babies off the Pears Soap calendars and put you on, instead. And on the cigar postcards. Who wants to look at this year's Grand National winner when they can feast their eyes on Jillian Morehouse?'

She fell back on her elbows and laughed, making her breasts jiggle and Kell scramble to think of more witticisms.

'I'll admit to being an improvement on a horse, but I do think you're overstating my charms.'

'Not at all. I don't deserve to kiss your shoelaces. Anyway, you'll feel better when you've had a bath.'

Jillian clapped and squealed. 'You have a tub?'

He threw out his chest a little. 'I have a tub, with a heater.'

Chapter Twenty-One

'Not sure what you did to deserve it, Jilly, my girl, but they asked for you. Are you payin' attention?'

'I am all attention, Madame.' She wasn't, really. Her mind was on what she and Kell had done a few days before, not the parcel of corsets Madame was wrapping.

Madame grumbled under her breath. Jillian wasn't sure if her employer was pleased or miffed that the assistant, not the shop owner, had been commanded by Marchioness Melton to deliver Lady Rosaline's finished bridal corsets. The assistant wasn't sure if she was pleased or terrified. True, she'd been a maid in a titled personage's house but that, to say the least, hadn't ended well. To be invited to enter a Belgravia address by the front door? That was almost as much of a horror.

It required several yards of salon ribbon for Madame to close the parcel. It was the size of a roast goose and held eight boxed corsets, two more than Lady Rosaline Melton really needed. Madame being Madame, she had talked the bride-to-be into the additional models after the marchioness mentioned the newlyweds planned a lengthy European honeymoon.

'Excellent for travelling,' Madame had coaxed Lady Rosaline, 'so lightweight and comfortable. I know you will wish every protection against the rigours of the road.'

Rigours of the road? Madame had somehow implanted a vision of trekking across Mongolia in yak carts. The new duchess and her spouse would, in fact, pass their *lune de miel* in first-class rail carriages moving sedately between first-class hotel suites in France and Italy. Perhaps the foreign cuisine would be rigorous.

Since Madame always got what she wanted, the two corsets were added to the six already ordered. For an entire week, the workroom had been given over exclusively to making Lady Rosaline Melton's *sous-vêtements*. That and snide commentary on the lifestyles of the idle rich, but mocking the rich was daily fare for the corset girls.

Madame kept talking as she worked the parcel's ribbon into an elaborate bow. 'Her Ladyship's told the butler, so you'll be admitted at the front. He'll be none too happy about it, I'm sure, but it ain't up to him to say who's let in and who's not. Let's 'ave a look at you, now.'

Madame's keen eyes scanned Jillian from shoe tops to hat. Knowing how particular Madame was about impressions, Jillian had donned the best outfit she owned, a forest green walking dress with cranberry trim. It was a two-seasons-past window model she'd bought on the cheap, then altered to look like a recent illustration in *The Lady's Modiste*, complete with a delicate lawn under-blouse and frothy lace jabot. Evie, brilliant with hats, used fabric and ribbon scraps to make her a neat little toque to match.

Madame gave a curt nod of approval, handing over the parcel. That made Jillian bold, so she asked a question. 'Madame, is the duke in residence?'

'Not from what I've been told. Mind you, I'm not handed advisories on a duke's where-habouts. But the clerk where I get our ribbon, she's the sister of one of the upstairs maids, and *she* said His Grace is in Ireland on some horse-buyin' junket, which is the kinda thing nobility gets up to. Anyway, His Grace has given his fy-an-say and her parents the run of his townhouse while he's gone. Makes it easier for 'em to shop London out, buyin' wedding frippery left and right, which is all to the good for us.

'Hark to me, Jilly. See you don't get above your station. Keep your voice low and your eyes lower. You're my ayd-ee-camp; Salon Sirena's reputation is on your shoulders.' Madame did a top-to-bottom scan of Jillian's clothing again. 'Is that the best frock you got? Oh, never mind, it's good enough. Just don't speak, sit, or sneeze unless you're asked to, understand?'

'They won't really ask me to sneeze, will they, Madame? Because I–'

'None o' your cheek, missy! Back in an hour, or I shall know the reason why.' Madame pushed her and her lavishly wrapped bundle out the door. 'The duke's carriage is at the end of the street. Get away with you, now.'

Ada would have had the *mot juste* for the carriage belonging to the Duke of Fells and St Andrews. Jillian's descriptive powers being feeble compared to Ada's, the best she could come up with was *great gold-garnished grandiosity*. It was her first ducal carriage, after all; she'd do better with her second.

The thing was blacker than a moonless night, except for the many curlicues and flourishes in gold leaf. Drawn by a pair of perfectly matched greys, it bore a footman at the rear and a driver up top, both liveried. The duke's coat of arms squatted fatly in the centre of each door, like a monarch wishing for a bigger throne.

Wonderment must have shown on her face. The driver leaned down from his seat and, with a kind smile, said, 'Are you in a rush, miss? Or would you like me to take a roundabout route to Belgravia?'

Jillian suppressed the urge to hop up and down like a five-year-old being offered a strawberry ice. 'Oh, yes, please! I'm a bit early for my appointment, and I should like that very much. As long as I arrive at the duke's residence by eleven o'clock.'

The driver touched his forehead with his whip hand. 'Right you are, miss.' Jillian was handed in by the footman and they were off.

Clearly, the driver knew just how to avoid London scenes that might distress aristocratic passengers. It was but a mile and a half as the crow flew from the salon to the heart of Belgravia, but the carriage took a long, meandering way that skittered around tenements and filth and overcrowded thoroughfares. Pleasant views passed by the window: Hyde Park, the Houses of Parliament, trees and statues and well-dressed pedestrians. The coach slowed as it joined the dense traffic along Park Lane, where it got many a sidelong admiring glance from the occupants of other vehicles. Once, a viscount's cream and maroon landau passed them. Jillian knew it was a landau and a viscount's because it had been in *The Times*. Viscount Randall Something and the Honourable Miss Somebody in Hyde Park.

The Park Lane walkway on the other side of the duke's coach was a parade ground for well-dressed Londoners. For a few minutes, while the coach was reduced to a crawling pace by traffic, a young man sauntered on the pavement just a few yards away. As Jillian watched, he lifted his hat to her. He had jet black hair.

That's all it took. Jillian was suddenly in the Hackney house, on the mattress on the floor with her own black-haired man, and her heart leaped like a hare under the moon. Trying to quell the tumult – she was working, after all – she reached into her skirt pocket for her notebook but felt only the pocket's lining. *Well, bother.* She must have left the book in her room. That wasn't surprising. She'd been so distracted by memory while she was dressing that it was astounding she hadn't left her eyeballs behind. The whole while, she'd thought only about undressing Kell.

He was her lover now. Just a few months ago she hadn't had any idea what a lover was. Certainly not when she was staring at herself in the mirror of that odious room at The Flower Garden, imagining hands and lips and breasts and...

Sex. Her sex, his sex. The sex they had together. Or was it love? She hadn't known either before, not really. She'd loved her parents, of course, flawed as they were. She loved Pon.

What she felt when she thought of Kell was very, enormously, different, and what they did in the Hackney house wasn't anything like posing in front of the mirror at The Flower Garden. The mirror was all surfaces and dreams.

Something different possessed her when she was in Kell's arms, and her *body* was the mirror of it. The body she hadn't really known at all until he greeted her parts with his. His mouth, his hands, the marvel between his legs that rose at a glance from her and died a twitching death of pleasure when she stroked it.

Away from that, away from him, had the clocks changed? Was time bent and twisted by the alchemy of their union? Every minute apart seemed longer, and every hour was an age. Next Sunday, Kell was taking her to the circus at Sanger's Amphitheatre, but Jillian wasn't sure she could wait that long to see him.

Him. Kell. *My lover.*

In the bedroom of the Hackney house after her bath, he'd turned up the gas lamp so they could both dress. Unfortunately for her *toilette*, the light meant that Kell could continue exploring her body from where he reclined, one leg in his trousers but otherwise naked, on the edge of the mattress. She tried and failed to bat away his hands while she wrestled with her underclothing.

'I let you look at me,' he taunted. 'Turnabout's fair play.'

'That's as may be, but my body's not as interesting as yours.'

Kell laughed so hard he fell right over on the bed. 'Jillian, my sweet Jilly, you have no idea how wrong you are.'

'But I don't have anything to show! No art, no–'

'What's this?' He sat up and reached for her leg, making it impossible for her to pull on her drawers. His forefinger traced a white crescent on her knee.

'That? I was six and fell out of a tree.'

'I knew it. You're the child of jungle explorers.'

'Hertfordshire has many trees, wiseacre. Pon, my brother, was always showing me up.' She mimicked a boy's husky voice, '"Look how high *I* can climb! Look how far out on this branch *I* can go!" So one day I shinnied out to the very end of an oak limb. It ended badly, I'm afraid.'

'A sad tale, I am moved. And this little work of art?' He grabbed her wrist and drew his thumb along a three-inch scar on the outside of her forearm.

'Oh, well, that was a tennis match.'

'A *tennis match*? Who was on the other side of the net, the Mongol hordes?'

'There was this despicable pair of sisters– never mind.'

'I do mind. A war wound deserves respect.' He lay back on his elbows, splayed and muscular like some Greek athlete on a vase. 'And that?' He lifted his chin toward her hip.

He'd spotted her only birthmark, a pink farthing-sized spot just above her hip bone. Jillian stopped dressing and looked nervously at him. 'I never noticed how marked I am. Do you mind?'

'Do you mind my tattoos?'

'No, I think they're wonderful. Not that I'll be running to exhibitions looking for tattooed men.'

'You won't be looking for any men and I'm not saying that because I want you on a lead.' He sat up, elbows on his knees. His intense expression arrested her.

'I want to be every man, all men, for you, my sweet and life-marked Jillian. I want to be everything you want, everything you need.' Something inexpressibly young and unsure crept across his face. 'Is that all right, Jilly?'

She abandoned her knickers and bent over the bed, her mouth seeking his. 'That... is perfect.'

It was perfect, in the moment. She would think about that and only about that. If she thought about tomorrow or the next day, if she thought about the *Plan*...

The ducal carriage turned off Park Lane and into Belgravia's streets, where any second it would bring her to the duke's residence. Jillian held up the tiny watch pinned to her bodice. Madame had loaned it to her. The watch read two minutes until eleven o'clock. Time to leave the magical coach with its velvet seats and burnished woodwork. A shame, but even enchanted princesses went back to their brooms the morning after the ball. She patted herself into order. They were nearly there.

Chapter Twenty-Two

Belgravia was everything she'd thought it would be. Mansions rising on either side, high railings of ornamental iron. Gardens she knew were the products of fleets of gardeners but that seemed to have always stood there, green guardians against a less privileged world. Ada would hate it.

The carriage slowed. Turning off the street into a narrow opening between tall hedges, it passed under a lofty ironwork arch bearing the duke's coat of arms, painted figures gleaming in the morning sun. The lane under the arch was so smoothly bricked that the carriage wheels made hardly any noise on it. Even the horses' hooves were muffled. A few dozen yards into the lane, a gatehouse appeared on the right. The coach pulled level with the gatehouse.

And stopped. There were noises from the top and back of the coach, almost like luggage being rearranged, and the vehicle rocked. Had there been cases on top when she boarded it? She hadn't noticed any. Why weren't the driver and footman descending?

Why were they even halting? Madame said the butler had been

told she was coming. Surely the gatekeeper had also been informed. Jillian peered out the coach window. There were hedges of very thick privet flanking the drive, which curved slightly. She couldn't see much of the house beyond the curve, only the peaks of the roof, some chimneys.

A man left the gatehouse and stood in front of it, a dozen feet from the carriage. He wasn't very well-dressed for ducal staff. Rough trousers, a collarless shirt that had seen better days, a soiled brown waistcoat. His face was rough, too, unshaven with a long scar across his nose and down one cheek. His cap was pulled low on his forehead, and he had a dirty red kerchief around his neck. To Jillian, he looked more like a gardener's man than household staff, but she had never been to a duke's residence before, so how would she know?

She put her head out the window, turning her face up toward the driver. She could just see the back of his livery. 'Hello there! Is there a problem?'

The driver didn't answer, and he didn't climb down from his seat, but the rough-looking fellow from the gatehouse strode to the coach door and grabbed the handle. Pulling open the door, he spoke to her in a voice as rough as he looked. 'Not one problem, Your Ladyship. His Grace send you escort to house.'

The man had a thick accent. Spanish? Italian? Why had he called her Your Ladyship? And why would she need an escort? She was just making a delivery. The man reached for her elbow with his other hand.

Jillian shrank back, confused. She gripped the salon parcel to her chest. 'I was told,' she began in a small voice, 'that His Grace is not in residence at the present–'

The man reached inside and yanked her out of the coach by her elbow, wrenching it so painfully she cried out. His lunge was so fast and violent she hadn't been able to get her foot on the carriage step and her ankle twisted painfully when she landed on the paving stones. The man batted the corset parcel out of her grip with his free hand. At the same time, she was seized from behind by other hands so strong they lifted her right off her feet. Arms belted her middle like an iron band, trapping her own arms to her sides.

She knew her only chance was to scream for help, but she forced out just one breathless cry, not nearly loud enough, before the man in front whipped the dirty kerchief from around his neck and shoved it into her mouth. The cloth reeked of tobacco and sweat, and her stomach convulsed.

Currents of fear coursed up and down her spine and she began to struggle, wildly. Kicking back at her captor's legs, she tried to twist out of the arms holding her. But the man behind had one thick wrist locked in the fist of the other, both fists locked hard against the steel busk of her corset. The pressure on her diaphragm made it nearly impossible to breathe, let alone scream again. Over her head, the man rasped something unintelligible, but a threat was clear in it.

At the edges of her vision, she saw two men being marched at pistol point across the drive, to the narrow grass verge. They were in their drawers and undervests. Her skin crawled when she saw their faces. The two were the duke's driver and footman, stripped of their livery. The man holding the pistol on them was shabbily dressed, like the one who had gagged her. Still another man appeared and began tying the hands of the duke's men behind them with lengths of cord. The captives' faces were chalk white and rigid.

The man with the cord finished his work, then pulled a thick, short truncheon from his trousers waistband. As Jillian watched in horror, he stepped behind the two servants and clubbed each of them in the head. The truncheon made a sickening smack as it hit. The men toppled where they stood.

Her stomach rolled and lurched, and she struggled harder, but her captor just tightened his hold until her breath was cut off completely. He hissed into her ear, ugly, garbled sounds, his breath revolting. Jillian strained behind the gag and worked her throat. All she managed to force out was a high-pitched whine. Feeble, but better than nothing, so she did it again.

The man whose kerchief was in her mouth stood less than a yard away, his eyes flint-hard and cold. He didn't say a word, just pulled back his arm and struck her hard across the face with his fist. First one way with his right fist, then the other with his left. *It hurts, it hurts...* The balled-up gag had caught her lip under her teeth, and blood gushed into her mouth. Mercifully, when the blows made her go dizzy and limp, the pressure on her chest eased slightly, enough for her to breathe shallowly.

The man who'd clubbed the driver and footman joined the one who struck her. He also had a kerchief around his neck, and he untied it. Wrapping it round Jillian's eyes, he knotted it behind her head. The last thing she saw before the cloth shrouded her vision completely was the parcel of Lady Rosaline's corsets on the bricks. The paper wrapping was ripped and some of the boxes had ruptured, spilling their snow-white contents. The corsets on the top of the heap were blackened where the men had trodden on them. Then, the kerchief was pulled painfully tight around her head and all she could see was a faint sheen of daylight under the edge.

A few seconds passed while the men muttered in their strange tongue. Jillian's left arm was abruptly wrenched from her captor's grip and pulled out straight, palm up. Someone's hands locked above and below the elbow joint. If she tried to pull her arm away, it would be broken.

She felt something cold, thin, and hard slipping under the bottom edge of her left sleeve, above her glove. Oh, God, a *knife?* Her arm was jerked upward as the blade sliced through her sleeve, almost to her shoulder. She heard and felt the fabric ripping and thought, absurdly, that it would be almost impossible to repair.

Nameless panic seized her and she pulled frantically away,

whining through the gag. She might have been a fox with its leg in an iron trap, for all the good her writhing did. A scream welled up from deep in her throat as something sharp lanced the inside of her elbow, burning deep. The fiery serpent struck again, then opened its jaws wide to reveal a throat of endless darkness.

She fell in and was swallowed whole.

Chapter Twenty-Three

When Lady Melton scheduled a delivery at eleven o'clock, she expected it at eleven o'clock. Neither one minute prior, nor one after. Her daughter's bridal corsets had not appeared on the doorstep by a quarter past the hour, and she paced the morning room in vexation. When it was half eleven and there was still no sign of the carriage that had been sent to fetch the 'assistant' from Salon Sirena, the marchioness was livid.

It only increased her ire that the late delivery didn't seem to bother her daughter at all. Rosaline was languidly draped on the sofa under the windows overlooking the garden. She had been there all morning, lollygagging over wallpaper sample books and making plans for the extensive redecorating of this, soon to be her, townhouse, which she had pronounced 'shabby, old, and drearily bland' the moment the duke was out of earshot. Rosaline's original plan had been to breakfast with friends. When the marchioness reminded her that her intimate trousseau was arriving at eleven, Rosaline changed her plans with a pout.

All for naught, since the delivery had obviously gone awry in some fashion. With an irritable cluck, Lady Melton dispatched a footman to the gatehouse to ask Higgins if there was any sign of the ducal coach. The footman pelted back to the house in under two minutes with a shocking report. There was no evidence at all of the duke's carriage and horses. His coachman, Sievers, and carriage boy Tom were barely conscious and moaning, laid out alongside the drive with Lady Rosaline's smashed parcel. The men had been trussed like chickens and were in their underclothes. Higgins had likewise been tied hand and foot behind the gatehouse and gagged. Whomever had been inside the ducal coach was missing altogether.

The footman thrust a soiled red kerchief at the marchioness. 'My lady, this was lying in the drive.'

The marchioness frowned at the kerchief but didn't touch it. Some political emblem, no doubt. Red neckerchiefs, revolutionary pennants. She'd read about such things in *The Times*. Those wretched Irish, probably. They were always stirring up trouble. Or Communists, jabbing at the social order. Might be thieves, she supposed, after the horses and coach, though the footman said the pockets of the gatekeeper and driver were untouched, while an exorbitantly priced bundle of corsets was left on the drive. As for the 'assistant' disappearing... The chit was probably in on the scheme from the beginning.

Well, the miscreants would find out soon enough what an assault on their betters would cost them.

Lady Melton glanced at the sofa again, her chest loosening a little with relief. Thank heaven for her daughter's corsets, or Rosaline might have been in the duke's carriage, returning from her planned breakfast. Still, the impertinence of the blackguards! To batter the duke's staff, to presume to threaten her family in her daughter's fiancé's own drive, to make off with the duke's carriage and horses! And the corset girl – something would have to be done about her. What a colossally vexing day it was becoming!

The marchioness sat at her writing desk and snatched up paper and a fountain pen. Scribbling a note, she shoved it at the footman.

'William, take this and that rag,' she pointed to the red scarf in the footman's hand, 'to New Scotland Yard. Now!'

William sketched a bow and nearly ran from the room, passing the butler, Soames, in the doorway. The marchioness flapped her hand agitatedly at him as he entered. 'Soames, I shall compose a telegram to His Grace and you shall see that it is sent immediately.'

The marchioness took another piece of paper and began writing. The fact that Fells and St Andrews was probably in some godforsaken Irish field, valuing horseflesh, made her annoyance rise to country-levelling rage. He could just leave off his hobby and deal with this affront to his, not to mention his fiancée's, honour.

As an afterthought, Her Ladyship gave Soames a few lines to deliver to her husband, the Marquess of Melton, at the House of Lords.

Ewan Exeter, who made it his morning business to view incoming messages whether they pertained to his borough or not, was doing just that at the Yard's reception desk when the marchioness's letter and the red kerchief arrived. Pocketing it, he pelted back to his office, where he shoved the note in his desk drawer, snatched his coat and hat off the rack, and tore out of the building and into the street. First, he needed to find Dague, who would get Kell. Then, God help them all, they needed to go to Salon Sirena.

CHAPTER TWENTY-FOUR

As he'd arranged it, Exeter arrived first at Salon Sirena. He hoped Dague's detour to The Flower Garden to rouse Kell had bought enough time for Exeter to find out just how bad the news was. Two out of four, those were the chances it was Kell's sister or the woman he was obsessed with who'd been kidnapped.

Either way, Kell would detonate like a Fenian bomb. That's why Dague needed to be there, too.

When Kell and Dague burst through the Salon door, Exeter and Madame were in the showroom with the corset girls. All except one, Jillian Morehouse. The look on Kell's face when he counted the three fear-taut faces – Min, Evie, Ada – was one of the most painful things Exeter had ever seen in a life that had conditioned him not to see pain anymore.

Exeter had already conjectured an answer for the question Madame asked. 'Why her? Why our Jillian?'

His answer was another question. 'You were all here, is that right, when the marchioness and her daughter visited?'

Madame's hands were clutched together and twisting. 'I dealt with the clee-on-tell, per usual. Jillian's my front-of-shop assistant. She took the daughter's measures.'

'This daughter, the Lady Rosaline Melton, what did she look like?'

'I was mostly occupied with the mother, so, let me think. I, *um*, I...' She trailed off, looking nervously at Kell. 'She was young. Fair-haired.'

'You've got to do better than that.' Kell's command was jagged as a handsaw.

'I saw her.' It was Min, her voice small but firm. 'Those of us in the workroom, we were, you know, curious. I just peeped around the drape while Jilly was taking Lady Rosaline Melton's measures.' Min looked at Madame and her lip quivered. 'I know I shouldn't have, Madame, but it's just, well, we don't often get to see the titled ladies and I heard you introduce Jillian to them, and I– I–'

Kell took a step toward Min. Before he could take a second one, Dague's fingers dug into his arm like crocodile teeth. '*Reste où tu est*,' he rumbled. *Stay where you are.* Dague smiled charmingly as he crossed to Min and took her tiny hand in his huge one. He brought it to his lips, brushing them lightly across Min's knuckles, while Madame's mouth fell open. Min's face pinked and then brightened like a candle.

'*Minerve*.' He said it the French way, *Meen-airve*. 'This noble young woman. What was her appearance?'

Looking only at Dague, Min answered promptly and firmly. 'She was a little taller than Jillian, but not by much. Ada's height, I think. She had blonde hair, just a touch of ginger in it. Very nice shape, a Number Six corset, I should think. Actually,' Min's large hazel eyes behind her spectacles darted back and forth between Kell and Dague, 'I thought she looked like... Well, she and Jilly could be sisters.'

The three men exchanged words in low voices among themselves, then left the salon. Exeter went one way, Dague and Kell another. Madame locked the front door and flipped the sign inside the glass from *Open* to *Closed*. She pulled down the shade.

They all sat morosely in the workroom while Evie made tea. Min unrolled ribbons and rolled them again. Ada's face was tight, her lips compressed.

Madame had a handkerchief in her hands, balling it up, spreading it out, balling it up again. 'I should never have sent her there. I should've told that flighty daughter that it's *my* shop and *I* deliver the goods.'

Ada reached over and grabbed Madame's hand while Min and Evie gasped at the familiarity. 'I know my brother,' Ada told Madame with the conviction of *the sun is hot* or *the ocean is wide*. 'He'll find her. He'll find her if he has to go to hell and cut Lucifer's head off to do it. He'll find her and he'll bring her back.' *When he does*, Ada thought, *he better keep her where she should have been all along: his house, his bed*. 'Until then, Madame, we need your help.'

'What– What should I–'

Ada stood. 'We need to gather some things. And take them to Hackney.'

Chapter Twenty-Five

In the servants' hall at the duke's Belgravia residence, Soames turned his fiercest glare, the one that reduced maids to tears and made footmen's lips quiver, on the detective inspector. How dare a policeman evade him by effecting an entrance from the service door, so the butler was denied the chance to refuse him at the front!

Whether at the front or back of the house, Soames had fixed ideas about admitting policemen of *any* rank. This one compounded his trespass by ordering Soames, William and another footman, and the housekeeper to stay in the hall and be interrogated like common criminals. At least the butler had been permitted to banish Cook and the maids.

'I have an important question,' Exeter began coolly, 'and you will provide a prompt and truthful answer. Has the Marchioness Melton or the duke received any communication from the men who took the young woman from His Grace's carriage?'

Soames whitened with indignation. 'I'm sure I am not party to private communiqués between His Grace or his guests and–'

Exeter put his hand on the butler's shoulder. It was not a

friendly hand. The eyes that drilled into Soames's were not friendly eyes.

The butler gulped before he spoke again. 'I do not believe there has been any communication whatsoever from… those persons.'

The hand stayed where it was. 'Well done. Now, where exactly in Ireland is your master?'

Telegrams raced between England and Ireland in the next hour. The marchioness might rush to attribute the violence in the duke's drive to political radicals or thieves, but Exeter knew the marquess was not so foolish. Why had no ransom demand been made? That was the question that nagged him as he wrote out the first wire. Jillian wasn't an accomplice; that meant she was the target of the abduction. Shop girl or marquess's daughter, she was still worth something as a hostage. Melton was a decent man; he would pay if there was a demand. The kidnappers might even make a run at the duke. But, thus far, they hadn't done either. That was worrying.

Exeter handed the filled form to the telegrapher.

> *His Grace the Duke of Fells and St Andrews*
> *Upon arrival ransom demand respectfully suggest ten thousand.*
> *DI Ewan Exeter*

The duke's reply was speedier than Exeter might have expected, given His Grace was at large in Ireland.

> *Exeter*
> *No ransom. Regrets but no longer my concern. Find horses and carriage.*
> *Fells and St Andrews*

Exeter scrutinised the duke's wire for a full minute, thinking. He'd been on the wrong side of the law longer than on the right, giving him a finely tuned sixth sense about crime and criminals. That sense was jangling now, as loud as a fire engine bell. He'd find the source of the alarm but not today, not with Kell in the vicinity. Keeping his former captain from exploding was enough of a challenge without murky hints and suspected subplots. Whatever came later, he'd have to attend to Kell first.

They were up the Embankment from the Yard, in a pub called The Judge's Tavern. None of them was drinking, but to keep a table long enough to come up with a plan, they'd ordered pints, which sat untouched before them. It was four o'clock in the afternoon. Jillian had been gone for five hours.

'I'll gut the bastard,' Kell snarled when Exeter showed him the duke's wire. Kell's expression was thunderous, his jaw set like stone. Dague sat next to Kell. His massive arms were crossed and his broad face impassive, like a watchful Buddha.

Exeter leaned forward. 'He's a *duke*. You'll hang if you lay hands on him, Stammer, and how will that help your girl? There's more to this than he's sayin', a blind bat could see it. When I find out what it is, I'll take him down, believe me.'

Exeter didn't want to show Kell the red scarf, but sooner or later it would come out. He pulled it from his jacket pocket and dropped it on the table. Kell gave it one glance. Then he shouted an oath and swept his arm across the table, flinging the scarf and his pint to the floor in a burst of glass and liquid.

Heavy silence followed, and then the sound of the publican's feet as he crossed the room, a dustpan and mop in his hands. Exeter nodded at the man, who nodded back his recognition. As he shifted shards and mopped, the publican slid a look at the detective's companions, the silent French giant and the Irish with the hair-trigger temper. His glance didn't linger. Instead, he picked up the soggy red rag and put it back on the men's table. The detective inspector reached out to shake the publican's hand, pound notes changing place.

Exeter was just as calm as the publican, just as ready to mop up Kell's anger. 'It's not the Cortellis.'

'The fuck it's not!'

'What it's *not,* is Raff. I wired him first thing, right after the duke.'

'Because you and he are such good mates.'

'Because he's not his old man and I'm not Scraper anymore. Now, it's business, Kell. Just business, and you've never really understood that.' Exeter leaned forward again, willing calm, willing agreement. 'If I'd wanted to stick where I was, where we all were, in the swill of Seven Dials, I would have. I would've fought Raff's father for every inch of that wasteland. No quarter, no compromise. And then I'd have ended up like most of Aurelio's men and ours. In prison or worse.'

He sat back, resting his hands on the table. 'I do things differently now. So does Aurelio's son.'

Kell snatched up the scarf, wadded it, and threw it at Exeter. 'This says nothin' has changed.'

Exeter coolly plucked the scarf from his forearm, where it had landed, and put it to one side. He brushed at a patch of damp on his sleeve. 'It says not everyone's onboard with the new way of doin' things, Stammer.'

'Are you sayin' Raff Cortelli can't control his own men?'

'Are you sayin' we always controlled ours?'

It was a lot for Exeter to admit. Some of the Jacks went straight when the gang disbanded. Some went over to the Cortellis, where they got a grudging welcome.

Some struck out on their own, and that didn't end well. *Jinks and Joe Lively.* The troubled faces of the other two men at the table said they were remembering the brothers just as Exeter was. Good lads, but with bigger wants than their brains could fill. Picked up within a year, both sent to Newgate. Jinks dead in another year, Joe still inside.

Careful of his spotless cuffs, Exeter lifted the red scarf and folded it, taking his time. 'What I'm sayin' is that Raff knows damn well that if any of his men go rogue on my patch, I'll take care of 'em. Permanently. And he'll have sod-all to say about it.'

Kell seethed, but silently. Exeter lifted his glass and drained it. The publican came over with two fresh pints, but Exeter waved him away. 'For your fine self, Archie. Cheers.' The pints and the man went back to the bar.

Finally, Exeter braced himself to be killed by Kell. They were eating up precious minutes and he had to ask it. 'Stammer, we need to know. Is she intact?'

'What the–?' Only Dague's outflung arm stopped Kell from diving across the table.

Exeter talked earnestly and fast. 'If she's intact, she's worth enough to keep alive. You know that.'

Kell shut his eyes, but pain was visible in every line of his face. 'She's a virgin,' he bit out between clenched teeth.

'There's this, Kell. I've heard of a place, a subscription club of sorts, where sick scum go to buy that sort of thing. Girls and women snatched off the street, taken from their homes, bought from cadets. They're left whole but stupefied on opium, morphine, cocaine. Then they're auctioned.'

Dague spat a series of oaths in French. Kell, only one word. 'Where?'

Exeter shook his head. 'Fuck if I know. For obvious reasons, it's kept under wraps. But you and me, Kell, we know somebody who might be able to tell us.'

'Who is he? I'll cut it out of his brain.'

'It's not a he. It's Theodora Arbuthnot.'

It was after five o'clock when they shouldered past the stuttering maid, up the staircase, and into The Flower Garden's drawing room. Mrs Arbuthnot, with a flicker of shock, shooed the three men back onto the landing and shut the door behind her.

'You're late,' she snapped at Kell. And at Dague, 'Who the hell are you?' And Exeter, but sweetly, 'Detective Inspector. Been a while. Not here officially, I hope.'

Exeter stepped forward and draped a long arm across Mrs Arbuthnot's shoulder. 'That all depends on you, Theodora.' Smiling, he gripped her shoulder and squeezed, hard enough that the proprietress winced and spoke hastily.

'Everything's in order here, Scraper.' *Scraper*. So, she'd known Exeter in the old days, the Jack days. 'I run a clean house, you know that.'

'It's not *your* house that interests us, Dora my lass.' He pulled a strand of Mrs Arbuthnot's brass-blonde hair from her coiffure and curled it between his fingers. Colour left the woman's face. 'We need a name and a direction.'

'I'm sure I can't help you, gents. I'm quite the homebody these days. Why, I hardly set a toe in the lane, don't you know, and I–'

Exeter tightened his grip on her shoulder, pulling her hard against him. The woman's eyes flitted from Kell to Dague and back again, while her throat convulsed.

'The Church.' Exeter spoke the words like a caress into Mrs Arbuthnot's ear.

Her mouth opened and she gawped like a fish. 'S-Scraper,' she finally forced out, 'you don't want to meddle with those– They're a nasty lot, they are, cut you as soon as lay eyes on you, they would. Sick bastards, too, all of 'em. What they get up to don't bear thinkin' about. You should–'

'Tellin' me what I should do, Dora? That's not like you. You've always been such a biddable filly.'

Exeter dropped the blonde curl he was holding and instead put his fingertips on Mrs Arbuthnot's pale throat. He made a low, animal noise as he pressed the throbbing vein. 'The Church, Dora, before I have to do something regrettable.'

The woman swallowed as though choking down ipecac. 'There's a– a fallen-down abbey, or monastery, or somethin'. St Duncan's or David's, somethin' like that. Nothin' now but a few walls and arches. It's on Tooley Street, hard by the old London Bridge. Some mad cove runs it, he's a lofter. Slave to the poppy, if you get my drift. They call him the Bishop.'

Chapter Twenty-Six

Night. More than night. More and worse, because night was inside, spreading like internal bleeding. Night pressed outward against her skin, distending it, trying to break through and succeeding in a dozen places. Her eyes bled night, her mouth.

Asleep, unconscious, she went somewhere else for a while. Then she came back, and it was worse than before. Sick. She was so sick, her stomach roiling and cramping! Where was she? Back in Hertfordshire? On the lake with Father and Pon? It couldn't but must be. The boat was rocking and rocking and– how sick she was! Father patted her back and Pon laughed.

She needed to be sick now, but she couldn't seem to roll over. If she was sick lying down, she would soil herself. She might choke. Why couldn't she roll over? Her parts weren't connected anymore, that's why. Legs and arms and head. Not hooked together the way they should be. She was missing parts. Or had too many. Were there two of her, now, two Jillians? One Jillian had arms and legs. One was just a head stuffed with wool. Black wool, smelling of sick.

She was moving. No, someone was moving her. If only they would stop moving her. Picking her up, putting her down, like luggage. Like bags they kept dropping. Didn't they know she was a person, not a–

She just wanted to sleep again.

Her mouth was so dry. She would ask for water. Water. There, she said it. Why didn't anyone answer? She would say it louder. *Water.*

Tired, she was so tired...

Everything hurt. Because they'd dropped her again. Now she was lying – on a bed? Such a hard bed. Hard and gritty and cold, not a nice bed at all. If only she could be warm. She wanted a blanket. *Blanket blanket blanket bl–*

Bad smells. Damp. Old things. Foul things. A foul place, a dirty place. *I don't want to be here. I'm so ill.*

Thirsty. Cold. Everything stinks, everything is wet and black. Someone is coming with light. She knew that face. A dark face with a scar. Him, oh God, *him. No, please, please.*

Don't. Don't. Don't hurt my arm again.

Something – bright light – woke her, searing her eyes. She didn't want to wake. She wanted the dark again, where nothing hurt. What was she wearing? Was she in her own bed? She was wearing a nightdress. Not hers and not a very nice one. Long. Scratchy. There was something over her eyes. Not very thick, though. *I can see shadow people through it.*

More light, more and more. It was– Why was there light between her legs? Why were her legs spread apart? She couldn't move them. *I don't want my legs apart.* There were men, men talking. They shouldn't be... *Why can't I move my legs?*

Cold, cold, cold. Outside and now inside, too. Inside her body. Something cold going inside her, pushing and pushing. No. No. *No no no no no no...*

Please, Kell, please come get me. Kell. Kell.

CHAPTER TWENTY-SEVEN

St Decumen's rose against the night sky like the carcass of an ancient sea monster. The moon, the same one from the time of sea monsters, was high and nearly full. The moon meant nothing to Kell. The cloudless sky and pitiless white eye were there for one purpose alone – finding Jillian Morehouse. No one, nothing, could hide from the moon or him. He was Ultio, the Roman god of retribution. Revenge with a beating heart.

Ten o'clock in the evening. Jillian had been gone for eleven hours. It could just as well have been eleven years or eleven hundred. Kell had aged and died in his mind, poisoned over and over by a brew he concocted.

Guilt. He hadn't prevented it. While he slept on Catherine Street, scum two miles away in Belgravia tore the heart out of his chest when they took Jillian from a duke's carriage and made off with her to some devil's lair. The scum had crawled out of Kell's own past, so the fault was his. Years since, he'd put down the dark tools of that past, but he'd picked them up now. He would cut the scum to ribbons.

Fear. The kidnapping was bad enough. To hold her against her will, treat her roughly, obscenely, possibly discard her like so much rubbish when they were done with her... A chunk of ice filled the space where Kell's heart had sheared away. The chunk enlarged with every thought of what might have happened, what was happening now, to the woman he loved, the woman he had *failed*.

Rage. Ah, that he welcomed. Craved, opened to it, let it flood his every cell and organ, his brain, his soul if he still had one. Michael Seraphin Kelly – that man was gone. No man combed through the fallen stones and shattered walls of this ancient church. Only a Jack, a famously brutal one, still whispered about in the rookeries. Stammer, the Jack whose fists were permanently stained with the blood of his enemies.

'We'll take it in sections.' Exeter pointed to the ruins ahead, roughly marking them into three parts. Exeter, Kell, and Dague split up, keeping within sight and hailing distance.

Finding what they sought might be easier with a dozen men from the Metropolitan Police. But that would mean witnesses to what they were going to do and that was never a good idea. Besides, the three of them were more efficient, not to mention quieter, than a squad of bumbling coppers.

Even so, it took them forty-five minutes of poking around in what remained of St Decumen's to spot it. Kell gave a sharp whistle to the other two. They clambered across broken stones to join him and then stood, looking into a tumble of bricks that nearly concealed the access point. A narrow, descending flight of stairs was free of rubble, speaking to recent and regular use. The three men lifted high the oil lanterns Exeter had brought from the Yard. They moved carefully down the steps into blackness.

While the church above had been a ruin since the Dissolution, the crypt below was intact. Kell's skin crawled as he surveyed the space that was and wasn't sacred. Solid Romanesque pillars held up the barrel-vaulted ceiling, and the chamber was long and lofty. There were newer touches of ecclesiastical splendour. Heavy crimson drapes hung on the walls, rippling subtly from hidden draughts. Kell's footsteps were muted by carpets, rat-chewed but rich in the half dark, covering ancient stone floors.

The air reeked of incense gone cold. Blood gone dry. Death gone – not very far.

He held up his lantern. His and the ones Dague and Exeter carried were the only light in the crypt now, but scores of guttered tapers in candelabra and wall sconces spoke to unholy acts lit by candles on other nights.

Their swinging lanterns threw monstrous shadows on the walls, the ceiling, and the floors as the three men went forward with the stealth of Hashshashins. Exeter was armed with a pistol, his *sgian-dubh*, and an American bowie knife at the small of his back. Kell carried a wicked blade that spoke death in its length and design, another just like it in the waistband of his trousers. No way to tell how many killing tools Dague had on his person. He'd never run out of them in a fight.

A mockery of an altar stood on a dais at one end of the crypt. Atop it, a central crucifix was mounted upside down on a gilt silver stand. Two rectangular stone tombs crouched in front of the altar, one angled to the left, one to the right. Red drapes, splotched and stained, lay on both. Kell's stomach lurched and bile burned his throat.

They found the horror who officiated in The Church in a curtained antechamber. The man was half awake, completely drug-addled, lying in a rickety bed. Around him the pedestrian goods of daily use were scattered: a chamber pot, a wooden table, a small oil heater. Those affirmed he lived there like a rat in a hole, when he wasn't pretending to be the High Priest of Sin, wearing the scarlet chasuble that hung on a hook beside the bed. He was so stunned with opium he hadn't heard them enter or seen the flickering lights of their lanterns. The sick-sweet smell of the poppy was everywhere, like carrion rot.

The first part of the interview was easy enough. His degenerate flock called him Bishop Black, but his real name was

Sylvester Wilkins. After the introductions, he became less forthcoming.

Dague, who'd let Kell handle the shaking and slapping until then, stepped forward. '*Mon frère*, please. Permit me the honour.'

Kell and Exeter stood to one side. Dague cracked his massive knuckles and went to work. There was screaming. There was also more information, all of it alarming.

The women who were brought to The Church came from one source, a man called The Viper, real name unknown. He operated with a squad of six. Not the usual dips and picklocks, toughs and bruisers that made up every gang in the city. These were specialists. Their specialty was abduction and ransom, which is why they'd not attracted the scrutiny of the police. Threats against the victims and their families tended to keep everything quiet. Most of the time, the families paid up.

'How many?' Exeter prodded. 'How many have paid up?' Kell looked at him sharply, but Exeter's face was unreadable. Even so, he clearly had a reason for such a specific question and wanted an answer. When Wilkins didn't supply it fast enough, Dague encouraged him. Wilkins's squeal became words.

'I dunno, I can't say! How would I know? I only get my piece and it ain't near enough. The Viper, he gets most of it. It's been goin' on for years and nobody's tumbled to it.' Wilkins's head lolled to one side as though he was sliding into unconsciousness, but before Dague could jolt him awake, the lofter's red-rimmed eyes snapped open. 'A bloody fortune!' he bleated. 'Thousands of pounds! Thousands and thousands!'

Thousands and thousands. Again, Kell saw something almost too subtle to be called emotion cross Exeter's face. If he had to hang a tag from it, Kell would call it *revelation*. There might be a time to pursue it, but not now. Now he was focused on the detective inspector's next question.

'What if the ransom's not paid?'

'Then, if they're *good* girls, they come to church, like good girls ought.' Wilkins's voice pealed off into a gale of wet laughter, stopped by Dague grabbing the lofter's greasy hair in his massive fist and shaking him until his teeth rattled audibly. When he could talk again, Wilkins choked out the information they were putting up with him to hear.

A young woman, Wilkins didn't know her name, had been offered to him that very day. A doctor had been summoned, one of The Church's flock with special proclivities that ensured his discretion. He'd examined the girl, pronouncing her *virgo intacta*. A high-ticket prize for the bidders at The Church's monthly auction.

Kell's control slipped when he heard about the doctor. No question that Dague and Exeter heard the murder sing in his blood. Exeter slid a glance at him, then shifted his hand subtly to the pistol at his belt, obviously ready to clout him if he charged Wilkins and tore out his throat before the man gave up all they needed to know.

But there was too much at stake for Kell to lose control. His question came out like a carpenter's level, not a bubble off calm. 'You took her, this young woman? The one you were offered today?'

'*Took* her? Not 'alf, I didn't! Viper's not the only one with operatives! I've got 'em works for me, y' know! Viper's lads got this girl from Belgravia, thought she was the bleedin' daughter of a marquess. They been watchin' the bint, see, and this one was her spit, so they figgered they'd got the genuine article. Worth fifty thousand quid, 'at's what they thought. Fuck me, what a larf!'

Some strangled phlegmy sound that might have been mirth escaped Wilkins's split and bleeding lips. 'But my nark seen the note the marchioness sent to the Yard, see? She weren't nuffin' but a shop girl, the one the lads took. From a soddin' corset shop!'

The note the Marchioness sent to the Yard. Kell looked at Exeter, both of them seeing the same thing. A turncoat. A spy. At Scotland Yard. Someone, whose days were numbered from this moment, read the note on its way to Exeter's hands or after it left them. There would be hell to pay at the Yard, but not tonight. Tonight, the demons were closer to hand.

Wilkins smelled like piss and fear, but Exeter crouched close in front of him. 'The woman The Viper's lads brought you, she came from a corset shop. What difference does it make? A virgin's a virgin. Your – parishioners. Surely, they don't care if they exercise their peculiarities on a shop girl or a friggin' blueblood.'

'I care! *I* care!' Wilkins was spitting, agitated. 'I care if the girl works in the same shop as the sister of a Jack! That's death, that is, *death!*'

From where he squatted, Exeter couldn't see Kell's reaction, but Kell knew the detective inspector smelled it, like the crackle and sharpness of ozone just before lightning strikes. Exeter straightened, slowly and carefully.

Kell cheated his old gang leader of the spectacle he might have seen when Kell was younger. No supercharged bolt hit Wilkins and incinerated him along with the crypt and most of Southwark. Kell's voice came out flatter, calmer, and more lethal than before. 'What happens if the women aren't ransomed or auctioned?'

'Well, then, they're no use, are they? No bloody use at all! Cat's meat! Offal! Get rid of 'em!' The bleeding mess on the cot extended a shaky arm toward the crypt and mumbled through chipped teeth. 'There's a tunnel.'

Kell bored holes into Wilkins's red and swollen eyes with his own. 'Where does the tunnel *lead*?' Wilkins's answer was cracked and strained, but they all heard it.

'Let's go,' Kell told the others.

Dague held up a broad hand. '*Un moment*. You may wish to look away.'

None of them looked away. It was done in a few seconds, brutal and wet. Exeter tsked at Dague, who was wiping his hands on a handkerchief he pulled from his always neat plaid suit.

'That tears it, you French lout. I could've run the fucker in.'

The lifted eyebrows in Dague's large, mild face told Exeter that wasn't an option, and the policeman shook his head. 'You'll have to go back to France now, you know.'

Dague shrugged, that Gallic gesture that drove both the other men round the twist. '*Eh, bien*. One pays for one's pleasures.'

'Stop talking,' Kell's voice was a sharpened blade, looking for a place to plunge, 'we're wasting time.'

Chapter Twenty-Eight

Kell checked his pocket watch. Just after midnight. Jillian had been gone for thirteen hours. He, Dague, and Exeter had just passed the junction of two tunnels. Both led away from the crypt. One, in which they now stood, appeared to have been an expansion of the crypt, probably added when burials beneath the floor and in tombs filled the older space to capacity. The overflow of bodies had then gone into a purpose-built tunnel, but any human remains were long gone, rotted away or reinterred somewhere else. The twenty-yard barrel vault was empty and swept clean.

At its end, the three men found the extension intersected another tunnel in a sharp right angle. In taking that, the three men surmised they were turning toward the Thames. There was no way to be certain, but Kell and Exeter both thought they knew where they were and what the second tunnel was or had been.

'This bit here,' Exeter raised his lantern to look at the brickwork above and around them, 'I'll give you odds it's part of the old pedestrian tunnel under the river.'

Kell went ahead, trying to see into the distance and failing since his lantern only shed light about five yards in front of his feet. His voice echoed. 'If that's what it is, it'll go under the viaduct, the one running to Stainer Street.'

The three men pushed ahead, their lanterns throwing feeble beams. Darkness closed around them like a fist the instant they passed.

Kell's hunch was right. The tunnel floor inclined as they went along it until, quite suddenly, the three men passed under a high masonry arch and found themselves out of doors, under the London night sky. A paved slope faced them, abruptly slanting downward into yet another tunnel, into blackness.

To a man, they recognised it at once. They were looking into the catacombs under Old London Bridge.

They moved forward to the entrance. It gaped and gave off a foul breath, as though to warn them away. Stagnant water, ancient stone, something worse. The smells of a disused charnel house. The bright moon made their lanterns redundant where they stood but, once inside the yawning hole, there'd be no light other than what they brought with them. They kept a tight hold on the lamps. As they passed the threshold and paused, the pale flames abruptly weakened, making barely a dent in the gloom.

Dague crossed himself. '*Sainte Marie sauve-moi.*' *St Mary save me.*

Even Exeter seemed nervous, changing his lantern from hand to hand. He reached under the tails of his jacket to touch the bowie – three times the size of the *sgian-dubh* he kept in his boot – at his back. Then he rested his hand on the grip of the pistol shoved in the front of his trousers waistband.

A dreadful stillness had Kell in its grip. Like his middle name, he'd become a vengeful archangel, stone cold and deadly. He turned his head toward Exeter. 'It's not your fight. You should leave now.'

A low chuckle from the detective inspector. 'And let you have all the jollies? Naw, I don't think so. Besides, it's like old times, the old Jacks.'

'One for all and all for one? A bit late in the game for that, isn't it, Ex?'

'Would be if I was here for anyone but you, Stammer. No more gob. Let's get your girl.'

Dague was examining a *poignard*, a twin-edged throwing knife. Even one of his had seen more action than the combined weapons of the other two men. He turned the blade this way and that in the uncertain light, assessing. '*Allons,*' he finally said, '*aux portes de l'enfer.*'

Kell looked into Dague's eyes, then Exeter's. 'To the gates of hell, brothers.'

Kell knew in his gut that if Satan had a receiving room, it would be the catacombs under London Bridge. They weren't under the bridge proper, but under the approaches. Graves, haphazard burials, and at least one crowded plague pit had been dug in the Thameside earth over centuries. Thousands of bodies had gone there. Hundreds had slid into the river, but hundreds remained, rotted to bones or less. Some were in vaults and crypts, some shelved like goods in a macabre death shop. Some lay underfoot, crunching sickeningly with every step.

About sixty yards in, the sloping tunnel forked. Kell raised his hand and they halted, utterly silent, listening. At first there was nothing but the rustle and squeak of rats, the faint sough of air coming from some place where the decayed walls broke through to the outside.

Two minutes passed while Kell died a little with each second. It would take but a moment for the kidnappers to destroy the only witness to their crime. A sharp twist of her head, a killing punch to her chest, a knife across her throat. Every second was borrowed from that narrow interval between the Jillian who lived and breathed, and the one who didn't.

Voices. Men's voices. Kell heard them, distant but identifiable as such. He jerked his chin toward the left-hand tunnel. They went forward with the delicacy of rope walkers, stopping now and then to shift rubble, one rock at a time. The last thing they wanted was to announce themselves by the sounds of snapped bones and falling bricks.

As they went, the walls to either side changed, becoming more finely finished, the shoddy brickwork yielding to square cut stones. Kell wondered if they'd passed into another crypt, or maybe the cellars of a buried building. He and Exeter knew London as well as anyone did, but no one knew everything under their feet. There were scores of ancient structures swallowed whole by centuries of city atop them. The voices ahead grew louder, nearer.

And then they were there, just feet away.

The Viper's men had more light burning than they needed, a feckless measure that meant they didn't see the faint lantern glow preceding the Jacks, but the Jacks saw their prey. Backs to the entrance of the high-roofed chamber, six men worked, bathed in a grotesque play of gold and black from a half-dozen torches in iron wall sconces, reeking of pitch. The Viper's men also had oil lanterns like the ones the Jacks held, and these were clustered close to where they laboured among a cluster of above-ground vaults. Fifteen, twenty, more. The chamber was full of tombs. There was no sign of Jillian.

Kell, Dague, and Exeter stood in deep shadow, just outside the chamber's mouth. They shuttered their lanterns and left them on the tunnel floor, dislodging not so much as a pebble as they did. Together, they drew their weapons, watching Kell as he silently mouthed a count.

On five, he nodded. Hell unleashed three of its own.

Already ahead in the kill count because of Wilkins, Dague entered the chamber and immediately smashed the skulls of two opponents. '*Desolé, mon frère,*' he said to Kell between heavy breaths as he readied his *poignard* to throw. 'They annoyed me.'

One of The Viper's men had a pistol. Exeter's bullet exploded the gunman's forehead as the man's single shot went wild, his trigger finger closed by a dead man.

A hairy boar of a man lunged toward Kell. Kell sliced off the man's knife-holding hand at the wrist with a downward slash, then opened his chest on the upswing to release a fatal gush of blood onto the stone floor. His next kill leaped, a knife in each hand, from the top of a vault. With a two-handed grip on his own blade, Kell met the man from below, gutting him before the two of them fell together, the death-spluttering man on top. Rolling the body off, Kell gagged at the stench of shit and blood that came with spilled intestines. He pulled hard to extricate his knife, stuck so deep in the body's torso that it had lodged in the spine.

The chamber went abruptly and profoundly quiet, as though the walls themselves were shocked at how much violence had taken place in so few seconds. The only noise came from Dague's captive, whose breath sawed and gurgled.

The Frenchman had the last abductor pinned from behind in a grip as powerful as the iron gates of a drawbridge. He'd already punctured a lung with his *poignard;* the handle of the razor-sharp weapon protruded from the man's chest. Kell and Exeter watched dispassionately as Dague dislocated one of the man's shoulders with a subtle jerk, then pulled back both the man's arms, hard. From the prolonged scream, the sensation was sheer agony, but Kell and Exeter looked on calmly. They might have been watching Dague knot his tie.

Kell approached the captive. The man coughed gobbets of blood down his shirtfront. A fresh knife gash at his hairline bled into an old scar on his face, merging with the blood from his mouth to drip off his chin. The stream was a brighter red than the kerchief the man still had knotted around his throat.

The blue of Kell's eyes had gone to black ice and his voice could have frozen water a mile away. 'Where is she?'

The man didn't speak – a mistake. Dague gave a fierce twist to the captive's upper body, tearing the second shoulder from its socket.

The man screamed again through the blood bubbling on his lips. '*Quello!* That one!' Wild eyes swivelled toward a tomb. Kell and Exeter ran to it.

It took all their strength. Straining and groaning, they shoved aside the monstrous stone lid, not enough to dislodge it completely but enough to expose the interior.

In a long, white linen shift like the burial shroud of a Saxon queen, Jillian Morehouse, pale and unmoving, lay inside the tomb.

The sound that escaped Kell was something none of them wanted ever in their lives to hear again. He and Exeter pushed frantically at the stone lid, moving it farther and farther until it toppled to the floor with an ear-ringing crash and an explosion of stone dust. Kell reached in to take Jillian's upper body, Exeter her ankles. Together, they lifted her from the tomb as though she was made of glass. Her body was limp and cool, unresisting, unresponsive.

As they lifted her, both men recoiled to see what she had been lying on. Bones, whole and in fragments, the rotted detritus of hundreds of years of interments, decay, grave openings, new interments. None recent in this tomb, but the smell of death was everywhere. The bodies in at least some of the vaults had been put there months, not centuries, ago.

They lowered Jillian to the stone-flagged floor, Kell despising it for its hardness, its cold and filth. He crouched beside her, holding her bloodless face in his bloodied hands.

'Jillian, Jillian.' His voice broke. He could barely force out the words. 'Wake up, love, please, wake up. Jillian, please.'

Exeter knelt beside him, holding out an opened flask that smelled of brandy. 'Just a little,' he said. Kell wiped one hand on his trousers and tilted the flask over his fingers, then rubbed the fiery liquid on the seam of Jillian's mouth, working it under her lips. So cold, she was so cold.

Jillian's eyelids quivered, then opened. Her pupils were dilated and her gaze unfocused. She breathed out a word so soft no one but Kell heard it. His name, and it was enough. He lifted her in his arms.

There was just one more thing to do before they left the chamber of death. Exeter went to the captive, moaning in Dague's implacable embrace.

'Answer and this can be easy and quick,' he told the man. 'Don't answer, and this will be slow and much, much more painful. Are you The Viper?' The man shook his head, grimacing from pain.

Exeter's long arm swept the chamber, taking in the five bodies cooling on the floor. 'Those men, any of them The Viper?' Again, the captive shook his head.

With Jillian in his arms, Kell came to stand next to Exeter, both men attuned to a verdict in Jillian's now wide open eyes. Vague and fearful, a spark of loathing still ignited in them as she looked at the captive. Exeter reached out and laid his palm as gently as a leaf across them. The queen had given the order to her executioners. All her enemies must die.

Kell nodded at Dague.

Chapter Twenty-Nine

Ada, who had the key, Min, and Evie were at the Hackney house when Kell brought Jillian back. Dawn was just pinking the sky as a hackney cab drew up to the kerb and Kell alighted, Jillian in his arms.

Ada held open the door. She and the other women were so shocked by Kell's appearance that none of them said a word. His coat was torn, one sleeve hanging by a few threads. His shirt and waistcoat, what they could see of them, were streaked and, in some places, saturated with blood. The knees of his trousers were ripped and gaped open; blood stained the abraded skin beneath. There was blood mixed with dirt on his cheek, his forehead, his jaw, the last darkened further by a two-day growth of beard. Tormented eyes burned in his ghastly white face.

Kell looked directly at the three women but seemed not to see them. Had he not been standing, with a woman in his arms, he might have been something left on a battlefield to die.

There was also the smell. It came in the door with Kell and almost knocked all of them off their feet. Rat shit, human shit, sweat, urine, Thames mud as foul as the River Styx. Something worse, too. Death, both ancient and fresh. Evie muttered something French under her breath. Min put the back of her hand against her nose.

Kell's voice was as shaky and hoarse as a ninety-year-old man's, the voice of someone standing at the edge of their grave. 'I need to lay Jillian down. I've been carrying her for an hour.'

Ada couldn't speak. She could only nod once and watch as her brother walked with his fragile burden to the stairs. He mounted them, his footsteps leaden and slow. There was no telling what condition Jillian was in, since Kell had her cradled to his chest, her face pressed against his soiled waistcoat. Ada didn't like the way Jillian's lower legs hung from the knees under which Kell's strong arm held her. The feet dangled lifelessly, so white Ada could see the blue veins.

She mouthed to her workmates, '*Train.*' Evie and Min nodded and went quietly out the front door. Ada closed it behind them. She trudged upstairs with dread in her heart.

It wasn't so awful when she saw Jillian on the bed, which she and the corset girls had assembled and made up with fresh linen. There was colour in Jillian's face – faint, but enough to contrast with the clean sheets and the bleached shift she was wearing. Ada could see the slow rise and fall of Jillian's breasts under the shift.

Kell made it to the bed but no farther. He sat on the floor next to it, his head hanging and his shoulders slumped. One of Jillian's hands draped over the edge of the mattress and Kell held it. Ada frowned at her brother's black nails, encrusted with dirt and only the Blessed Virgin could say what else. Someone's blood, she was sure of that.

'I'll go for a doctor,' she began, but Kell shook his head.

'No. She's been under too much morphia for a day and a night. I know what to do. I don't want anyone touching her but me.'

There'd be no argument and no further discussion; Ada knew better than to try. She also knew Kell, knew not only what he'd been, but what he was now, the raging, protective animal he'd become where Jillian Morehouse was concerned. He would care for her, no one better. She looked at the wrecked shape he was in and hoped he'd also care for himself, but that wasn't Kell's way and she couldn't change that, either.

She settled for a mild admonition. 'You should at least wash. If she comes to and sees what you look like now, she'll think she's in Hades.'

'If I'm there, she is.'

The weariness in Kell's voice, the desolation: they were worse than if he'd argued with her. Ada forged ahead, anyway. 'There's food in the kitchen. Try to eat.'

Kell didn't reply, so Ada left the room and the house, locking the door behind her on the way out. Whatever happened now was up to her brother and the woman in his bed. As it was always meant to be, she reflected as she briskly walked toward the train.

Chapter Thirty

The chills came first. Jillian curled into herself and shivered. The shivering became violent, nearly seizures. Kell took off his clothes and got in the bed with her, pulling the blankets over them both. He covered her as completely as he could, wrapping his arms and legs around her and tucking her head under his chin. She huddled against him while tremors ran through her, again, again. The whole bed shook with her agitated limbs, even with him weighing down the mattress. He chafed her arms, trying to force his heat into them. Kissed her, spoke to her, told her she was safe, told her it was over, told her he had her and would never let her go.

'I'm here, love. I'm here.'

As suddenly as the chills came, they fled, and the sweating started. She soaked her shift and the bed linens and couldn't stand anything touching her as she thrashed and tore at the sheets. He stripped her and washed her body with witch hazel, putting cool compresses on her forehead even though she kept pulling them off. She was feverish and delirious, calling for her parents, her mother.

He raged and wept when she called to him but couldn't hear him answer. He kept answering anyway.

'I'm here, love. I'm here.'

She'd been badly treated. Her fair skin, softer than a doe's, showed every place she'd been grabbed, wrenched, restrained, and ill-used. Her wrists were circled with dark contusions where brutish hands gripped her. She had bruises on both sides of her jaw, the kind that came, as he knew too well, from being punched in the face. Her left inside elbow was a huge purpling wound where a needle had gone in and in and in.

Kell had seen every sort of damage from fight rings, from street scrapes, from all-out gang wars. Damage left on the bodies of others, on his own. But when he saw what the abductors did to Jillian, he barely made it to the washroom before he retched into the basin. As his stomach emptied, a corrosive shame took its place.

He'd vowed to protect her, but he hadn't.

It was a small mercy, but at least there was no blood. She had abrasions and rashes in many places, but her skin wasn't truly broken, apart from where the needle punctured her. His own blood combusted with fury when he thought about whether she might have been violated. According to that doped-up bastard Wilkins, a doctor had examined her to confirm her virginity. Bared her vulnerable sex to the eyes of strangers. Used a tool, perhaps, to spread her innocent flesh.

If that was the worst that was done, it was still too much, a world too much, a universe. He would find the doctor. He would debase and then kill him. Slowly.

He'd said he would keep her safe, but he hadn't.

Sponging Jillian's fevered and battered body, Kell replayed the slaughter in the catacombs, again and again. Five times, ten, twenty. He brought Jillian's captors back to life in his mind, devising new scenarios of death for them. There were many ways to make men suffer prolonged, revolting, and unbearable pain. His imagination applied them all to each of the men whose bodies were now rotting in the stinking cavern where they would have let Jillian rot.

The Viper. He wasn't among the dead men, but he was the engineer of the whole filthy scheme. Kell would make it his life's work to find the man and take him apart, piece by excruciating piece.

Jillian called to him, bringing him back from waking nightmares of revenge. He kissed her face and hands, telling her over and over he was beside her. She didn't seem to understand or to recognise him, his voice. He thought he would lose his sanity, then. To think of her trapped in her mind, in pain and entombed, calling his name, and he not able to go to her...

He'd made himself her champion, and he failed.

She was rarely conscious, even more rarely lucid. When she was, he made her sip water. Sometimes she kept it down. Sometimes she retched painfully and he had to wait until she was calmer to try again. A spoonful. An hour later, another.

He checked her eyes, taking a candle to the bed and lifting her eyelids so he could measure the dilation of her pupils. They seemed nearly normal, but she still lingered in some distant dream world where he couldn't reach her. Where no one could.

'I'm here, love. I'm here.'

A day passed and then a night, followed by most of another day. Finally, late in the second full day after she was rescued, Jillian sank into a normal sleep. Kell carefully worked the shabby linen shift over her again, so she wouldn't be cold, and pulled the top sheet up to her shoulders.

Then he let himself become unhinged. He fetched a bottle of whiskey from the kitchen and brought it upstairs. It was all he knew to do to keep his ghosts at bay. Sitting in the armchair he'd pulled close to the bed, he drank straight from the bottle until the ghosts stopped screaming. Screaming his uselessness, his guilt, his bloody worthlessness.

After an hour of steady drinking, he fell forward onto the bed, one arm folded under his head, one stretched out with his hand on

Jillian's shoulder, in case she stirred. For the first time since he'd brought her home, he let his eyes close.

CHAPTER THIRTY-ONE

Ada arrived late in the evening, using her key. She stumbled up the dark stairs, cursing. The bedroom was even darker than the stairs, and she fumbled with the gaslight on the wall.

The first thing she saw when she could see anything was the near-empty whiskey bottle on the floor by the chair. She picked it up with an angry cluck, shaking her brother's shoulder until he lifted his head. He looked like a man who'd been snatched back from fiery Gehenna, but not before a hundred devils had chewed on him.

Ada sloshed the bottle in front of his face. 'What d'ya think you're doin' with this, you eejit? She might wake and need you, and where would you be? Off in some whiskey-soaked fairyland.'

Kell turned drenched and bleary eyes on her. 'If she– If I lose her, I'll die, Ada, I will.'

'You won't lose her. She's tough, our Jilly. Now go wash yourself and shave. You look like a bear and you stink like one, too.'

He got to his feet slowly and walked toward the washroom.

'Kell,' Ada called after him, and he turned to look at her. She'd made a promise to Min and would keep it. 'Dague?'

Kell's face went blank for a second, as though he couldn't remember who Dague was. Then the light went on, dimly. 'France,' he mumbled tiredly, and left the room.

As soon as Ada heard the tap running in the bathtub, she unpacked the contents of the large basket she'd brought and went to work. Clean sheets, for starters. Jillian slept through Ada changing them, though she made a small noise of protest when Ada rolled her over and back again.

Next, the coarse linen shift the kidnappers had put her in. As she worked it off Jillian's slack body, Ada made a mental note to cram it into the first dustbin she came across.

She'd said Jillian was tough. Ada thought of herself as tougher until she saw the bruises – purple, blue, and yellow like necrotic blooms – on her friend's arms, shoulders, breasts, back, hips, jaw. Ada kept working, but tears rolled down her cheeks and onto her busy hands.

She took a bottle of lavender water from the basket and sponged her friend down from scalp to toes. Jillian's hairbrush and comb were also in the basket. Ada applied the comb to the snarls in Jillian's hair, then brushed it until it gleamed.

The last thing Ada pulled from the basket was a folded garment of fine French cotton. Shaking it out, she admired the pin tucks on the bodice, the rows of soft lace, and the tiny mother-of-pearl buttons at the neck. Madame had given Evie the cloth and the nimble seamstress had made a lovely nightdress. Evie had stayed awake an entire night to sew it.

Jillian murmured something that sounded reassuringly like irritation when she was made to sit up so the nightdress could go over her head. Easing her back down, Ada straightened the gown and spread Jillian's hair over the pillow.

Kell came from the washroom. He was bathed, shaved, and

barefoot, wearing clean trousers but shirtless. Ada had seen the tattoos before.

He stared at the vision on the bed. 'Is she– Do you think she–'

It wasn't her usual style, but Ada could speak softly when it was called for. 'I think she'll be fine. All she needs now is you, brother. And all you've ever needed is her.'

She pecked his cheek brusquely, picked up her basket, and left the room and the house. If she hurried, she could catch the last train.

Kell climbed into the bed next to Jillian. Taking her hand, he interwove his fingers with hers and plunged headlong into sleep.

Sometimes heaven rained grace on bad people but only because they were lying next to good ones. That was the way Kell explained it, since he was sure God didn't owe him any favours. Jillian woke with no memory at all of the three days after she left Salon Sirena and stepped into the coach belonging to the Duke of Fells and St Andrews.

'Have I been ill?'

Those were her first words when she opened her eyes and looked at him. He'd been stretched out next to her, fully clothed, dozing off and on. He thought he was dreaming at first when Jillian, in her new nightdress, sat up and smiled at him.

He wanted to crush her in his arms. He settled for letting his eyes and then his fingers caress her poor, bruised cheek. He'd had three gut-wrenching days to fabricate answers to her questions. Now, if he could just propel them past the lump in his throat.

'You were in a carriage accident, darling. Do you remember anything?'

She shook her head as she looked down at the white gown. 'This isn't my nightdress.'

'Evie Broussard made it for you. Ada brought it while you were... sleeping.'

Kell's heart came out of darkness like sun on a cloudy day as he watched Jillian smile. 'Evie's so kind,' she said, fingering the lace on the gown. 'May I have a bath, please?'

'You may have the Crown Jewels. Just give me an hour to bring them to Hackney.'

She laughed. Kell thought that if he had to trade an eternity in hell for that sound, it was still a Petticoat Lane bargain.

Chapter Thirty-Two

Now what? It was a two-note song Jillian couldn't get out of her head. *Now what now what now what now what now.*

Twelve days ago, she'd stepped into a bottomless pit when she entered a ducal coach in Mayfair. Now, it was a deceptively normal Monday after all those days, the ones she'd slept through, or couldn't remember, or tried to forget, and she was back at Salon Sirena.

The worktable and the women around it seemed familiar but newly strange, as though she'd never really seen them before.

Needle in through the ribbon, out through the ribbon, pull the thread tight... Her hands, at least, remembered their way around the work. With all her other woes, she didn't need to lose her position.

Maybe *she* was the strange thing, the new thing, sitting with a fixed smile on her face. Trying to concentrate on the corset in her hands but thinking only of the parts of her life that had flown away, like uncaged doves, in such a short time.

Kell had made an effort to delay her return to the salon, but

Jillian insisted she was perfectly well. Her bruises and scrapes were healing. She was bored.

He tried, as well, to make her stay on in the Hackney house. But he wouldn't stand for her being there alone and she wouldn't stand for his missing his own work any longer in order to stay with her. She might not like it that he was employed at The Flower Garden, but she wasn't going to let anyone label her the invalid wife.

Wife. She was sure no one would label her *that*, so she'd better face up to it. The soaring, passionate Sunday she'd spent in Kell's bed – where had that landed her? She couldn't feel less tethered to that day and that bed if she'd floated away in a balloon with Phileas Fogg.

Kell had barely touched her since she woke from her long sleep. Yes, he was gentle and solicitous. Doctored her wounds, checked them every day for signs of swelling or festering. Quizzed and questioned her until she clenched her jaw not to snap at him. Did she feel any pain? Was she warm, cold, agitated, dizzy, hungry, thirsty? Did she want a blanket, a shawl, a window open, a window shut?

He took her for meals and short walks. Watched her, stared unnervingly at her, sometimes, for signs of tiredness or discomfort. At first, she hadn't noticed the change in him. She slept much of the time. But as she grew less drowsy, she became more confused.

Because they hadn't really talked. For a couple of days at the beginning, her thinking was disordered and fogged. She wouldn't have made much sense if they *had* conversed, since she tended to forget the end of a sentence before she got there. A result of the accident, Kell told her. Later, when her brains stopped rattling around like a jar of buttons, she and Kell only talked about everyday things. What would she like for lunch? Did she want the coal fire lighted?

At night, he held her until she fell asleep. That was lovely, she liked that. But his touch and his kisses were chaste. The man who'd fairly torn off her clothes and his own to get at her body, who'd kissed her in ways that set her aflame from her lips to the soles of her feet...

Where had that man gone? What had driven him away? Would he come back? What would she do if he didn't?

Ada and Evie were laughing about something. Jillian looked up and smiled. She'd not heard a single word they said, but she didn't want them to know how completely lost in her own mental circus she was. *Tiny stitches, nice and neat, Jillian. Gather the trim around the curve...*

She supposed she could have reached for Kell, taking the touch he now seemed reluctant to give. She didn't think it was wrong in the moral sense for a woman to reach out for a man. No, what held her back was something else. Shyness. Doubt. When her thoughts cleared enough to ask Kell about more serious, more intimate things, she couldn't seem to do it. The words got stuck between her heart, that wanted him so much, and her brain, that said there must be some terrible reason for him not wanting her in return. Not as he'd wanted her before.

She began to feel slightly mad and wondered if that was a result of the accident, too. Had she hallucinated those glorious hours in his arms? Was her memory of them a delusion, a fantasy from a disordered brain? Kell might just be waiting for her to come to her senses and say, 'Oh, I had the oddest dream! I thought you and I had...'

But it wasn't a dream, it was *real*. If it wasn't real, then nothing else was. Not the salon, not Ada sitting next to her, not the corset in her hands.

All she could say for sure was that things had disappeared, and she was the only one admitting it. The carriage accident wasn't just a few missing days. It was a blot, an erasure, a strike-through in her life, especially the part she thought she had with Kell. When she tried to reconstruct the missing days to see what went wrong, it gave her a headache.

It was making her head hurt now, so she put down the corset she was trimming in Alençon lace and rubbed her eyes. She needed to think of something else and look at something else, too.

The workroom appeared as it always did. A clutch of new orders pinned to the corkboard. Evie across the table, singing softly in French. Ada next to her, making faces at her work as though she could frighten it into submission. Min, a few yards away, making tea for their break.

Perhaps there was one difference. Evie and Ada were their usual selves, but Min seemed subdued. Not just shy but – despondent.

'What's the matter with Min?' Jillian whispered to Ada.

Ada cursed under her breath. Jillian couldn't tell if she was cursing the thread she just broke or the question.

'The Frenchman,' she whispered back.

Jillian thought for a few seconds. 'The– Dague? Him?'

Ada nodded. 'There was some trouble. He had to go back to France.'

Trouble. 'You mean, trouble with... the law?'

Ada nodded again.

'Well.' Jillian returned to her sewing. 'I warned her that he wasn't the sort of man someone like her should... I mean, you know how Min is. She's so, so–'

What *was* Min? Naïve? Trusting? Jillian halted in mid-stitch. Maybe she'd been naïve and trusting, too. Why *was* Kell behaving so strangely? Had he lost interest in her? She was no adventuress, but she knew enough about the world to know that men did that. Pursued a woman until she yielded and then, when they'd tasted her, turned their interest elsewhere. But *Kell*?

She focused on her needle. *In through the lace, measure the interval, out through the lace...* She fought it, but her eyes filled as they'd been doing for days when she thought about the change in Kell. As hot tears spilled over, she blinked, then brushed them hastily away before the others could see. It would be unbearable if they saw, if they knew. *Breathe, Jillian.* She tried, shakily.

Comprehension hit her like a blast of cold air. What an idiot she was. At the time, she hadn't considered, not even for a minute, what would happen after that Sunday in Hackney. Shouldn't she have foreseen that she could never tell anyone? Just as she could never tell anyone why she was going to pieces now. She knew what happened to women who admitted they'd done what she'd done. The names, the scorn, the ridicule. None of those were ever attached to the men, only the women.

Ada was her closest friend, but she couldn't even tell her. Jillian knew how Ada felt about Kell's job, about the women who worked in places like The Flower Garden. The *specials*. Money hadn't changed hands when she and Kell had done... what they'd done, but did that make it any different, really? The specials took men into their beds. Was there some point at which they were whores, but she wasn't? A matter of numbers? Five? Twelve? They'd all started just like her.

With one.

Jillian, you're a stupid, stupid girl. Kell never promised there would be anything after that Sunday in Hackney. Oh, yes, he'd said some flowery things about being all men to her. But only a really, truly, *colossally* stupid woman would have taken those things at face value.

What was the other thing he'd said? He didn't want her on a lead. Unflattering metaphor, that. Did he think she was a dog? Or was that his poetic way of saying they weren't really attached, and she shouldn't think they were.

It all made sense, now. Things weren't as they were a hundred years ago, when a man had to marry a woman if he deflowered her. But even so, even now, Kell might think she would expect marriage if they... completed the act. He'd been careful not to let that happen. Because he might've liked her at first, but what man wants to marry the sort of woman who leaps into bed after *her first kiss*?

Not even a bed, just a mattress. On the floor. How tawdry.

She should've thought it through beforehand. Did other women? Probably. She wouldn't have had to think at all if she'd followed *My Plan for Life*. Saints in heaven, she gave more thought to buying a pair of stockings than she had given to what she'd done on that mattress. What she'd done was a big step in a woman's life. But in Kell's? Not so big. Maybe for him it was a very small step, a bump, a pebble. Not something he wanted profound consequences from. Not something he'd want to risk a second time. Not when she was doing *nothing* to stop him.

Stupid Jillian. All Kell's tough talk about her parents, and his mother, and rent collectors, and how she wasn't a china doll.

She certainly had a few chips in the porcelain, now. He'd put them there. She'd let him. No, she'd *encouraged* him. Immodest, improper – those were kind words for how she behaved. Wanton, debauched – that's what most people would call it.

Now she was crying and couldn't stop it. Ada was a foot away and would spot the tears any second. Jillian turned her chair toward the corkboard and pretended to count the new orders. Five, six, seven.

She sniffled cautiously and felt Ada stir. Still facing away, Jillian said thickly, 'My hay fever's terrible this year. I need a handkerchief.' She dropped her sewing on the table, lurched out of her chair, and went to her coat, hanging with the others on the wall hooks. Face half buried in wool cloth and eyes streaming, she sniffled harder and dug in her coat pocket.

She should've resisted Kell, that's all there was to it. She should've– she didn't know! Demurred, denied, refused, put her foot down. Said, *Take your hands off me this instant, Michael Kelly. You're mistaken if you think you can do whatever you want with me. Just what sort of woman do you think I am?*

But no, she'd wriggled and sighed just exactly like one of those abandoned women at The Flower Garden.

What she'd let him do to her, his mouth on her–

What she'd done to him, her hand on his–

Oh, God. No wonder he wouldn't caress her, kiss her, barely wanted to touch her after *that*. He did the decent thing after her accident, cared for her, and that was laudable. But that's all it was, a gesture of kindness to a woman he probably never wanted to see again.

She needed air. She needed *out*.

She snatched her coat off its hook and flung it around her shoulders. Coughing into her hand, she cleared her throat and addressed Ada as casually as she could. '*Modiste* should be on the racks by now. I'll just pop round to the newsagent.'

Thankfully, Ada replied without looking up. 'We can buy it on the way back to the room. It's only an hour till we're done here. Why don't you–'

'No, no! I need to stretch my legs and I'm tired of fighting that wretched lace. I won't be a minute.'

Her friend looked up, startled, and opened her mouth to say something, but Jillian was out the door to the alley before she heard what it was.

Now what now what now what now.

CHAPTER THIRTY-THREE

T*he Lady's Modiste* wasn't at the newsagent, but something else was.

MISTAKEN FOR A MARCHIONESS
A Violent Abduction in Belgravia

The headline blared from the front page of *The Illustrated Police News*. The centrepiece of the pictorial collage below was the ducal coach, the one with the matched greys and the liveried driver and footman. The coach that took Jillian to Belgravia to deliver bridal corsets to Lady Rosaline Melton, the duke's fiancée. The coach Kell told her was in an accident, an accident that erased three days of her life and left her purpled with bruises.

Most of the article was inside the paper, but there was one damning line of text at the bottom of the front page.

On the morning of Wednesday the 8th June, an innocent shop girl was snatched by ruthless abductors from the very doorstep of the Belgravia residence of

```
His   Grace   the   Duke   of   Fells   and   St
Andrews.
```

It couldn't be and yet it was. In black and white, for all London to goggle at. Jillian went numb for half a minute. Then she was electrified by the need to read more, to read all of it. She supposed she should count herself lucky there were copies of the penny dreadful at the stall. It came out on Saturday and usually, by mid-week, the popular paper was sold out. As it was, there were only three left. The studied blankness of the vendor's face when she handed over a penny for one of them said he thought it wasn't reading matter for a decent woman. *Well, sir, if you only knew what an indecent woman I am.*

How blank would the vendor's face be if he knew she was the subject of the newspaper's lead article? He'd probably give her the rest of the papers for free. He might ask for her autograph. She felt like screaming, or hitting him with the newspaper, or yelling, 'It's me! It's me!' Jillian had to get out of the stall before she started raving on the spot.

Fifty feet away, reaction set in. She halted on the pavement while Mayfair bustled and chattered around her, but she was befogged, everything hazy and muffled. She couldn't stand there and read the paper in full view of the world, nor could she return to the salon with it under her arm. She folded the paper and put it in her coat pocket. All she could do was go to her and Ada's room.

Not their room, Kell's. The room where everything reminded her of him. The bed he'd slept in and the chair he'd sat on. The window he'd looked out of. The wardrobe he'd built.

The man she'd held in her arms, and who now felt as far away as the moon.

'Here you are! I brought your hat. Where'd you go? I was worried, we all were. Except Madame, of course. When I left, she still wasn't back from the–'

Jillian, sitting on the bed, held up the paper. The front page faced Ada.

Ada walked over and scanned it in Jillian's hands. 'Jesus, Mary, and Joseph.'

'You knew, didn't you?'

Tense seconds went by. 'Yes,' Ada finally breathed out, 'I knew.'

'And the others?'

Ada nodded, miserably.

'Everyone knew. And no one told me.'

'Kell–'

'Kell wasn't the one who was–' Jillian rattled the paper in her hands, '"mistaken for a marchioness". They didn't even get that right.'

Ada spoke in a rush. 'They prob'ly got everything wrong, the papers usually do. There ain't no way to tell it's you, Jilly! That front page, it don't even say you're a corset girl. Look at the drawin', it'd make a stuffed bird laugh! She could be anybody. A clerk, a waitress–'

'What would a waitress be doing in a duke's carriage, Ada?' Jillian slapped the paper on the bed next to her, then curled her hands into fists in her lap. She kept her eyes on them.

Ada sat on the bed. *The Illustrated Police News* was between them, a wall fifty feet high. Guilt-studded silence kept the wall in place.

Jillian finally broke through the silence but kept her scrutiny on her hands. 'What did they do to me, Ada? The men who took me. I woke up with bruises all over. Kell said they were from a carriage accident. Those men, did they... interfere with me?'

Ada's shoulders went up with a deep, shuddering, intake of breath. 'I– We don't think so.'

Jillian levelled a flinty stare at her friend. 'You don't *think* so, Ada?'

'Do you remember anything at all, Jilly?'

Jillian unclenched her fists and brought her fingers to her forehead, rubbing it as though she could urge memories out. 'Sometimes... sometimes I have a kind of vision. I'm in a dark place. I'm cold. There are voices.' Her hands fell again to her lap, and she looked helplessly at Ada. 'Who brought me back? If it wasn't an accident, which it wasn't, who took me from those men and brought me back?'

Ada hesitated, then told her. 'Kell. With Dague. And Ewan Exeter.'

Dague and Exeter. Dague, who'd smiled at Min, and held a bag of sweets, and juggled almonds in the alley behind Salon Sirena. Exeter, who'd taken her to the park, to lunch and the theatre, and about whom Kell had warned her. Two more people who knew everything. Two more who conspired to tell her nothing.

Jillian wasn't sure she'd ever used the voice that next came out of her mouth. A hard voice, cold and unforgiving. 'Tell me, Ada. Tell me everything you know. Now.'

Ada did, at first haltingly, then all in a rush, as though she needed to get rid of it. Jillian was sure the story lacked some gore, either because Ada wanted to spare her or Kell didn't share it. But his sister made it clear that there'd been seven criminals operating under the ruin of St Decumen's when her rescuers went below, seven alive and breathing. None, when they emerged.

Jillian listened quietly. No hysteria, no interruptions, no comments. At the end, she was too drained even to cry. Tears overflowed her eyes anyway; maybe they hadn't stopped when she left the salon. She couldn't say because she didn't feel them anymore. They just fell, one by one, onto the hands in her lap.

Ada saw them fall. She violently shoved the paper off the bed, splaying it on the floor. Edging over, she gently put her arm around her friend. When Jillian didn't resist, she pulled her close and they sat that way for a while, heads tilted toward each other and touching. Emptied by shock, it was just the way they'd sat in the filthy shed in Whitechapel after they fled Larches. After Jillian killed Sir Hubert Alloway. Before she met Michael Kelly.

Jillian finally sighed out a few words. 'He won't touch me.'

Ada's head snapped up.

'Kell won't touch me. I thought it was something else, but now I think it must be because of those men. They must have done something and now I'm– ruined. Or maybe he's afraid I'll say *he* did it, or...'

Ada squeezed her shoulder. 'Jilly, there ain't been serious talk about ruined maidens since white wigs. And you can't say that's what happened, no more'n the rest. I can tell you this. Even on his best days, my brother's a nut you can't crack with a hammer. You don't know why he's... hangin' back. Chances are he don't, neither. And you don't know those men did anything more than takin' you away, which is bad enough.'

'No, I don't. But now, I know they did that. If there was something else... I have to find out, Ada. Maybe I can go to a doctor.'

Ada's arm came off Jillian's shoulders and she bolted to her feet, hands on hips. Every inch an East End girl. 'We don't need a flamin' doctor. We've got my mam.'

Chapter Thirty-Four

A half hour later, they were on a short reach of Upper Thames Street, hard by the Hour Glass Brewery. Before Ada motioned her inside, Jillian stood at the kerb and tilted her head back to take in the curious and very old house. It was three storeys and built, Ada said, for a gentleman in the Jacobean age, and now sliced into flats. Ada's mother lived in four rooms on the second floor.

The stairs were narrow and unlighted. Jillian had to keep one hand on the stairwell wall to keep from losing her bearings altogether. When they got to the flat door, Ada opened it without a knock. A slim, black-haired girl about fourteen, a younger version of Ada, slipped out with a silent smile as they squeezed past.

Ada flapped her hand toward the girl's back. 'My sister Eileen.'

Light welcomed them when they entered the flat. Along one side of a neat, open space, a long row of casement windows with tiny, ancient glass panes poured bluish rays into a sort of kitchen-parlour. A sink and coal range sat stolidly on one wall, a red tufted sofa opposite. In front of the sofa, a red and blue hooked rug displayed somebody's needlecraft. Two mismatched armchairs were cosily planted before a broad hearth, its wood mantel blackened with age and smoke. A few commonplace framed prints dotted the plastered walls. Ducks in a farmyard, a castle on a hill, Jesus with a crown of thorns.

The main feature of the room was a square table – oak, with a white linen cloth – and four straight-backed chairs. An oil lamp, unlit, hung over the table.

Introductions went around, brief ones since Ada's mother seemed to already know who Jillian was. They sat at the table. One of the four corners of the tablecloth brushed Jillian's knee. She lifted and examined it. The corner was embroidered with a cluster of shamrocks in green thread.

No one said anything for a minute or two. The room seemed to settle around them, unasked questions drifting in the bluish air like dust motes. Since there'd be no progress, otherwise, Ada handed the penny dreadful to her mother, who took it with one hand. With the other, she extracted a pair of spectacles from her apron pocket.

Mam Kelly read the paper slowly, spectacles on the end of her nose. She looked a little like Madame, large-bosomed, middle-aged, not fat but solid. Her hair must once have been jet, like Ada's and Kell's. Now it was streaked with grey and braided neatly, the braid pinned to her head. She wore a plain dark dress under her striped apron.

Jillian couldn't look away from Mam's hands. They were strong and broad, chafed and reddened by work, with clean, neatly trimmed nails. She tried not to think about one of those hands balled up and headed for the face of a sixteen-stone rent collector. What on earth would a woman like that think of a foolish corset girl, one who'd let herself get into the mess she'd brought to the kitchen table?

Minutes crawled by, marked by the ticking of a china clock on a shelf over the coal range, while Jillian fought rising panic. Ada's mother was examining the front page of *The Illustrated Police*

News like a jeweller with a suspect gemstone. Touching her finger to her tongue, Mam turned to the full article inside, and Jillian's panic slid into something like numbness. Worse. A dank sludge of despair.

Her chant of *now what* changed to something pathetically worse. *Please Kell, let me go to you.* No. *Please, please, Kell, come to me.* Not that, either. Either way lay danger. Either way, the growling beast of rejection crouched between them. The rejection she saw, or thought she saw, or imagined she saw, in his eyes.

Was she in love with him? Was that why she felt this way? Did she even know what love was, or was she being naïve and stupid again? The only thing she could say with certainty was that she couldn't say.

It wasn't as though her past had given her leisure to form ideas about love, not the kind of ideas she supposed most girls and young women had. They learned about love from romantic novels and sentimental poems in ladies' magazines. Just when was she supposed to read those?

They weren't allowed romantic novels at St Margaret's. 'Occasions of sin,' Mother Winifrid called them. According to Mother Winifrid, novels were the top of a greased slope to the Abyss. The girls had to find what love they could in the classics, and even Shakespeare was rigorously policed. *Romeo and Juliet* was out. *A Midsummer Night's Dream, As You Like It, The Taming of the Shrew...* all forbidden. They were given *Macbeth,* guaranteed to put you right off love forever.

Magazines? Love serialised in twelve issues a year. What barmy philanthropist was going to donate back issues of *Juno's Review* or *Her Own Companion* to a load of orphans?

From the little she'd read or the girls whispered about when the lamps were dimmed, she supposed love was soaring joy, the triumph of being courted, the thrill of being desired. Paper Valentines and bouquets of roses. The gallant suitor, the blushing maiden. The white wedding.

Not this. Not this room in Whitechapel, this baring of her possible ruin only to find out none of it mattered. Not if the man she might indeed love, didn't love her. Maybe he'd never loved her. Or if he had once, he couldn't love her now, because of something she'd become that wasn't even her fault.

If this was love, she didn't want it. It was sordid and clinical. It was *pain*.

And if her heart wasn't breaking, it was the closest thing. Jillian could hardly understand how it continued to beat, to pump blood. How could there be any blood to pump when hurt filled her chest so completely?

The room swam and her eyes flooded. Again. Would she ever stop crying? She reached out a trembling forefinger and traced the tablecloth shamrocks. She refused to let the pain overtake her. She refused to fall apart at a kitchen table in Whitechapel. Kell had told her she was strong. She would be strong.

At last, Mam put the paper down. She looked over her spectacles at Jillian. 'You'll be tellin' me, now, why I'm readin' this.' If there were traces of Ireland in Kell's voice, his mother's was the rich earth of the western isle.

Jillian opened her mouth, but nothing came out. She swallowed and tried again. 'It's me.'

'You bein' the girl they took?'

Jillian couldn't meet those sharp blue eyes, so like Kell's. She picked at the tablecloth and nodded.

Mam folded *The Illustrated Police News* and put it to one side. She took off her spectacles, folded them, and set them carefully on the paper. Her weathered hands, fingers interlaced, rested on the table and she waited out the silence while her visitor counted green-thread shamrocks. Jillian knew it was her turn to say something, but she was longing to be in the Hebrides, Canada, South America, even on the high seas, like Pon. She was here, painfully and now, so she'd better speak.

'Kell– Michael. He and I, we– we're...'

'I know about you and my son.'

Jillian nodded again for no reason. Mam knew about her and Kell, and that wasn't surprising. She'd been married, she'd made children with her husband. She knew about the physical things that pass between a man and a woman. But she couldn't know what Jillian and Kell *felt.* Couldn't know the things Jillian was so sure had passed from her heart, the heart that was breaking now, to Kell's, and from his to hers. How could she make the woman across from her understand that? How could she make her understand that she might as well die if Kell never took her back. If he never again held her against him, kissed her, *wanted* her?

She began clumsily, brokenly. 'He must think– I mean, what happened, it's all a blank. I don't– and he won't. And if he doesn't, I just don't know if I can...'

Ada came to her rescue, pointing at the newspaper. 'Jilly don't remember nothin' of that. She's got amnosia.'

'Amnesia,' Jillian corrected bleakly.

'Right. And my fool of a brother thinks she might have been– that the men who took her might've, you know, *done* somethin' to her. So now he won't– an' Jilly can't rest until she knows if she's still–' Ada didn't finish, but was there really any need to?

The room quieted while the clock ticked. Half a minute. A minute. Mam spoke, only to Jillian. 'In Ireland, there was never doctors for folk such as us. Whitechapel's no different. We do for ourselves. We do what needs to be done.'

She stood. Ada and Jillian did the same.

Mam folded the tablecloth – newspaper, spectacles, and all – and put it on the chair where she'd been sitting. Jillian stared blankly at the bared table, bleached by scrubbing and use.

'Ada,' Mam told her daughter firmly, 'boil the kettle. We'll be wantin' tea.'

Mam stumped over to the sink and poured water from a pitcher into a basin. She laved her hands, then dried them on a clean dishtowel hanging over the edge of the sink, talking to Ada all the while. 'Pull the curtains. Light that lamp over the table, and fetch a candle, too. An' get the whiskey bottle out of the dresser. By one road or the other, we'll be needin' it later.' She looked pointedly at Jillian. 'You and me'll be talkin', girl, and not just about what you come here for. Now hike up your petticoats and get on the table.'

She flung a last order over her shoulder at Ada, who was holding a corked stoneware bottle in one hand and a tea tin in the other. 'When we've finished here, Ada, get a message to your brother Michael. Tell my son he's to come see me, the second the doors close in that sin factory where he works.'

CHAPTER THIRTY-FIVE

It was half six, too bleedin' early in the morning to be sitting in a chair at his mother's kitchen table, but that's where Kell sat. He was exhausted and surly. If he didn't soon get some tea, he might throw something. Knowing Mam, she'd pick up something bigger and throw it back, so he tamped down the impulse.

The Flower Garden had been Bedlam from opening to closing. Drunk and disorderly custom all night and he'd had to toss two men, one an earl's middle son, out on their ears. All he wanted to do afterward was sleep. But the tone of Ada's message made it clear that his presence was demanded in Whitechapel at first light, no arguments and no delays.

He'd have thought his own mother would give him a cuppa. But the minute Kell saw the look on her face, he knew both tea and resistance were lost causes. Whatever bee had got into the old girl's bonnet, he'd just have to—

His mother unfolded a newspaper on the table and pushed it across to him.

The front page paralysed Kell for ten heartbeats. Then he leaped to his feet, knocking over his chair. Profanity that was foul even by rookery standards rent the air in the room. The story could only have got to *The Illustrated Police News* from one source. He would tear the arms and legs off Ewan Exeter with his bare hands.

His mother was unmoved by his reaction. 'Before you're after askin' me any eejit questions, she's seen the paper and I've seen her. She was in this very room yesterday, in the chair you just toppled. Now, set it straight and put yerself in it.'

Weeks of fatigue hit Kell all at once. He righted the chair and sagged onto it.

His mother kept talking. 'And before you're after givin' me any eejit answers, think twice. Have you forgot that I bore six of your father's babbies?'

'Two died.'

'Four lived. Did you think any of 'em, yerself included, was brought to your father and me by the pixies?'

His mother apparently took his silence for dissent. 'As I thought. So, havin' got as far as you did with the girl, explain to your mother just what about that shambles in the duke's drive stopped you from takin' her back to your bed? Or did you think she forgot you bedded her, along with the rest of it?'

There were any number of things Kell knew he needed to say, but his mother didn't wait for his tired brain to sort them out. 'I see,' she nodded, 'you was plannin' all along to use her the once and never again. Her losin' her memory made it easier to put her out with the slops.'

'*No!*' Kell spat the word with such violence, he was surprised not to see blood fly out of his mouth with it.

'Let's have nothin' but the truth, son. Did you, in your tiny suspicious mind, think the men who took her used her ill and, her being dirtied now, she ain't good enough for you?'

'*No, no, no!*' Kell's elbows went on the table so hard it quivered. Moaning, he put his head into his hands, scrubbing at his hair. He forced himself to look up and to speak, cracked and desperate. 'It wouldn't matter to me if she'd been had by the Royal

Regiment of Fusiliers, don't you understand? What matters is that I wasn't there to stop it. I vowed I would protect her; I promised her; I *swore*.

'But I didn't protect her! I was dead to the world in my bed at the back of that sodding whorehouse while those filthy bastards put their hands on her, knocked her about, shot her full of poison, locked her in a putrid, stinking–' His voice broke as he dropped his forehead to the table with a heavy thud. Once, twice, three times, while the table shook. He crossed his arms on the table and buried his head in them. With a spasm that rippled across his upper body, he began to weep.

Mam waited while his shoulders shook. The clock ticked as it always did, and a few homely morning sounds from the street filtered into the room. Somewhere in Whitechapel a tree survived just so a bird could trill in it, which it did. Its song was oddly beautiful against the sounds Kell made, sobbing as he'd not sobbed since he was a child. Since he was nine, the last time he'd been beaten in a fight.

He mastered himself to the extent that he sat back in his chair, roughly dragging his hand across his face. His forehead stung from where it had met the tabletop. He got his voice to work again, but it felt and sounded like he'd swallowed tacks.

'Everything I've done,' he said, his eyes blank with disbelief, 'every hellish thing I've done, but when she needed me, I wasn't there for her. What was the point of it, Mam? Of Seven Dials, and the Jacks, and the money, and the vice? A woman like her, like Jillian, she can find a better man any day of the week. A richer man, a finer one, a man who won't soil a wife and children with his black history. A man...' He spread both hands flat on the table. They were meaty, big-knuckled, scarred. Carmine painted the knuckles of one, from the blow he'd had to give the earl's son to get him out the door of the brothel. 'A man who doesn't have blood up to his wrists.'

He made fists and raised them. 'The only thing I've got is

these. And what good are they? I can't be with her every hour of every day, can I? And I won't lock her in a box until she dies for want of light and air.

'*That.*' He pointed at the newspaper, then let his hands fall into his lap. 'That just shows I can't keep her safe. I can't do what needs to be done to lay claim to a woman like her. I'm just not good enough, not man enough.

'She'll forget me like– like she forgot the hours when those bastards had her. It's the only thing I can do for her. Let her go.'

His mother rose, pushing off from the table with a creak from her stays, followed by a sigh. A mother's sigh, one filled with decades of sufferance. She crossed to the range and put the teakettle on the burner, then fired the coal. Opening the tea tin, she ladled a few spoons into a Rockingham pot. When she came back to the table, she didn't sit, just stood, hands on her hips, staring at her son.

'You know,' she began, 'it's a shame and a pity your elder sister Constance run away. If she hadn't, if she was here, I could ask her, "Con, did you drop your wee brother on his head when you was supposed to be mindin' him?" Cause if she didn't, Michael Seraphin Kelly, I can't for the life of me figger what's wrong with your brain.

'Your father wasn't always a drunk and a brawler. When we was first together, when life pressed down on us so hard we felt the very breath bein' squeezed out of our lungs, we still had each other. To hold, to comfort, to make a place inside our arms where nothin' could get at us. He was a man of only a few fine qualities, was Liam Joseph Kelly, but there was that.

'In that place inside our arms, we had dreams, Himself and me. Now he's gone and they're gone. No more to be said about it.' The light of dawn through the ancient casement windows shifted, tipping her faded dark hair with gold like a gilder's brush.

'But you, my handsome fool of a son, you're *alive*. You're alive, you're young, you've riches. And crownin' that, you've a dear little girl who, for some lunatic reason, thinks the world of you despite you doin' your best to make her as addled as you are. You and her, you should have twice the dreams me oul' fella and I had. There's nothin' stoppin' you from makin' 'em come true except your own blockheaded notion you don't deserve 'em.

'Go to her, *mo stór*, my treasure, my son. You should've taken her to wife before you took her to bed, but go to her now and finish what you started.'

Steam whooshed from the teakettle's spout and Mam went to the range. As she did, she directed five words over her shoulder at Kell, five words that went straight to his deepest fear.

'Before some other man does.'

CHAPTER THIRTY-SIX

On his way to New Scotland Yard, Kell nurtured murder in his heart. Another man would never finish what he'd started with Jillian Morehouse, because he was on his way to kill that man now.

Not openly. He didn't want to spend his honeymoon in prison. After he killed Ewan Exeter in some dark corner, he'd go to the offices of *The Illustrated Police News*, drag the scribbler who wrote MISTAKEN FOR A MARCHIONESS into the street, beat him senseless, and roll him into the Thames. Next, he'd go for the scratcher who did the front-page drawings. Then, the man who set the type for the article. The one who ran the press. The editor of the paper. The publisher. The newsagents, every single one who hawked the stinking broadsheet from one side of London to the other.

Before doing all that, though, he needed answers. For those, he went to The Talbot, the smallest, dimmest, oldest pub on the Embankment near the Yard. En route, Kell left a message with the Yard's desk sergeant. Exeter's presence was required. Immediately.

Exeter had been waiting for the summons. That was evident from the moment he crossed The Talbot's threshold. As always, he carried himself like Scraper, the arrogant king of the Jacks, barely cloaked now in the skin of a Metropolitan Police detective inspector. Impeccably groomed and tailored, he still wore the same faintly bored, fully dangerous air he wore when he ran Seven Dials. Only someone who knew him as well as Kell did would have seen the slight hitch in the walk, the tension in the close-shaved jaw.

Kell had ordered a shot of whiskey and a pint of bitter for them both, and the full glasses stood on the table. Ex went straight to them. Standing, he downed the whiskey with a grimace, then tipped back his head and drank the ale. All of it, at one go.

The barman, watching the show, nodded when the policeman pointed to his two empties. As he took a chair, Exeter addressed the man across from him. 'Ta for that. The condemned man's last meal, was it?'

Kell's anger burned so hot he was fairly sure he could start a bonfire with his eyes alone. His voice burned even hotter. 'Tell me about *The Illustrated Police News*, Ex. Now, while you can still talk. Because when I'm done with you, you won't move your jaw for a month. Maybe never.'

'I didn't give the story to the *Police News*.'

Kell started to his feet.

Exeter held up his hands, palms out. 'Listen, Stammer, before you lose your rag like you always do. I did *not* give the story out.'

'And I should just believe you?'

'You should. I've lied so much to so many people I can't remember what I said or who I said it to, but I've never lied to another Jack. And you know it.'

The fire in Kell's eyes continued to shimmer, but he kept his seat.

Exeter went on talking. 'The note from the Marchioness Melton. The one where she told the Yard that the duke's carriage and horses had been stolen, his men abused, and a girl taken. Remember that? That note's how I first found out. I thought I was the only one to have seen it.

'I was wrong. I knew that as soon as Dague forced the truth out of that maggot Wilkins, in the crypt. That's when I knew there was an even bigger maggot, an inside man, at the Yard.

'He's a clever one, he is. At first, I thought he was just a bent copper, trading in information. Whatever makes him the most brass, yeah? If he makes it on the right side of the law, that suits him. But the wrong side suits him just as well.'

The publican brought Exeter his drinks and, as before, he downed the whiskey the instant the glass touched the table. He put down the glass, raising slate eyes to Kell. The eyes were as clear and sharp as if he'd not inhaled two stiff shots in rapid succession.

'See, now, I think this nark's more complicated. More of a problem. And maybe not workin' alone.' Exeter wrapped his hands around his pint glass. 'I had a little chat with Jimmy Sullivan.'

'The reporter from the *Police News*.'

Exeter's chin barely dipped. 'Jimmy hung back at first, you know how they are. "Protecting my source" and all that blather. I promised him something, though, an exclusive on the biggest story he'd ever have in his pathetic, ink-pushin' life. He gave up the snout.'

Kell leaned forward. His whiskey and the pint of ale were still in front of him, still full to the brims. The contents of both glasses were seconds away from landing in Exeter's face, followed by Kell's fists. He knew it, and Ex knew it. 'Give me the name.'

'That I will, Stammer. Just... not yet.'

Kell stood, fast. So did Exeter. The inspector was an inch taller, but Kell outweighed him by more than a stone, all of it pure muscle. Ex's haste to avoid a fight came out as a hissing command.

'Sit *down*, you mad fucker! If you punch a detective inspector, you'll go inside, and then you'll never get your hands on the bleeder. I said I'd give you the name and I will. But there's a dozen things I can use him for before you take him out, so just give me a chance to squeeze the cull till he's dry. Then you can have him. Put his head on a pike on London Bridge, for all I care.'

Exeter sat warily, keeping Kell in his sights. Kell finally sat, too, sensing the publican's sights on them both.

'First things first, Stammer. Tomorrow's Friday, the first of the month. That's when The Church holds its services. What you, me, and Dague did there... A couple lads I trust helped me clean up the mess and that's good as far as it goes. But tomorrow's our only chance to put a stop to these verminous sods before they tumble to their high priest of shite bein' dead.

'Friday night we empty the pews for good, and you're comin' along.'

Kell let the wheels turn for a few seconds. 'The big story you promised Jimmy Sullivan.'

'The biggest.' The king of the Jacks raised his pint. 'To the wrath of God.'

Kell bolted his whiskey. *I'll drink to that.*

CHAPTER THIRTY-SEVEN

Kell knew Exeter wouldn't be able to resist a dash of theatre and the policeman didn't disappoint. The scarlet chasuble of the late, unlamented Sylvester Wilkins stretched across his wide shoulders as he stood on the dais, facing the upside-down crucifix. The detective inspector looked comfortable there, expanding into the moment and the role. Between the tunic, his stance, and the low light, no one entering the crypt could have said if Exeter was Sylvester Wilkins or the Archbishop of Canterbury.

Kell checked the chambers of the detective inspector's revolver and pressed deeper into the shadows. Twenty bluebottles were cached in the shadowy recesses of the crypt. All carried truncheons. Four detectives were also in the squad, all in dark clothing and all armed with pistols like Kell.

The detective inspector had turned up at the crypt with a prossie. His story was that Theodora Arbuthnot, after Exeter stressed the advisability of helping the police with their enquiries, had loaned the force the youngest and most innocent-looking of her Flowers. With a scrubbed face and in a plain white nightdress, the girl, Sally, looked as much of a virgin as any prossie in dim lighting could look.

Two bluebottles heaved her onto one of the red-draped tombs in front of the altar, then pulled a white sheet up to her breasts. Sally had a tendency to sniff due to adenoid trouble, but Exeter made it clear to her that her remuneration was dependent on her neither moving nor whuffing for the duration. Kell also heard Exeter flatter her, saying she should think of the night as a theatrical debut. Sally's face lit from within, and she comported herself like Sarah Bernhardt playing Camille.

The Yard men and Kell waited in cold silence for nearly an hour. All the candles in the crypt were burning and the tall, wobbling shadows were the only signs of movement. At the quarter hour before midnight, Kell heard low conversation and footsteps on stone, coming from above the crypt. The Church's faithful were descending from the ruined St Decumen's.

They were a prompt lot, or maybe just an eager one. In fifteen minutes, around twenty-five men gathered before the dais. They were all ages, from young adults to greyheads, all well-dressed and of apparent respectability. There was very little talking and no visible camaraderie in the group. Many men were hatted, keeping the brims low over their faces. A few made a circuit of the tomb where Sally lay. Kell fingered the grip of his pistol, ready to charge if the ruse should be discovered. But the girl was as still as a saint's effigy, and none of the men moved to touch her or disturb her drapery.

At the stroke of midnight, Ewan Exeter turned to face his flock. He made the sign of the cross grandly and his greeting rang in the vaulted space.

'Blessed be God, Father, Son, and Holy Ghost. Gentlemen, you are under arrest.'

Some hours later, Kell and Exeter stood under a streetlamp, just up the Embankment from the Yard. The Black Marias had finished disgorging passengers – some stunned, some loudly proclaiming their innocence, one weeping – to be processed. Dawn was a shy glow in the east.

Exeter held a small, leather-bound notebook and was reading names aloud from it. Kell listened intently. The detective inspector didn't look up until he got to the last of the names. Then he closed the notebook and smacked it against his palm, raising satisfied eyes to his old gang mate.

'Three peers, an Anglican bishop, some of the City's biggest merchants, a cabinet official. A Scottish earl, though he's a dubious article if ever I saw one. A French *comte* – it'll be a pleasure to send him back to Dague's pitch; I'll wire him in advance. Oh, and Marcus Wallenden, the head of London-Kowloon Shipping.

'I was likewise pleased to extend warm greetings to that fistful of blue-blooded younger sons. The Yard knows most of them already. Gambling debts, unpaid tradesmen, fisticuffs in bawdy houses and the like. A good haul, Stammer.'

'And the doctor.'

Exeter's face creased in a sarcastic smile. 'That paragon of British medicine, Sir Jeremiah Checkley, F.R.C.S.'

It had taken three bluebottles to restrain Kell when the Harley Street specialist who'd examined Jillian in the crypt was taken up and identified. Exeter made haste to get the man into the Black Maria. Public ruin would be the least of Checkley's worries until he was out of Kell's reach.

'*The Illustrated Police News* put in telephones a few weeks back. I'll ring up Jimmy Sullivan today, so he can get a running start on next week's edition. It'll make history in Jimmy's little world. The Yard's, too.'

Kell was certain the Yard and the papers weren't the only sectors that would reel. London's gossip machine would run noisily for a year on the scandal. 'What about the families of the men you collared?'

Exeter shrugged in a 'don't give a hang' way. 'I'll post them a little notice so they can flee to their country houses before London shite rains on their heads.'

Kell had nothing to say to that. Philanthropy wasn't in Exeter's nature. He'd reassure the prisoners about their families, but only as a bargaining chip in his game of arrest and punishment.

Kell knew better than to ask if he could be present at any of the men's interviews. Apart from his barely contained urge to exact bloody revenge, he couldn't know what deals were made between Exeter and his well-placed captives. Whatever they were, he was sure Exeter's career would be advanced and his pockets enriched. Running the Jacks, rising in the Met, answering to 'Scraper' or to 'Detective Inspector' – all the same to Ex.

One loose end dangled. 'The Viper?' Kell asked.

'Ah, yes. The Viper.' Exeter put the notebook in his coat and extracted his cigar case from the inside pocket. He opened the case to Kell, who shook his head. Ex took his time cutting the end and lighting a smoke for himself. The first few draws released vapour that mixed surprisingly well with London's early morning smells. Burning coal, Thames water, horse manure, baking bread.

Eventually, Exeter spoke around the cigar. 'I have the keenest anticipation of that line of questioning.'

No surprises there. Kell knew exactly what made Exeter keen in an interview, keen as mustard. At first, his questions would be put formally, persuasively. Then rudely, threateningly. Finally, accompanied by heavy blows to the face and punches to the gut. By any means and any road, untiring, relentless.

There was something else Kell could make book on. If the interrogations didn't produce what Exeter wanted to know about The Viper, the hunt would continue. Exeter would keep at it because he couldn't allow such a flagrant operator to range London on his watch. Kell would stay on the trail because, when he found him, he would take the greatest pleasure in dismembering The Viper alive.

One of the new safety bicycles whizzed by, the rider threading through horse-drawn conveyances in a daredevil manner that belied the two-wheeler's name and raised shouts and panic. In the half hour Kell and Exeter had been standing and talking, the Embankment had gone from dozing to dinning. It was time to part.

They'd never been much for fare-ye-wells and Godspeeds. Conversation over, they simply exchanged nods and pivoted to go their separate ways. Just before he was out of earshot, Kell called to Exeter, who stopped in his tracks and turned around.

'Ex, where do you buy jewellery for Reenie Storme?'

Exeter's effort to squelch a mocking response was almost comic, but with a relatively straight face he called back. 'Leitermann's, Bond Street. Use my name.'

Exeter strolled toward the Yard, smoking and thinking about truth. He'd never lied to another Jack. And, for the moment, he didn't know much more about The Viper than Kell did, so he'd told no lies today. Knowledge could expand, though, and he'd keep it to himself until he saw a reason to share.

There weren't many nobs Exeter could say owed him anything, but that changed the instant he lobbed six younger sons of titled personages into the Black Marias. The baron's son was a sprat he could toss back. But with the other five in his net, he'd scooped up their fathers – two marquesses, two earls, and a duke.

Aristocrats were nowise as numerous or fertile as they once were. Fewer heirs, fewer spares, and each one valuable. Too valuable to rot in prison.

Exeter lingered fifty paces from the Yard, smoking his cigar and watching London wake up around him. When he finished his smoke, he would step over to a café that served up a fine breakfast with excellent coffee. Today called for a full pot. He'd been up all night and would need it. *Busy hours await you, Scraper.*

First, he'd pay some social calls, starting with the marquesses. The higher his place on the precarious social ladder, the less likely the noble was to nark on his kind. But drop just a rung or two, and the toff clinging to it would cheerfully give up the goods on those above, those who'd looked down their noses at him a few too many times. Add to that a little incentive from the detective inspector who had the toff's son behind bars, and useful things fell into his hands.

Yes, that was the ticket. He'd definitely start with the marquesses. All he needed from them was everything they knew about the Duke of Fells and St Andrews.

CHAPTER THIRTY-EIGHT

It didn't surprise Kell that the second time he and Jillian took the train to Hackney, they conversed even less than the first time. Kell prayed it wasn't because he'd made such a hash of the past few weeks that Jillian couldn't forgive him. There was no bigger fool in Britain than him, to have made the woman sitting next to him feel spurned and despised, instead of what she was. His life and his future. The breath in his lungs. The pulse in his blood.

It was a leaden, wet day. Jillian had the window seat but wasn't looking at the view. She sat quietly, eyes cast down and ungloved hands folded in her lap. Very still, she was perfect and pale as a lily, with no idea of the storm raging in the man alongside.

Kell looked past her at the rain-streaked landscape and thought about what his mother said, that Jillian loved him for some lunatic reason. Maybe she was a little unbalanced to love him, haunted as he was, as they both were. He'd accept any reason, madness included. They could be mad together. Lunatics in Love, it had a ring to it.

There would be no more mistakes. He'd sorted his mind and heart and put the slavering ghosts of his past to rest. They hadn't gone easily or completely. That might take a while, years, even. They'd leave things behind, traces, doubts, bad dreams. But as soon as he'd brought Jillian into his life, the ghosts began to lose their power. From here on out, they would be like the Jacks, dead and gone.

Kell dipped his thumb and forefinger into his inside jacket pocket and brought out a tiny box. Jesus, it was surely too small to have his whole life in it. He'd find out soon enough what that life was worth to the person whose opinion meant everything. Good thing he was on a train. If the next few minutes didn't go the way he hoped, he could throw himself under the wheels.

Jillian saw his movement and turned to look, not at the box but at his face.

Kell opened the box and took out the ring. He reached across Jillian's lap and lifted her left hand, then slipped the gold and emeralds circle on the third finger.

She didn't say anything, just spread her fingers and looked at them while Kell looked at her. To his horror, a single tear gathered and slid from the corner of her eye, making a slow path toward her jaw.

Alarm grabbed Kell's heart and shook it like a rat in a terrier's mouth. 'You don't have to– I know you probably don't want– Please, don't cry, Jilly. I'll take it back, I–' He reached for her left hand.

With her right, Jillian slapped his wrist so hard he winced. 'Touch that ring, Michael Seraphin Kelly, and I will break your fingers.'

Kell grinned like what he was, the veriest lunatic ever to be in love. Right then and there, in full view of a dozen scandalised passengers – and one old duffer who kept huffing 'I say, there!' – Jillian threw her arms around his neck. They kissed for two minutes straight.

'I didn't want to hurt you.'

Jillian felt herself blushing so deeply she was sure Kell could see her cheeks redden in the half light of the bedroom. She wriggled closer to him under the blanket. 'It was only for a few seconds. You made me ready.'

His lips brushed hers. 'Light of my life, I'll make you ready any time you let me.'

Their mouths joined, tender and deep. With every kiss, Jillian discovered something new. The way it tickled when he licked the hollow of her throat. The way his sucking her earlobe sent wetness rushing between her thighs, because it was so like him sucking the sensitive trigger at her core. The way he growled possessively when he thrust his tongue into her mouth.

Despite multiple enticements of that sort, she rolled toward sleep. She was almost there when Kell whispered against her ear.

'Jillian.'

'*Mm-hmm?*' The storm outside had passed, and the moon was high over Hackney. Just enough light came through the bedroom window that she could see the blue of Kell's eyes. And the tattoos, coiling and rippling across his shoulders and chest.

'Jillian, there've been a hundred times I could have told you about my past. A hundred times I couldn't make myself do it. It's just that you're everything pure and lovely, everything that I– and I couldn't come straight out and say– oh, hell and damn.' Even in the scant light, Jillian could tell he was scowling.

'Jilly, when I was young, I made decisions that started wrong, stayed wrong. I should have told you right from the start. But because I knew I didn't have any right to want you, I never thought I'd have to explain.'

Jillian tried to stifle a yawn, but it came out anyway, her jaw cracking. 'Is this about Seven Dials and the Jacks?'

Ten long, fraught seconds passed. 'Because if it is,' she went on, 'I already know about all that. Your mother told me,' Jillian poked him in the chest, 'since *you* didn't seem to be getting around to it.'

'My mother, she– my *mother*?'

'You remember her, nice older lady, lives next to the brewery. I'm sure she left out a few of the most unsavoury bits, but she did a fine job, overall. Gave me the gist, as it were. The shilling edition.

'Michael Kell Seraphin Stammer Kelly.' Jillian took his hand, putting it on her heart and pressing it there. 'It's time for you to listen and listen well. I'm a murderess. Ada, you, your mother, for all I know half the people in London know what I did and what I am. Can you live with that?'

'Jillian, what you *did* was defend yourself.'

'Sir Hubert Alloway is still dead, and I killed him. Are you saying your crimes are worse than mine? That it's quantity over quality? Lord love a duck, Kell, if our history ever does catch us up, we'll have to jockey for position on the steps to the gallows.'

'Don't even joke about that, Jilly.'

'All right, I won't. But I'll ask you again, can you live with what I did?'

'If you'd killed a hundred Knights of the Realm, I could live with it. I'm just sorry I wasn't there to do it for you, to take that sin on my back with all the others.'

'And I'm sorry, sorrier than I can ever say, that I wasn't around to take your sins on mine. Because I may not be very big, Kell, but when it comes to you, you were right. I'm strong. You can shift half your load onto me, any day, any year, any lifetime.'

'Don't you understand? I could never hate you for what you did, what you had to do then, or later, or even now. My parents–'

'I'm sorry for what I said about them, Jilly.'

'No, you were right about them. And about me. I made the past a fairy tale and tried to write myself into it, like a princess in a tower. I was a fool about that. But I've never been a fool about you. I've loved you from the start, even though I couldn't explain it. Does it need explaining? Does the wind or the stars? I can't imagine the sky without stars, can you?

'I can't imagine the world without you, Kell, my centre, my heart. For me, that's all there is. I don't need a single thing more.'

Jillian felt more than saw him bring her hand to his lips, kiss it, then put it against his own heart. His voice was velvet, like the night around them. 'Jilly, I can't bring back your parents. I can't bring back that other life, that beautiful life, whether you had it or only imagined you did. That's beyond my or anyone's reach. All I can do is make a new life for you, maybe even a better one. If you'll let me, if you want me. I can start by giving you my name–'

She gave a low laugh. 'Which one?'

'Any one you like. I'll come up with a new one. The Count of Monte Cristo.'

'Taken.'

'Ichabod Crane.'

'Taken, awful, and American.'

'Uriah Heep.'

She laughed again, louder. 'I refuse to be known as Mrs Heep!'

Kell lifted his arm and she slipped under it, nestling against his firm chest with a happy sigh. His words were low rumbles under her cheek.

'Well, then, Mrs Kelly, I can give you a house. This house, for a start. I'll fill it with anything you want, even a piano. Two pianos, one upstairs and one down.'

'And how will you get a piano up those stairs?'

He shrugged. 'The way I've done everything else, Jilly. On my back.' He rubbed his fingers across hers and they both smiled at the rasp of his callouses. Callouses he got working on the house that held the bed that held the love that held them together.

'Anything, Jillian. Just say it and I'll move heaven and earth to get it for you. Tables and chairs and sideboards and– what-nots.'

It might be a good time to tell him she didn't really care for what-nots. There *was* one thing, though. 'I want a dog.'

Surprise and then eagerness in Kell's voice. 'Lurcher? Spaniel? French Bulldog? Dague says those are very–'

Jillian shook her head. 'Cairn terrier. Well, part, at least. If he's still at Larches, he lives in the scullery yard. His name is Tige.'

271

Chapter Thirty-Nine
Eighteen months later

Kell and Exeter reconsidered their proximity to the practice ring when blood splashed on their clothes. It was Kell's boxing academy and his ring, so he didn't mind, but Exeter cursed as he viewed the spatter on his silk necktie.

Inwardly laughing, Kell apologised. 'Sorry, Ex. You wouldn't think two viscounts could go at it with such vigour.'

'*Vigour?*' Exeter used his handkerchief to swipe at the blood, giving him a bloodied handkerchief as well as a tie. 'They're fuckin' pit dogs.' Surprisingly, Exeter's sharp features rearranged in a grin. 'You do good work, Stammer.'

Kell wasn't a man who blushed, but at the rare compliment and rarer smile from his former gang leader, he came damned close. Clearing his throat, he went back to what they'd been discussing before sparring viscounts distracted them. 'The duke. Fells and St Andrews.'

'I enjoyed that,' Exeter drawled, a cat with a saucer of cream. 'Took months to work it all out, but revenge served cold is as tasty a dish as ever was.'

'Careless of His Grace to forget he was already married. With three children.'

'Shockin'.' Exeter's eyes could never be said to twinkle, but a spark of humour lit them. 'Ireland's not nearly far enough away to hide a thing like that.'

'Sloppy, the man, very sloppy.'

'A pernicious rotter. Maybe if the wife hadn't been *Eyyye-rish...*'

Kell punched Exeter in the arm and the policeman guffawed, then groaned theatrically as he rubbed the spot where his one-time captain's powerful fist had landed.

'The Viper?' Kell pressed.

'Right. Well, the public undressing of the duke's private life was ruination on wheels, but what really got everyone's attention was *The Illustrated Police News*.' Exeter framed a headline with his hands. 'Viper Duke Masterminds Abduction and Murder!'

'You leaked the story?'

'With the greatest pleasure. When I slipped Jimmy Sullivan the brief on The Church, he nearly choked on his own slobber. For once, young James beat the coppers to a crime.'

'And the Marquess Melton?'

'I told Melton everything before the story came out. Not his daughter's fault she got in the duke's crosshairs.'

Kell nodded, wishing no girl or woman had ever gotten in those crosshairs. Lady Rosaline's near *mésalliance* might have cost her a notch or two in society, but some of the duke's other victims paid with their lives. 'It was all about the money, wasn't it?'

'All about the brass, yeah. The duke was skint, had been skint for years. Not that it stopped him from generally livin' like Midas. Lady Rosaline's dowry was big enough to choke a whale, but it would barely have put a stopper in what Fells and St Andrews owed from here to John o' Groats.'

Kell watched the viscounts swipe at each other for a minute, then mentioned, almost casually, 'The nob takin' the easy way out saved a lot of bother.'

'A labour-savin' gesture. And it made a grand sequel in the

paper.' Exeter's hands framed another headline. 'Criminal Duke Turns Pistol on Self. How's that for–'

A heavy thump jerked both men's faces toward the ring. One of the boxers was on his knees, shaking his head dazedly. As Kell and Exeter watched, his opponent took a step toward the downed man.

'Oi!' Kell hitched his foot onto the platform and fisted the rope, ready to vault over.

The aggressor retreated, gloves raised. Kell let go of the rope and stood down from the platform but kept his eyes on the fallen viscount until the man got unsteadily to his feet. Kell looked a question at him and the viscount nodded back. The bout resumed.

'*Oi?*' Exeter's face mingled incredulity and amusement. 'Not 'My Lord', or 'Your Lordship', or even 'Sir'?' Kell didn't respond, so Exeter crowed in his old voice, his Jacks voice. 'Me an' you, bruv, we ain't so diff'rent. You fiddles the toffs your way an' I fiddles 'em mine.'

Pointedly not rising to the bait, Kell changed the subject. 'A little bird told me that in place of a reward from Melton, a certain detective inspector asked only that Lady Rosaline become the patroness of the East London Pugilists Academy.'

'Ah, well, Stammer. You can't trust birds.'

'Hmmn.' Kell said no more. For now, it was enough to know that funds would keep streaming in for the Academy and its East London Youth programme. That younger versions of himself, Exeter, and Dague would be given different choices. That the Jacks and gangs like them would stay dead and gone, forever.

The viscounts finished their practice bout and tapped gloves in the centre of the ring. Kell knew they'd change their clothes and move to the Patrons' Club on the floor above, where they'd continue sparring, without blood but with snifters of brandy, in deep armchairs before the fire.

Kell lifted his chin in the Club's direction. 'Care for a drink, Ex?'

'Ta, Stammer, but can't do it. It's the last night of *The Merry Monarch*'s run and Reenie's draggin' me to some *aprés-soirée*. I've got just enough time to get into evening dress.'

Kell coughed into his fist to keep a derisive snort from escaping. The king of the Jacks, dropping French expressions. Fussing over silk ties. Rushing home to don evening dress. Exeter was definitely back with Reenie. He'd be wearing an ascot next.

Exeter and Kell shook hands – effusive, as their farewells went. The policeman settled his hat and started away from the ring, almost tripping over three women – Evie, Min, and Ada – on their way to the street door. All three were gabbling nineteen to the dozen and laughing like loons. Evie and Min waved at Kell, hardly glanced at Exeter, and then scurried toward the exit. The third of the noisy trio lagged behind.

Exeter touched his hat. 'Adaline.'

She gave the policeman a curt nod. 'Ewan.' She turned to Kell. 'Hopscotchin' vicars, Kell. Jilly worked us up to death's doorsill in the Lady Pugilists, today.'

Kell's grin was one part approbation, three parts pride. 'Glad to hear it. Where's my slave-drivin' missus now?'

'Havin' a bath.' Ada looked in the direction Evie and Min had gone. 'I'm off.'

Exeter stretched a long arm toward the street. 'I'll walk you, Ada.' After a second's hesitation, Ada nodded, and the two set out.

Kell watched how they went, a foot and a half of space between them. *Good.*

His Jillian was having a bath. All by her lonely self in their flat at the top of the building. Pining away in that deep copper tub of warm sudsy water. Kell should do his husbandly duty and comfort her. He set out for the stairs at a lope.

'Have I told you recently how pleased I am that my husband is rich and successful?'

Husband. Kell would never tire of hearing Jillian say the word. He would never tire of lying half-dressed on the bed, watching his wife while she bathed. It made him feel like an Oriental potentate, savouring his beautiful, beloved, harem of one.

The tub was just a few feet away and neither of them ever bothered with the flimsy bamboo screen. It was folded to one side, giving Kell a delicious view of a shapely, soap-slick leg, draped over the edge of the bath. He shifted the tightening mass under his trousers placket. 'I suspected from the beginning you were a fortune hunter.'

'You can hardly accuse me of that. When we met, you were wearing patched shirts and working in a brothel as a–'

'Floor man.'

'Door man.'

'Chucker-out.'

'Bouncer,' they said together.

'And that terrible room at the back where you lived!'

'Your lodging wasn't exactly Buckingham Palace, my dear.'

'Do try to remember it was you gave it to Ada and me.'

'Trying to establish common ground, is all.'

'It was common, all right.'

'Had a very nice wardrobe, didn't it?'

'It did.'

The devilishly tempting leg went back into the tub and *holy martyrs,* Jillian began washing her breasts. Lifting one, so the nipple tilted toward him. The soft cotton rag circled it, creamy suds sliding across the cherrystone peak and over the full, round–

Was she still talking?

'There's no way I could have known you were a wealthy man. Certainly, I'd never have believed you had the wherewithal...' Jillian took her hand from under her breast and waved it airily. 'For all this.'

Kell had no trouble believing. Every skinned knuckle and hardened callous on his hands bore witness to the building of it. A defunct rope factory in Poplar, the East London Pugilists Academy began life as three dusty and debris-littered floors. Once cleared, cleaned, and converted, it was lavishly outfitted. The ground floor now held gymnasiums and boxing rings, a hell of a job to build. The top floor was a fine flat, with a fully plumbed bath and a sitting room whose tall windows gave views of the Thames. And, of course, a large bed.

Kell lifted his hands and examined the lasting evidence of the middle floor conversion. Half was given to Jillian's idea and domain: the Institute for Lady Pugilists, where women were trained in fitness and self-defence. When Kell asked her where she got the notion, she only smiled and said, 'A buckram corset.'

The other half of the middle floor became the Patrons' Club, an elegant den with a staggeringly expensive subscription. At first, Jillian worried that Kell set the fee too high, but when he upped it, the list of member-hopefuls responded by expanding greatly.

Jillian was singing in the bath. That made Kell think of the piano in their other residence, where her fleet fingers darted from Schumann to 'Sweet Rosie O'Grady'. Never Chopin.

'Hackney this Sunday?' he asked.

'Hackney this Sunday.'

Could they buy a different house? Something newer, larger, grander? They could, but they didn't care to. They savoured their Sundays and holidays in Hackney, just far enough away from The Smoke, the noise, the crowds, and the demands of the business. Since Baby Andy arrived, the house was a shared fantasy. For Jillian, a new incarnation of the cottage in Hertfordshire, snug and secure, vined with roses. For Kell, the family home that might have been his, had he been born anywhere but Whitechapel.

Jillian rose from the tub. God, she was a picture. Standing there, water glistening and streaming off her ivory skin, pale copper hair loosely pinned up, wet strands curling against her forehead and neck.

'Come to bed, wife.' No matter how manly Kell tried to say it, why did it always come out as begging?

'I've just bathed!'

He unbuttoned his trousers and his cock sprang out, as ready for action as it always was when Jillian was within sight. Or scent. Or hearing. Or, generally speaking, anywhere. 'In my present condition, we'll be done before the water cools. You can bathe again.'

'And what about *my* pleasure, hasty husband?' She turned around and braced her hands against the tub, lifting her leg over the rim to step out. Kell almost rose off the mattress like an airship.

He got out of his trousers, quickly. 'I'll fill another bath for you.' Flopping back on the bed, he lay with arms spread. 'Please, Jilly, darling...' Begging again, even less manly than before.

She came to him, patting herself with a Turkish towel. 'All right, my impetuous love. But we mustn't lose track of time. Your mother and Eileen will be back with Andy in an hour.'

'Do you doubt my ability to make you scream with ecstasy twice in an hour, madam?'

'I do not.' She climbed onto the bed and straddled his thighs. 'Numerous proofs have been provided and the product reliably performs as advertised.'

'Besides,' Kell struggled to speak as his wife gripped him, easing him between her legs, 'Tige'll delay them. He's such a charmer, every second person in the park has to pet him and– *ahhh, Jilly...*' Speech fled, thought fled.

Love stayed.

Acknowledgements

The author acknowledges with gratitude the privilege of working with Bloodhound Books' gifted, diligent, and expert team.

About the Author

A career historian, Annie R McEwen has lived in six countries and under every roof from a canvas tent to a Georgian Era manor house. Winner of a 2022 Page Turners Writing Award (Romance Category), Annie garnered both a First and Second Place 2022 RTTA (Romance Through the Ages Award), the 2023 MAGGIE Award, and the 2023 Daphne du Maurier Award. Her short fiction appears in numerous anthologies.

When she's not in her 1920s bungalow in Florida, Annie lives, writes, and explores castles in Wales. Find her online at: www.anniermcewen.com

A NOTE FROM THE PUBLISHER

Thank you for reading this book. If you enjoyed it please do consider leaving a review on Amazon to help others find it too.

We hate typos. All of our books have been rigorously edited and proofread, but sometimes mistakes do slip through. If you have spotted a typo, please do let us know and we can get it amended within hours.

info@bloodhoundbooks.com

www.ingramcontent.com/pod-product-compliance
Lightning Source LLC
Chambersburg PA
CBHW061527210726
48287CB00006B/1869